WHITE WITCH DOCTOR

White Witch Doctor

LOUISE A. STINETORF

Decorated by Don McDonough

Philadelphia
THE WESTMINSTER PRESS

PRINTED IN THE UNITED STATES OF AMERICA

To my husband
HENRY LOEL WILSON
who has given me every encouragement

Foreword

No, I am not the Little White Witch Doctor. Nor is Ellen Burton, whose story this is, a "real person."

Perhaps I should include here the customary statement that "all characters in this book are fictitious"—but that would not be true either. For a novel, if it is a sincere picture of a way of life, often comes nearer to the real truth than mere factual reporting ever can.

In writing the story of Ellen Burton, I have done what every fiction writer does—drawn upon direct and vicarious experiences. Many of the incidents in this book are based on actual fact. The rest is true to life of the people of the Congo Territory as I have known them, but shaped to the best of my ability in order to make a logical whole of the story. Very few things are ever created out of complete nothingness. And any missionary who would, or could, loosen up with you, could surpass anything I've put into my story.

LOUISE A. STINETORF

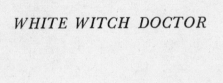

WHITE WITCH DOCTOR

CHAPTER
1

Y OU'RE going home!"
My work is over, my affairs are in order, and my co-
workers have been saying good-by, wistfully and sometimes a
bit enviously. "You're going home now!"

Yes, soon I shall cross the Atlantic and travel halfway across
the United States until I am back again in the little Indiana
town of my birth. But I shall not be going home. For Africa is
my home. Here in the Congo Territory is where the people I
love were born. This is where my work was done.

Yet after a quarter of a century of the best years of my maturity, my only years of personal fulfillment, I am being exiled,
because that is the usual fate of aging missionaries. But my
heart will remain here with the children that I brought into the
world, and with their children, and with the white-haired
women and the gray-bearded men for whom I opened up new
vistas of life after their own people had cast them into discard.

Henceforth I must tread paved streets and sleep under shin-
gled roofs, all in the name of care and kindliness being shown
an old woman. But my calloused feet will miss the soft mold of
jungle trails. And how can I fall asleep at night without the
subdued rustle in my ears of a thatch roof inhabited by a thousand tiny creatures? When I look about me at the pallid faces

of those who will be solicitous of my physical health, will I dare share with anyone, even my own flesh and blood, the fact that I love and honor an old black woman as I have never loved or honored another human being? Or that I, who never married, mourn an African stripling as my own son?

No, I am not going home. At the end of life I am being uprooted. I must live among people who will be strangers to me, because they believe the center of the universe is in their own back yards. And having known self-sufficiency, I must now somehow step back into the rather pathetic position of a family dependent. That is what life was for me before I went to Africa; that is all that the remaining years seem to offer.

Can I do it? I must. How, I don't know. I can only pray, as I did so often in the middle of some dank jungle, "God, please help me."

My youth was spent in the Middle Western United States. I came from what is called "missionary stock"—that is, although my parents were humble farmer folk, I had aunts, uncles, cousins, then a brother and sister, and now nephews and nieces, scattered all over the world in Christian service. From earliest childhood I took it for granted that I too would become a missionary. My parents were sympathetic. Mother encouraged me to memorize great sections of inspired literature, including whole books of the Bible, while Father saw to it that I received well-rounded instruction in the basic academic subjects, most of it at home under his tutelage.

"A good foundation for specialized training later on," he insisted when I was inclined to rebel against Cicero's interminable orations or the theory of differential equations. Even at the ripe old age of sixteen I felt ready to get on with that specialized training. Whatever it would be—pedagogy, medicine, evangelism—I knew exactly where I wanted to go. Africa!

Moffat, Livingstone, Krapf, Stanley, Burton, Hannington—I knew the lives of all the great missionaries and explorers of the Dark Continent as well as I knew our village grocer, postmaster, or pastor. I read everything I could find published on Africa, and folk like Tippu Tib, that crafty slave runner, and Mutesa, powerful and villainous beyond belief, personalities that enthralled me more than any elfin creature Andersen or the brothers Grimm ever dreamed up.

But the years went by and I did not apply for missionary appointment, although it was always in the back of my mind as a step I would take as soon as the immediate situation in my family cleared up. We were a large family—I had four brothers and four sisters—and there was always some good reason why I should stay at home "just a little longer." This sister was getting married and, instead of buying the indispensable household equipment for me to take to Africa, the money must be used for furnishing her new home on the farm next door. Or that brother, just finishing his hospital internship and already appointed to the mission field in China, had the opportunity to buy a really splendid set of surgical instruments for "next to nothing." And so it went.

I was glad to do what I could to help, and if anyone had spoken of my efforts as sacrifice, I would have called him crazy. My life was full and happy, and I did not notice the inexorable flight of the years. Then, when I was in my very late thirties, my mother died, and six months later we knew that Father too was leaving us. As is so often the case with devoted couples, he simply pined away from sheer loneliness. He had reason to be proud of some of his children; and as for the rest of us, I couldn't see that the problems we faced were any greater than those of all right-intentioned, hard-working, moderately intelligent people. Shortly before Father died he spoke to me as he had never done before. I was sitting beside his bed, reading because I thought he was asleep. Something made me look up suddenly, and I found him staring at me, wide-eyed and perplexed.

"Are you comfortable?" I asked and patted his hand. He

3

grasped my fingers with more strength than I had supposed he possessed.

"Ellen dear— Ellen, you're a good girl," he murmured just as though I had been four, or fourteen, instead of only a hair-breadth from forty.

"I've had good parents," I smiled.

"We've tried, Mother and I," he answered calmly. "But, Daughter— What's to become of you now?"

I was dumfounded and my face must have shown it, for after a moment he went on.

"Your mother and I always worried about you, Ellen. I could go to her now with an easy heart if only—you—were—provided for."

"Why, Father, you've told me I'll always have the income from the farm while I live!" I exclaimed. "You know I'm not extravagant. You needn't worry; there'll be more than I need."

Even as I spoke, he shook his head. "That's not what I mean. You shouldn't live here alone. But don't go to one of your brothers or sisters, Daughter. You've served as hand-maiden to each one of them long enough. Where will you make your home? How will you occupy your time?"

His eyes demanded an answer. But how could I tell my father what was in my heart without seeming to say, "Your death will be my release"?

He took the words out of my mind. "You think you'll go to Africa, don't you?"

"Why I—I—" I wasn't stammering, but rather searching for the right words.

"Ellen, Mother and I have prayed for you oftener and more earnestly than we have prayed for any of your brothers and sisters. Not that they are any better than you—sometimes I've thought you were the most deserving of the whole lot. But—well—you've missed a lot out of life and the years ahead are going to be difficult. How difficult, only God in his infinite wisdom can know. You'll come through, though, in spite of your

4

lack of advantage and privilege; Mother and I have never doubted that for a moment. But when the going is difficult—God bless you, Ellen. God bless you and be with you always."

I shall be eternally grateful to my father for that benediction. Not only was it deeply sincere, but I knew at the time that it had long been in his mind. I saw it in his eyes every time he looked at me thereafter.

Eight days later we laid him beside Mother in the little rural cemetery where so many of his friends and relatives already slept.

Before the funeral, brothers James and Robert had offered me a home with them. Each had assured me that his wife would welcome me into their family life. I knew that was the truth, but I declined, and neither one pressed me.

"You've got a right to your own life, Sis," James remarked dryly.

Robert merely nodded agreement, but I thought I heard him remark to James as they walked away together, "What there is left of it."

I think that was the first time it ever really dawned on me that I was no longer a young woman. And even then I did not realize that my lack of youth could be held against me.

Sister Alice was not nearly so considerate as James and Robert—but perhaps there was some justification for her attitude. She was the youngest of our family; in fact, there was eight years' difference between her age and that of the last before her. As a child she had been petted and babied, and with other parents than ours she probably would have grown into a brat. Even so, she was a self-centered little egotist. She married young, and the babies came—one, two, three, four, five, six— with scarcely more than a normal gestation period between them. Sam, Alice's husband, was a steady, hard-working man, but he had not been able to make much headway, and I knew that both he and Alice had counted on her probable inheritance from Father. There would be a tidy sum for Alice and

5

Sam, but I was sorry for both of them when they learned that Father had left the home place to me.

I was honestly sorry, but scarcely prepared for what happened. All morning at the house before the funeral Alice hovered over me like an old hen with one chick. I noticed Sam watching her, and I wondered if he was striving to restrain some sort of outburst on her part.

After the prayer at the house, Alice said to me suddenly, "You're riding with Sam and me in our car." It was a command, not an invitation.

As soon as Sam's car had taken its place in the funeral cortege, she came to the point without mincing words. It was unthinkable that I should live alone, something smacking of the indecent. "People would talk." Nor was it Christian that I should move into the nearby village and live a life of idleness, even though I could easily afford it now. "People would talk" about that too, especially since she, my own sister, slaved from morning till night. Now the sensible thing for me to do would be to move in with her and Sam. Or, better yet, have them move in with me at the home place. I could help with the six children; they and the work would keep me from being lonely and bored. And I could contribute enough to the family income so that I wouldn't feel a burden on anybody. Didn't I think it a good idea? Didn't Sam?

Sam didn't answer. His knuckles were white against the black of the steering wheel.

The family sat in the first four rows of the church. I was wedged between Alice and my brother John. Father lay just before and below the altar. As I stared at his face, calm and gentle-looking as always, it seemed to me he was just on the point of shaking his head and murmuring: "Not in Alice's home, Ellen. You've been her handmaiden long enough."

John patted my knee with one of his big, work-hardened hands. Alice saw the movement and seized my arm. I felt resentful, and tried to pull away, but she only tightened her grip.

6

John bent forward a trifle and looked past me at his youngest sister. Her face crimsoned, and for a moment she quailed; then she recovered and whispered to John, her eyes darting from his to mine and back again, "A beautiful sermon, isn't it?"

A week after the funeral, I made a trip into the city to the office of the Mission Board. Alone! But getting rid of Alice, who by now was in my house oftener than in her own, was far more difficult than many a farm chore I'd helped Father with. At the last moment, she doubted if I should take the car out alone.

"For heaven's sake!" I exploded. "I've been driving for ten years and you know it."

"But—the traffic, you know. Traffic in the city is terrible nowadays," she put in hopefully.

"Alice, I've driven into the city in stormy weather, with sleet on the road, through Christmas traffic, and, after all, I'm not a child, you know."

Two hours later, in the office of our Mission Board, I had to eat those last words. Staring openmouthed in spirit if not in fact at the executive secretary, I could scarcely believe my ears. In spite of her own white hair and the cane which she always used, she was saying: "But, my dear, at your age! You're not a child, you know."

No human being with any backbone at all gives up the sustaining dreams of a lifetime without some struggle. I was tense and perhaps on the defensive. Her words made me bluntly, obnoxiously aggressive.

"I've always been a member of our local missionary society, and I've served several terms on your Board, as you well know, but never, not to this minute, have I realized that it was children we send to our mission fields," I burst out.

"Now, not *children*, my dear. But, after all, there are age limits which must be met, you know," she began placatingly.

I did know. I had known all along, but I had never thought of their being applied to me. "The word is yours," I stormed.

7

"I'm not a child, you said, and thereby implied that only the very young should be sent to the mission field."

"But the difficulties a missionary must face are such—"

"Since when has maturity incapacitated one for facing difficulties?" I demanded.

"Now, my dear, let's face this thing calmly," I heard our secretary pleading.

I suppose *she* was calm. It was a part of her job to face other people's disappointments with poise. As for myself, I neither pulled her hair nor spit in her eye, but I did get across to her that, with or without the blessing of the Mission Board, I was going to Africa. Our interview ended in a compromise—the secretary would call a special meeting of the Committee on Foreign Appointments to consider my case.

In due time two of the members of the Board came to call on me. They were obviously too embarrassed to put much heart into their mission—namely, to dissuade me from wanting to go to Africa. By then I was saturated with that terrible, calm temper which listens to the reasoning of others with the quiet impregnability of a mountain cliff. How could I give in now? I had gone through an additional two weeks with Alice perpetually underfoot and, after living with my dream for at least three decades, I was not going to give it up now that reality was within my grasp.

Suddenly, I realized that my callers had been given instructions for an alternate argument. Finding me obdurate, they brought up the matter of specialized training. The day had long gone by when zeal in the heart and a Bible in the hand were all the equipment a missionary needed. What could I do? they asked me. Educational work without formal college training? Ministerial work without seminary study? Medical work without the long years in both classroom and hospital that are requisite?

"I can go as a practical nurse," I answered suddenly.

"But, my dear—"

I have always wished violently that people would not begin "my dear-ing" me whenever they disagree with me. Or treat me like a child while assuring me that I am no longer young.

"My dear, according to the reports of the workers on the field, almost every village woman is a practical nurse of sorts. Now if you really had nurse's training, that would be a different matter."

"Then I shall take nurse's training," I promptly answered.

"At your age!" They exclaimed in a crescendo duet.

"What are three years compared with the time I have already waited?" I replied. I can remember with more than a little amusement now how lighthearted and triumphant I felt at the time.

CHAPTER
2

I'M not going to dwell upon my stint in the hospital. Suffice it to say that I had to ask friends of my family to use their influence to get me into one—at my advanced age. When the admissions committee turned down my application, I went to the town banker, who had gone to school with my father; to a prominent lawyer, whose son wanted to marry one of my nieces; to one of our richest local industrialists, who, without any security to offer other than his character, had once borrowed money from my father with which to erect his first insignificant factory building. From that day to this, whenever I hear any of the numerous platitudes about wealth's being nothing, I listen with my tongue in my cheek and recall a favorite quip of my father's: "It's true that money won't buy happiness; but if you have a little money, you can be just as unhappy as you like—in comfort."

Oh, yes! I was admitted to the hospital, and in many ways the difficulties of my period of training were lightened for me. Still it seemed that I, who had done housework all my life, spent that first year bending over cots "learning" how to smooth and tuck in sheets, or on my knees scrubbing floors which could have been cleaned just as well in one half the time and with one tenth the effort, given proper equipment. I don't know whether or not all hospitals are alike, but the abasement of the flesh of the early Christian had nothing on the institution where I was supposedly trained.

After my three years' training, I was duly awarded permission to write "R. N." after my name. Then, like many another missionary, I left the hospital loaded down with broken, castoff equipment. I wondered at the time what in the world I could do with the trash, but more was sent me from time to time throughout my terms of service and almost all of it was put to good use.

I was also commissioned a missionary by our Board. There was not much else they could do under the circumstances. Finally, with an incredible amount of luggage, I took a train to New York and there boarded ship for Léopoldville on the Congo.

Around the entire coast of Africa there are towns, with excellent cosmopolitan shopping centers. But every Mission Board of which I know anything at all, insists to this day that appointees bring with them all the appurtenances, domestic and professional, necessary to the maintenance of a moderately well-regulated home in Middletown, U.S.A. And they are further loaded down with similar supplies for every missionary family they are likely to meet within the next six years.

I have heard it argued that prices are higher in Africa than in the United States, but, while that is generally true, they are not enough more to make up the cost of freighting bed linen, simple furniture, and pots and pans across the Atlantic. However, I did exactly as I was told because I was as ignorant of the land that was to be my home for the next quarter century as were my employers. So, when I arrived in Léopoldville, I looked like a traveling circus bereft of all its performers but one. The head of our local missions who met me in Léopoldville shared my reaction, although it was an old story to him.

"I always hope against hope with each new appointee that this won't happen," he groaned. "But it really doesn't matter;

you new ones will always come loaded down, so I reserved the top deck of the boat we take upriver just for you and me—and your luggage."

At first sight Dr. Early, the mission head and my boss from now on, made me think of a russet apple. He was certainly as squat, plump, and round, and, in spite of the sola topee he invariably wore, the African sun had parched his skin to the hue of a prime russet. Whenever he took off his helmet, an absurd cowlick, springing stubbornly from the crown of his head, could have passed for a stem. His belt, an elaborate affair of okapi hide, had been presented him some years earlier by a native tribal council of old men. I learned later that no African wears an okapi hide belt except those who have earned the right by some act of signal bravery, but Dr. Early always laughed off any questions as to how he came by this badge of honor. Cinched as the belt was at the man's point of greatest girth, it gave him a humpty-dumpty look, and I frequently found myself wondering what kept it from slipping up, or down.

But Dr. Early's most remarkable feature was his eyes, and yet, for the life of me, I can't tell you now what color they were. They were tired eyes—tired and disillusioned—but still they showed no loss of faith. It was as though he thoroughly understood human weakness and somehow had managed to retain his faith in the ultimate triumph of that spark of eternal good which God tucks away in the heart of every human being.

Before I left the United States I had made arrangements with the bank at home for credit with the Bank of Belgium in Léopoldville. Dr. Early took me first to the office of the American consul, with whom I registered as a fellow countryman looking forward to indefinite residence in the vast territory known as Upriver. Then I asked Dr. Early to go along with me to the bank, to identify me if that were necessary, and help me establish my claim to credit.

I hadn't finished speaking before I knew that something was

wrong. For a moment he looked as though I had stepped on a sore toe. Then he stared speculatively at me for several seconds, under perfectly level brows.

"H'm," he grunted finally. "So you're one of *those*."

"One of what?" I demanded.

He gave me no direct answer, then or ever. But I learned, very quickly, that independent means were as much of a stumbling block on the mission field as my age had been at home.

When I first went to Africa, my salary totaled the magnificent sum of $25 a month, which was the rate in our denomination for missionaries, regardless of age, training, and years of service. Married couples received $50 per month and an additional $10 for each child under sixteen years of age. Thus, $100 a month was considered sufficient for the maintenance of a man, his wife, and five children. And the amazing thing is that missionaries do get along on whatever they are paid. Not after the fashion of "African explorers" who travel about in motorized caravans, or even by air, with a retinue of hundreds of servants. But the missionary gets along and, ironically, often smooths the way of the highly press-agented "explorer," who shows his gratitude by caustic reports of the stupidity and bigotry of the religious workers he has met on the field.

But poverty is never easy, regardless of cultural background or spiritual incentive. And my co-workers were so poor that, even though their reaction was subconscious, every one of them was deeply resentful of my financial independence. There were times when I surprised stark hatred in the eyes of women who called me "sister"—hatred because I could discard a worn-out undergarment and replace it with a new one from the stores in Léopoldville.

Dr. Early was a friendly enough man, and normally even a little garrulous, but he seemed tongue-tied as we stalked along to the bank. When I finally demanded an explanation, he flushed, but informed me that, in his opinion, an employee could scarcely be expected to give the most conscientious service if his employer were not able to take away his bread and butter at a moment's notice.

I stopped stock-still in the middle of the street.

"Why—how absurd!" I burst out when I could manage words at all.

"You think so," my companion murmured in a white-lipped fashion. "H'm."

"Do you think that at my age—" I stopped abruptly and almost laughed as I heard my own tongue shaping the expression that had become so odious to me in the past three years. "Do you think that at my age I would have gone through all I did in that hospital and—and—and elsewhere?" I couldn't speak to him of sister Alice or of the executive secretary in the home office. "Would I have scrubbed floors for a year in a charity ward if I had not intended to do all I could to give satisfactory service in—in my chosen work?"

He looked up the street and then down the street, and then took my arm and motioned toward the bank, but I stood firm until again he came out bluntly with, "You're not the first middle-aged woman who has thought she had the health and vigor and—" he cleared his throat—"and mental flexibility to make a life for herself in a new environment."

Believe it or not, it was the first time I had ever been called middle-aged; that first time always makes a woman mad whether she shows her temper or not. I could feel every nerve in my body tightening and my words sounded brittle in my own ears as I answered, "I don't know that I came to Africa to make a life for myself."

"Why did you come, then?" he asked.

I expected to see a sneer on his lips, to hear sarcasm in the words, but there was none of either. I was very much on the defensive at that moment, but I was also conscious of the conviction that, in spite of anything and everything, I would like and respect this man.

"Why?" he insisted gently, and seemed as unaware of the foot traffic eddying about us as I was myself.

"I believe," I began, speaking slowly, "that Christianity can be made to work. And that, if it is made to work, we can evolve such a civilization as—as, perhaps, only a very few men have ever grasped."

"Here in Africa?"

"Yes. Why not here in Africa? Religion isn't geographical, or racial."

"Sister Ellen, a long and difficult row stretches out ahead of you." Dr. Early spoke as slowly as I had done. "But, God helping you, you may be able to hoe it."

Suddenly he laughed like an impish child. "Do you know, when someone like you is sent out to us, we hope for the best, and pray—" He was speaking in a confidential tone as though sharing a delightful secret, but after a sidelong glance at me, he broke off.

"Pray for the best and take whatever comes," I supplied lightly. We both laughed, I briefly and in order to be polite, although at the time I did not entirely understand the humor. Then we turned and went into the bank, where I established my identity as that rare and not altogether desirable bird, a financially independent missionary.

The bulk of our time in Léopoldville was occupied with getting my mountainous luggage on the little tram which carried passengers and freight bound for the interior up around the rapids that break the "Great River," as the Congo is commonly called. At the end of the tramline, it was not the train crew, but Dr. Early, myself, and two *"boys"* who got my bales, boxes, and miscellaneous bundles off the train and onto the boat.

It was a wearing task, but I didn't think too much of it until my companion muttered irritably, "Why you new appointees always feel you have to bring an entire department store with you is beyond me."

15

I turned upon him in blank surprise. I didn't have a thing with me that I had not been assured many times over I would need and that I could not get in Africa. And at least half of my luggage was for others. The memory of the Léopoldville department store windows was still puzzlingly fresh in my mind —windows filled with the same odds and ends that jammed my luggage. Odds and ends on which I had paid freight from the middle of the United States to Léopoldville, then duty, and for which I must still pay transportation several hundred miles Upriver.

Hot and sticky and tired, I replied irritably: "Why is it that you who are already on the field asked me to bring you so much? Things that I saw for sale right here in Léopoldville?"

He gave me a look that I never forgot, and I hastened to explain, "I haven't minded in the least, you understand, but, after all—"

Suddenly abashed, I stammered into silence. He seized a bale, gave it a jerk, and called to a *boy*. Naturally I didn't understand a syllable of the native dialect he used, but the *boy* jumped as though someone had stung him with a whiplash. My irritation grew. Why should Dr. Early take such offense? It was he who had given way to temper first. Then he began to speak, slowly and ever more slowly as he continued until finally his words came in reluctant jerks. I was still too inexperienced in mission ways to understand fully the effort the statement cost him.

"What we buy here in Léopoldville we must pay for ourselves out of—of—our own salaries. What is sent us from home is—is in the nature of—of a contribution—above and beyond our salaries."

Three times after he had closed his mouth, he opened his lips as though to speak, then closed them again without a sound. At last he turned back to the *boys* who were wrestling my luggage about. I was shocked. Bewildered.

Slowly, through the confusion of my reactions, resentment

16

began to burn within me. Here was a college man who could easily have multiplied his monthly stipend by ten, or twenty, or more, if he had stayed at home. No wonder his words stung when he released his pent-up vexation on a black *boy* who could not answer back. I certainly believe that the "first fruits" belong to the Lord, but I also think it is a travesty on the spirit of religion to lay the best upon God's altar—and leave it there to wither and rot.

I am not going to describe the Congo. It has been done before, many times, by those more skilled with words than I. Yet this mighty waterway is like the sky above us, the desert, the ocean, ever changing, ever new. Distance in Africa is not measured in miles or kilometers, but in terms of difficulties to overcome and time consumed. It took us three major rapids and almost a month to reach the confluence of the Congo and the Tani Rivers. The river boats, all of them stern- or side-wheelers, ply between rapids too furious for them to negotiate. Thus, three times we unloaded, portaged rapids, one of which was over ten miles in length with a sheer drop of almost a half mile, and then camped beside the river until the next boat we must take meandered into view. Our boat hugged the bank because of the force of the midstream current and several times freight piled up on the top deck was scraped overboard by overhanging branches. When that happened, the captain anchored and waited until black *boys,* more fish than men seemingly, retrieved our belongings.

The Great River was too treacherous for travel at night. The boat always anchored not later than sunset, and I soon learned that tropical Africa has no twilight. The sun sinks below the horizon, there is a rosy afterglow which quickly shades into purple, and then, before one expects them, the stars are twinkling away, tangled in the branches of the tall jungle trees.

Perhaps I should explain here that male servants in Africa

are always called *boys,* whether they are *totos* of anywhere from six to twelve, or white-haired grandfathers of sixty or more. Our two *boys* cooked for us over a nest of coals which they kept glowing in a shallow jar of sand, and washed our clothes, somehow managing to smooth them almost free of wrinkles.

As soon as the boat swung in to a landing the black passengers who occupied the engine deck below us swarmed ashore, and for the next hour scurried up and down a rude gangplank loading fuel. Although they had paid their passage the same as we whites on the captain's deck, this *corvée* was required of both men and women. When the engine deck was piled high with wood, they cooked their suppers on shore, no two using the same campfire, but no two campfires more than a few feet distant from each other.

"Why do they crowd together so close?" I asked.

"Cats," was the terse answer from someone behind me.

"Cats?" I echoed, my mind picturing the succession of fat tabbies which had purred industriously on my lap many an evening as I darned socks or read aloud to Father.

"Leopards," another chance companion explained. "Now and then one will carry a child off, although they hug the fire as tight as they do."

"And lions too?" I queried, in a light attempt to show my knowledge of Africa.

"Not here," was the reply. "We won't run into lion country for about two weeks yet."

"There used to be a lot of them where we're going," Dr. Early broke in. "Why, I remember when I was a young man—"

But I never knew what happened when he was a young man, for he stopped and peered at me curiously for a moment before continuing: "You don't need to worry much about *simba;* just leave him alone and he'll do the same to you. Any self-respecting lion prefers zebra or a fat buck to man meat—

18

unless he's old and toothless and has turned man-killer out of the helplessness of age."

Our mission head and I shared the captain's deck with five other people—a Belgian official and his wife, a trader, a white hunter, and a prospective rubber planter. They were pleasant enough companions except that the official and his wife and the prospective planter spoke no English and my French was extremely sketchy.

Madame l'Administrateur, as I learned to call the official's wife, and I slept in one cabin; the five men shared the only other. The captain slept, ate, and guzzled a perpetual highball in what approximated a wheelhouse. I seldom saw him, but I know about the highballs because the trader bought all the bottles he emptied. As ornaments for favorite wives, they brought a good round price in ivory, goats, and kola nuts—one goat for an empty pint bottle, two goats for a quart, while a demijohn rated a tusk of ivory, a tusk which might bring anywhere from $250 to $500 later on the coast.

This extreme value placed on trifles, even trash, was impressed upon me one day when I tossed an empty tin can overboard. It had held some candied ginger and I had made a mess of opening it. It certainly never occurred to me that anyone could possibly want it, but it had not yet struck the water when a half dozen *boys* were overboard after it. The captain stopped the engines, stuck his head out of the wheelhouse, and demanded an explanation in tones that would have put an enraged bull to shame. Then he began calling out odds on this or that swimmer. His bets were taken immediately and others made between the passengers. In less than ten seconds I saw at least five hundred dollars waving in the air ready to change hands for what seemed to me no reason at all—five hundred dollars, almost the equal of my salary for two years.

It was scarcely a minute before the winner was back on board, waving the empty can triumphantly and grinning from ear to ear. His prize was promptly confiscated by the trader, with the full approval of the captain, and then given back to me. I protested that I had no use for it, and that under the circumstances I thought it belonged to the men who had risked their lives to retrieve it.

Risked their lives? What did I mean?

I pointed to the Congo, rough with great, swelling rolls and with a current that, on more than one occasion, seized us from the bank's edge and shook our boat like a puppy with a slipper. I, having done all my swimming in a waist-deep, placid pool in my father's pasture, would have contemplated a plunge into that vast expanse of turbulent water as certain suicide.

A howl of laughter greeted my explanation. The Congo black *boys* were as much at home in the water as out of it, everyone assured me. I had to admit that none of them seemed to experience the least difficulty from the time of the first splash until they had pulled their dripping bodies back over the lower rail.

But in any case, I had thrown the empty tin away as valueless, and whoever picked it up should have it, I maintained doggedly. Dr. Early remained silent throughout the entire fracas, but he watched me unwinkingly—weighing, appraising, perhaps laughing inside. I knew that he shared my feeling, but he dropped his eyes when I finally turned to him.

"My work is here, and Africa is my home. Why should I risk being expelled by the Belgian authorities for the sake of an empty tin can?" he told me later.

"Expel you?" I exclaimed. "You don't mean they'd do that just because you disagreed with them?"

"Oh, wouldn't they? You're new here, but if I, knowing the country as I do, still interfered with any Belgian subject's profit, I'd be kicked out so quick it would make my head swim."

"But what about the principle involved?" I asked him.

"Which principle?" was his reply. "Life is seldom so simple, even on the mission field."

But at the time, the captain, the prospective planter, and the

trader were all explaining to me, with a great deal more volu-
bility than logic, that while Africa is probably the richest
continent in the world, its people, by and large, are the most
poverty-stricken. There is little if anything a white man throws
away that does not seem riches to these folk. And I, personally,
had no right to devaluate trade. Even if I had no use for the
empty tin can, I must not give it to a "stinking nigger." Why?
Somehow that simple act would lower "white prestige" and
render my black brother even more odoriferous to greedy
nostrils. The trader offered me first a franc, then a shilling, and
finally an American dollar for it, which was more than it had
cost full of ginger.

"What will you get for it?" I asked in some amazement.

"A goat, maybe. Oh, I won't lose!" he assured me, apparently certain of my approval of his ability as a trader. His
companions laughed.

"I think I'd like to keep this tin can," I answered, on a sudden impulse.

Again laughter.

"A souvenir of your introduction to the Dark Continent?"
the trader queried lightly, and his companions nodded understandingly.

I still have that can. I keep threads and needles in it now.
It has become a symbol of Africa, Darkest Africa as I first knew
it. A continent whose most somber shadows were not inherent
but superimposed by the enlightened civilization of my fair-
skinned brothers.

I undressed and went to bed, but surprises weren't over for
the night. My bunk, like Madame's, had a four-poster sort of
superstructure. This was not any attempt at boudoir chic, but
was for the practical purpose of supporting the immense enve-
lope of mosquito netting which even I knew was necessary for
health as well as comfort. I crawled between the sheets, sat up,
and untied the lacings that held the netting out of the way
during the daytime. As the filmy cloth cascaded about me, I

giggled—it made me feel like a gigantic baby in a monstrous bassinet. Carefully I shook the folds of the netting onto the floor at the foot of my bed and pushed it into a mound above my pillow and against the wall at the back.

I had settled down to sleep when I heard Madame and Monsieur l'Administrateur outside the door. They chatted a few seconds, then Madame entered. Monsieur did not go away; I could smell his cigar and hear him pacing back and forth on the deck. Madame started for her bunk, stopped midway, and came over beside my bed to shower me with an excited volley of French. I was sleepy and confused, and the only thing I caught from the one-sided argument was a deep sense of her disapproval. But the only phrase of my high-school French I could corral at the moment was *"Parlez vous français?"* Even in my befogged condition, I knew that query did not fit the occasion.

Finally she gave up and started undressing. Madame came from the provinces, as I learned later, and while she was very Parisian, even chic, on the outside, she was definitely French Basque beneath the thinnest outer layer. Never have I seen such underwear, or so much of it on one human being. I lost count of the petticoats—with a camisole to match each one—as Madame stood and shed garments. Even so, I think she went to bed in more clothes than I ever wore in my life.

I was just wondering if I should venture a *"Bon soir,"* when Madame shouted, "Pierre!" Evidently Monsieur l'Administrateur had been awaiting that summons, for he instantly opened the door and walked in. Even in faraway Indiana, I had heard furtive whisperings of the lax moral behavior of the French, and for a few seconds I stared with the naïve curiosity of a child.

Monsieur walked straight to Madame's bunk, whispered something, and Madame squealed, *"Non, non,* Pierre!" But Monsieur was not to be deterred. He raised his right arm and brought his palm down with a resounding smack on Madame's plump buttocks. Good heavens! Was the man going to beat his wife? But both of them were laughing, Madame in a thin falsetto, Monsieur with great gusts of raucous merriment.

I would have liked to turn over, but I was too embarrassed to do anything so obvious. Instead I shut my eyes as tight as I could and wished desperately that I was any place else than on this Congo River boat and that the noises at the next bunk would cease. Presently they did. Then there were footsteps, but the door of our cabin did not open as it should have. I opened my eyes and almost shrieked; there the monster stood, not more than two feet away, staring down at me through the gently swaying net. Suddenly he flung his arms wide in that expressive, typically French gesture and again I was flooded with explosive language, and all I understood of it was, *"Non, non, non, Ma'amselle!"*

Then he bent over, and for one terrified instant I thought he was going to smack me too. But, instead, he seized the mosquito netting, shook it out, and, bending almost double, carefully tucked the filmy stuff in all around me. Then, satisfied that not even the most persistent mosquito could reach me, he clicked his heels together and saluted like a stage Prussian, and in three strides was outside the door.

Madame giggled, and I noticed that she too had been tucked in with the same care. Suddenly I had a premonition that I would see more of these two people and that I would like them both very much.

"Bon soir, Madame," I called across the room.

"Bon soir, ma petite chérie," she answered.

The next day I could not make up my mind whether or not I should tell Dr. Early about what I considered Monsieur l'Administrateur's "prank." I mentioned the netting on my bunk and, while I was searching for words, found myself listening to a bloodcurdling account of how very deadly the mosquito can be.

"We are passing through the worst malaria belt in Africa

23

if not in the world," Dr. Early informed me. "Be sure there isn't the tiniest rent in your netting, and that it is tucked in well under the covers and pillow at night. A little care now may save you untold suffering later—may even save your life."

In the end I kept my own counsel. I did not even write home about the "adventure." Sister Alice would have thought me an abandoned woman. In her world strange men simply do not tuck women in bed, even when their own wives are sleeping in the same room.

CHAPTER

3

THE next morning I saw my first naked man. I use the term loosely, of course; there were naked women and naked children also. We saw them by twos and threes in fishing boats, by tens on sandspits, and by the hundreds at the fuel docks. It merely meant we had passed out of the narrow belt surrounding Léopoldville where legislation protected the Victorian sensibilities of colonial females. Some people have hooted at the missionary's early attempts to clothe the native. By doing so, he was merely carrying out the will of those at home who subsidized him, and both groups were only living up to the social mores of their day. Even so, the missionary was infinitely less successful at draping the Negro than the mercilessly greedy white trader, who swapped moth-eaten silk hats and discarded dress coats for a thousand times their value in ivory and kola nuts.

It seemed a lifetime by various river boats, and then an additional week by *shimbeck,* before we reached our station. The *shimbeck* belonged to the mission, and because all missionaries are poor, it was only a small one, not more than thirty-five feet long. Dr. Early told me that it had been hollowed, by fire and obsidian adzes, out of the trunk of a single tree whose diameter was perhaps five feet.

25

Dried out by the fire and adz work, the shell was then plunged into a pool, weighted with stones, and left to soak up enough water to make it slightly pliable. After this it was raised and a number of forked sticks were wedged over the edges on each side. These were tied to nearby trees with lengths of thick, wet rawhide which, upon drying, shrank and spread the sides of the boat a few inches farther apart. This process was repeated until the finished boat was almost eight feet wide. But during the process of widening the trunk curved upward until each end of the boat stuck out of the water like the caricature of a Chinese junk, while at the point of greatest width the water lapped within six inches of the gunwales. Over the mid-section was a roof of green bark, stripped in one piece from some jungle giant.

This *shimbeck* met us about a hundred miles from the confluence of the Tani and Congo Rivers, two hundred miles perhaps from our central station on the Tani. At my first sight of this jungle cockleshell, dancing crazily on the swelling, side-slapping Congo waves, I laughed as delightedly as a child.

"Real, primitive local color," I told myself. "I must write home about it." As I stared at the boat and the twenty-one black *boys* in it, I noticed that each *boy* wore an ample loin-cloth. My first unthinking reaction was, "How silly!" I glanced at Dr. Early, but he was leaning over the rail of our boat, waving his arms and shouting at the top of his lungs.

I turned back to the *shimbeck* in time to observe an unforgettable spectacle. Every oar left the water at the same instant, described an arc, and halted before each black nose as stiffly erect as the bayonets of a crack regiment of the King's African Rifles of British East Africa on dress parade.

Once, twice, three times the oars were plunged into the air and the butt ends brought down with a resounding thwack on the bottom of the boat. On the fourth upward thrust the men rose to their feet and stood holding their oars as high overhead as possible. The *shimbeck* dipped and rolled crazily, shipping

26

water like a sieve, and the *boys* swayed like willow branches in the wind, in perfect balance. Then, oars still aloft, they broke into a sort of choral recitative, the only word of which I could catch was "*bwana*."

"They are calling you 'master,' " I murmured, proud of knowing one word.

"That's the way some people translate it," Dr. Early answered. His words were noncommittal, but something in his tone made me look at him.

"Has it another meaning?"

"It can mean brother, if the brother is older or well-beloved." He hesitated a second, and then went on: "Do not be surprised if you hear yourself called '*bwana*.' Only respect will be meant."

It really hadn't occurred to me that I was to ride in that *shimbeck* until I saw my boxes, crates, and miscellaneous luggage being tossed into the arms of our mission *boys*. Then suddenly I was frightened, and for one awful moment terrified, lest I should become hysterical and refuse to follow my luggage. But before I knew what was happening, I was seized by the forearms and just above the knees by four brawny hands and tossed as lightly and almost as unceremoniously as one of my suitcases into two big, black waiting arms. Then, very gently, as though I were not a robust farm woman, but something delicate and fragile, I was deposited upright on a bedding roll. A trickle of sweat plunged down one side of my nose and I pulled off my sun helmet and mopped my forehead. That operation over, I looked up into a wall of green water, and then soared as dizzily as though I were a bird and peered over the edge of the *shimbeck* into a frothing trough where the wall of water had been only a second before. If everything had not been so utterly new, I am sure I should have given way to hysteria. As it was, I could only stare and stare. I was in the middle of a new world, and I did not know how to react. Strange, overpowering things were happening too fast.

27

As I sat—"stupid as a hen," as I was to hear woman described so often in the days to come—again there was a burst of the choral recitative. And again the only word I could distinguish was "*bwana.*"

"Well, you made the first grade," Dr. Early remarked, sitting down beside me on the bedding roll.

"What do you mean?" I shouted above the roar of the Congo.

"You didn't squeal and kick and make a fool of yourself, and our mission *boys* are proud of you. If you had been hysterical, the black *boys* on the Congo boat would have laughed and our *boys* would have felt personally shamed."

"But I—I—" Unable to go on, I thrust out my hand at a wall of glassy water rising beside us.

"It makes one feel small, doesn't it?" Dr. Early answered calmly. " 'The Bosom of *Muungu,*' the natives call the Congo. *Muungu* is the greatest and most powerful of all the jungle gods. All the other gods are merely little fellows, fearful of him. If these, our people, Christian and pagan alike—even Mohammedan—believe you are favored of *Muungu,* there is nothing Africa will hold back from you."

Compared with the Congo, the Tani River, on which our Central Mission Station is located, is a mere trickle of water. There is no place, even at its greatest width, where both banks cannot be seen at once. I felt comparatively safe in the *shimbeck* after we had turned up the Tani. Of course we still tossed about like a dead leaf on a thaw-swollen creek, but I no longer had the feeling of being sucked into the vortex of a whirlpool that everyone experiences the first time he rides the Congo in a native boat.

We spent a week in that *shimbeck,* camping at night on the banks of the Tani, where I slept under a lean-to of bamboo and palm, only a blanket between me and the hard-packed earth, and a handful of blazing logs to ward off those animals that hunted and came to the river to drink under the cover of

28

darkness. Except for occasional traders and ivory poachers, we had passed beyond the usual range of white men and their high-powered rifles, and we began to see wild life other than the omnipresent monkeys, and the crocodiles forever basking half in and half out of shallow water. But the animals were shy, and more often than not my untrained eyes followed a pointing finger to some spot where a gazelle or zebra or rhinoceros, or even giraffe, had just been.

One afternoon, as we rounded a bend in the river and stampeded a herd of bushbuck which had been drowsing on a sand bar, our oarsmen shouted furiously and then fell into a sad lament.

"Ordinarily the Government expects a white man, or woman, on safari to shoot game for his porters," Dr. Early remarked.

"Are they asking us to stop and shoot a buck?" I asked.

"No, this is just a sort of dirge outlining some of the difficulties they endure for the sake of their religion," my companion answered. "And not without humor!" he added dryly.

I waited, but Dr. Early did not go on, and I had to prod him. "I don't understand just what you mean. What are they complaining about? What is it that is so difficult about being— They are Christians, aren't they?"

"Oh, yes! Every boy in the boat is a communicant. But they like fresh meat."

"And we don't give it to them?" I insisted.

"They have their own chickens, and they are skillful fishermen. And we buy them a goat or a sheep sometimes from a neighboring chief," he answered, clearly on the defensive about something. I did not let up.

"We *buy* sheep, with game like that feeding at our doorsteps?"

He looked me over again, carefully, coldly, as he had done on the street in Léopoldville when I had asked him to take me to the bank.

"There is a severe penalty for shooting game without a license, and a license costs two hundred dollars a year. A good dependable gun is as much more. Then there is ammunition."

He opened his lips as though there were more he would like to say; then shut them like a vise. He did not need to remind me that his yearly salary was exactly three hundred dollars.

The middle of one morning, after we had been in the *shimbeck* a week, a strange uneasiness seized me. For the next half hour I suffered more fear than I had ever known before. At first I was only mildly uncomfortable, and then waves of nausea gripped me and I felt my pulse hammering at every vein in my body. After three years in a hospital I knew just enough about medicine to fear everything, and yet I was too ignorant to recognize a simple case of the jitters, too unacquainted with Africa to hear the jungle telegraph the first time its curious sound waves pulsated against my eardrums.

"Good heavens!" I whispered under my breath. "Am I going to have a sunstroke? Or is it possible that I just can't stand this dank jungle air? I simply can't have picked up malaria so soon." Dismal thoughts of a forlorn return to the United States, beaten before I even had a chance to begin my work, filled my mind.

"Oh, no," I groaned. Anything but that! I could face savage tribesmen, jungle beasts, primitive living conditions, but I could not return to Alice, to our Board secretary, to the kind friends who had pulled the strings that had opened the doors of a hospital to me when I was old enough to have been the mother of half my fellow students. "No! No!"

The words were distinct in my ears, and I looked up in quick embarrassment. Dr. Early was smiling.

"Don't let them get you down," he said. "After you get used to them— Well, no white man or woman ever really gets used to them, but when you know what they are and understand how and why they're used, they aren't so bad."

His words didn't make sense. How could he know of the

throbbing in my temples, of the tension throughout my entire body, of the nausea that left me weak? Suddenly he laughed. "I don't believe you realize that you're hearing the big drums for the first time in your life."

African drums! I had read so much about them. I cocked an ear to listen, but Dr. Early laughed again.

"Oh, no, you don't hear them that way, not the big fellows, the jungle telegraph. We're too close to them for physical sound in the ordinary sense. You feel them."

I looked about me vaguely. "Where are they?" I asked.

"In the last village we passed. They're sending word to the Tani Station that we'll be home in a few hours."

"Did we pass a village? I didn't see it."

"You never see the river villages from the river itself. That would have made them too easy to attack in the days before the white man's policing, and the custom has hung on. They are always back a bit, hidden by the jungle. But you can usually see a well-defined path leading up from the river; that means a village. The Africans have a saying that can be translated, 'Every path leads somewhere, but the broadest path leads to the king's table.' Remember that if you ever get lost in the jungle."

Then we rounded a slight curve to the right and it brought us into an elbow of the Tani. Unlike most such curves, the river was broad here, and placid as a mangrove swamp between rainy seasons. One bank was a solid wall of green, looming a hundred feet into the sky. The other was a series of unbelievably luxuriant gardens, planted on a flight of natural terraces where the black "cotton soil" was caught and held by a series of outcroppings of uptilted rock strata. I held my breath from the sheer beauty of it while a strange, tantalizingly familiar fragrance almost stung my nostrils. I sniffed openly.

"The coffee trees are in bloom," Dr. Early remarked. "We experiment with all kinds of agricultural products that might be grown profitably here, but Tani isn't right for coffee. The

31

trees grow and bloom, but they don't bear more than a few berries. The soil lacks something, I suppose, or maybe it's the climate. Coffee seems to need colder, drier air and volcanic ash in the soil. Now oranges, lemons, custard apples, papayas—"

But I no longer heard what he was saying. So this was my *home* in Africa at long, long last. Without thinking of what I did, I rose to my feet as though that would give me a better view. Instantly an oarsman arose and, holding his paddle upright like a spear in one hand, clutched my forearm firmly with the other, but I had already sat so long in a *shimbeck* that I scarcely needed this help in order to keep my balance. The other oarsmen suddenly varied their rowing. Between strokes they clicked their paddle handles against the edge of the boat in a curious kind of syncopation, and the *boy* who was head porter on land and coxswain by boat, struck up a wailing primitive minor chant which the oarsmen repeated in chorus.

"They are broadcasting to the world that they found the new little white *mama* on the big river boat, and that they have brought you home to love and care for them for the rest of their lives," Dr. Early translated.

"That seems like a pretty big order," I answered.

"Yes, it is," he agreed. "But you'll be surprised at how close you come to doing just that."

The first cluster of huts I saw—"mission buildings," I should have called them—were dwarfed under a clump of tall palm trees. Their round, whitewashed walls gleamed in the sunshine, and the cone-shaped thatched roofs were so high-pitched that it looked as though they could easily split raindrops.

"Dollhouses!" I exclaimed.

"That is where the unmarried workers live," Dr. Early explained. "Each one of you has a house as your personal bedroom, living room, and study. Then there is a cookhouse, a storehouse, a bathhouse, and a dining house. You girls have your staff of servants separate from the households of the married couples."

He pointed out the hut that was being built for me. There had been much rain and it was not finished yet. I would sleep in the guesthouse, near the Earlys until the anthill and cowdung plaster of my hut had been applied and become dry.

"Cow dung!" The nonchalant statement that I was expected to live in a house plastered with dung made me gasp!

"Anthill clay, pulverized and wet down, has many of the qualities of cement and plaster," he said. "The dung gives it a harder set and a smoother finish, and it's the best termite repellent we've found yet."

The entire official staff of the mission, black as well as white, was at the landing to greet me. From the way the whites patted me on the back, not once but repeatedly, I realized that, for the time being at least, I was a breath of variety in the social monotony of their lives. In the Earlys' parlor, they pressed countless cups of tea and mounds of canned biscuits upon me. One asked wistfully if by some accident I had ever met her brother in Omaha—a good thousand miles from my home. Another, the sweat ever ready to trickle down her forehead, seemed transported to a nostalgic seventh heaven because I had once been in Boston in the wintertime. Massachusetts was her home state, and she measured for me proudly the reported depth of the snowfalls of the past two winters in the western part of that state. Suddenly I felt that these people were experiencing, in meeting me, an exhilaration akin to a night at the theater or a trip to a state fair. But I was not to understand until much, much later the honor done a guest when precious packages of cookies, carefully hoarded in tin boxes sometimes over an entire term of service, were brought out and spread before her.

The tea and the welcome warmed me, body and spirit, and presently I was dozing in my chair. Someone suggested that perhaps I would like to lie down and rest awhile. I tried to keep a discourteous eagerness out of my voice, but the tea party broke up immediately. Still, even as Mrs. Early, official hostess

33

of the mission, showed me to the guesthouse, a half dozen voices followed me.

"Oh, don't think I want you to bother with it now, but—did Aunt Clarissa send the bundle she has mentioned in several letters?"

And: "Brother Edward mentioned a crate. Tomorrow will do for it, but—did it come?"

Nobody wanted to trouble me with personal things "right at this moment"; everyone was solicitous about the rest I obviously needed so badly. But in the end we traipsed in a body to the boat landing, where my luggage was still piled high, and a confused sorting began which lasted until dinner.

I bathed in the Early bathhouse with the Early children that evening. A little old black gnome with a face like a nutcracker and the dulcet contralto voice of a grand opera diva scrubbed our backs—and our fronts too if she thought we had not done a sufficiently thorough job at any point. Then she sloshed water over us from the biggest gourd I am certain any vine has ever yet produced.

At dinner there was a great abundance of fruit and vegetables and a shred of chicken meat for each one of us. For some curious reason, domestic fowls in the Congo are miserable creatures; I never saw a chicken there larger than a scrawny pigeon. And it is not a matter of breed or attention; eggs brought from England and America with the greatest care produce healthy chicks with enormous appetites that seem to get them nowhere. As I tried to cut my mouthful of white meat into at least two or three bites, I wondered why any cook bothered with such a fowl when the jungle was full of game birds.

Further drugged with food, I could hardly keep the lids of my eyes apart. But there was no respite. After a few minutes of chatter, through the open door of the hut I saw two figures approaching, each bearing torches, and wearing what looked like white nightgowns.

Dr. Early opened a tin box in which he kept his Bible safe from mold and the ravages of white ants. "Time for prayer meeting," he announced simply.

For a moment I wondered desperately if I might not plead extreme fatigue and so be excused, but while I was searching for words, my host went on.

"For days our people have talked of little else than your coming. They will all be at church tonight to see you and to talk with you afterward. I have told them that you will have a message for them."

"A—a message?" I stammered.

"I shall read a chapter from the Bible and there will be a hymn or two, and then we will turn the meeting over to you," Dr. Early was saying.

It had never occurred to me that I, of all people, would be expected to preach. I gasped out as much, ending with a lame: "Why I—I have never even gotten up and testified in meeting. Goodness knows, I'm not a preacher or any other kind of public speaker."

"Now don't begin by making a mountain out of a molehill, dear," Mrs. Early admonished. "When Lemuel introduces you—of course they all know who you are to begin with so he won't tell them *everything* about you; it'll just be a sort of formal introduction you know—when he introduces you, you just get up there and tell them whatever is in your heart. You needn't take more than a half hour or so. Lemuel will translate for you."

A half hour in which to say absolutely nothing! For a panicky moment I wished desperately that the torches would go out and that I could slink away into the bushes. I wonder if I actually babbled something like this, for the next moment Mrs. Early was telling me that the torches were to scare away any leopards that might be lurking about.

Naturally I had heard countless sermons, but I should not have known how to prepare one had I been given all the time in the world instead of the few minutes it took us to walk from the Earlys' parlor hut to the rectangular chapel made of sun-dried brick. That chapel was pretty by anyone's standards. Even in the torchlight, I could see banks of shrubs and masses of blossoms that would have turned any American landscape gardener green with envy. I said as much, and Dr. Early grunted.

"Bad business."

"Why so?" I asked.

"Snakes. It makes an excellent hiding place for them," he answered.

Instinctively I stepped a little nearer the exact center of the path and shivered.

"Has anyone ever been bitten by them?" I managed to force a little false lightness into my tone.

Dr. Early stopped stock-still and faced me directly to emphasize his words. "Sister Ellen, when you have been in Africa as long as I have, you will know it is not what has already happened that one has to fear and guard against, but the improbable—if not the impossible—and certainly the unbelievable. Even the Arabs' kismet can't explain the things that happen here."

We stared at each other for perhaps ten seconds, then he put his hand on my shoulder and pushed me through the open door of the church.

The next half hour was a confusion of shining black faces and of hymns sung in nonsense syllables. I opened my mouth and tried to carry the familiar tunes in a string of la-la-la's but my tones were an embarrassing falsetto against that background of guttural sound, and finally I stopped and merely listened. Everywhere I turned my eyes, gleaming faces broke into smiles.

Then I was standing behind the pulpit with a hundred faces before me, each one upturned in bright expectation. And there wasn't a thing in my mind except the memory of the flowers just outside the walls and the torchlighted path and, beyond the dancing shadows, perhaps a hungry leopard. I looked down at my congregation helplessly; it was banked in tiers, according to age and sex. First the very old men, then the middle-aged ones, then the boys. Then the elderly women, the middle-aged ones, and the young girls. And behind the banks of black polls, most of them shaven clean, a thin row of white faces. Through the open door I could see many torches flaring, their handles driven into the soft soil beside the path. And beyond the dancing shadows, God only knew how many hungry leopards were lurking.

"There is a tribe of people who live far away across many miles of jungle and sea," I began, and before my voice had died away, Dr. Early, who was standing beside me, translated my words into Hausa.

"These people are fond of an old saying which runs: It is better to light a candle—a torch, I mean—than to curse the darkness!"

I am a nurse and not a preacher. But surely God was with me that evening and put words into my mouth—or else my people at Tani, black and white, for all their human frailties, are the most gracious in the world. On countless occasions since, when I have had to stand before a group of men and women in a strange village, one of my safari *boys* has whispered in my ear: "Tell them what you told us that first night in Tani, *mama*. That a woman over her cooking fire in the evening, although she is nothing but a pair of hands and stupid as a hen, is safer than the strongest man who rails against the night but does not gather sticks for a blaze. Then tell them that love of others lights up the soul—"

That first night I couldn't have said all the things for which they later gave me credit because I was too ignorant of Africa. But before I left the Tani Station, the women no longer sat behind the men in church. The benches were divided with an aisle running down between them, and the women sat on one side, the men on the other. We made that much social progress in a little over a year, which is phenomenal speed for any primitive community. People have told me that my first sermon was the starting point, and the statement always warms my heart.

Half the congregation escorted me to the guest hut. There they left Mrs. Early and me, all except two torchbearers who squatted on their heels outside waiting to "light" my hostess to her sleeping hut.

The guesthouse was lighted by a pressure lantern which hung from the center of the roof and shed a mellow but still quite good reading light up to ten feet. "Isn't the oil expensive here?" I asked.

"Twenty-five cents a gallon in Léopoldville, and then we have to bring it up the river."

Twenty-five cents a gallon! At home we had been paying six and seven cents. "I'll be careful not to burn the light any longer than necessary," I volunteered, hoping to show her that I did not intend to be extravagant of mission funds.

"I'll adjust it for you after you get in bed," she answered.

I assumed that she would turn the light out, but, once I was between the sheets and smothered in billows of mosquito netting, she merely turned it down to a soft glow.

"Leopards, my dear," she explained laconically. "We've had a scourge of them lately, and the best way to keep them out of a hut is to leave a light burning."

"I've never slept with a light," I almost protested. "Couldn't we, tomorrow, put bars at the windows?"

"Leopards are cunning; they rip bars out as though they were straw," she answered. "And then these walls, you know, nothing but mud and wattle."

Fine! I thought. If a leopard doesn't visit me perhaps an elephant will blunder through my mud and grass castle.

"We've assigned a *boy* to sleep outside your door so—so an alarm can be raised in case—anything happens," she was saying.

Mrs. Early's seriousness impressed me. Perhaps there was—there really must be—danger or she wouldn't talk like this!

Mrs. Early had reached the door, but she came back to pick up my shoes and place them on top of my other clothes piled high on a chair. I shuddered slightly. I am not a fussy old maid; still I do not like the dust of any street or path on my petticoat.

"We have to be careful about snakes and other things," she explained with a sigh. "Always look over your bed-covers before you shake them out in the morning, and always look under the bed before you get out of it, just—just to see what might be there. And always turn your shoes upside down and shake them hard before you put them on. Sand vipers seem to love to have their babies in the toe of a shoe. And no matter how tiny a sand viper is, it's terribly poisonous—even if it's no bigger around than a string."

Finally she was gone, and I lay staring at the pressure lamp, for the first time in my life thoroughly scared of the dark. At last, stupefied by exhaustion, I closed my eyes. Then I heard it the first time—a soughing, scraping sound. I sat up in bed—wide-awake. My terrified eyes searched every nook and cranny of that small hut. There was nothing there, nothing but my trunk and bags and bales piled up against one side of the hut, my bed, a washstand, and a chair covered with my clothes. Then I heard it again, almost directly overhead. Lying back, I scanned the muslin ceiling spread out like a tent fly under the thatch. All huts occupied by whites in our part of Africa have this cloth ceiling. It prevents the spiders, scorpions, rats, snakes, and other vermin too numerous to mention, all of which move into the grass thatch as soon as a hut is roofed, from dropping directly onto the occupants' heads. My ceiling that night was peppered with beetles and insects which made darting excursions toward the light. But there was nothing else, except a heavy-looking bulge directly over my luggage.

"Probably a piece of rotten thatch fallen on the muslin," I told myself, and felt curiously proud of my knowledge of

39

Africa. The thought or the pride—I don't know which—was comforting, and I lay back on my pillow, calmer than I had been for some time. Then the heavy bulge moved slightly, and again that soughing, scraping sound. Slowly, slowly it neared the edge of the muslin ceiling, and I stared like a hypnotized hen while what looked like a looped shadow oozed over the edge. Slowly the loop grew until it struck the circle of light from the pressure lantern. For a second it sparkled like a fold of jewel-encrusted cloth, and in that second I knew what had been sleeping literally over my head.

Then I let loose like a steam whistle. Even in my panic I was surprised at the volume and penetrating quality of the sounds I made. They told me later that they heard me clear across the mission compound, not only in the *boys'* dormitory, but even beyond that, in the native village.

And why not? There was a "plop" like a ripe apple falling in a puddle of September mud, and an enormous python landed half on, half over, the side of a bale of medical supplies not more than three feet from the foot of my cot. Still shrieking, I catapulted out of bed and leaped for the door. My watchman must have thought I was an evil spirit as I rushed past him, flailing with desperate arms at the cloud of mosquito netting which enveloped me.

A pair of eyes gleamed in the darkness and I gave a last despairing shriek as unseen black arms closed about me in the night. The next thing I remember was staring up into Mrs. Early's face from the settee in her living room hut. Behind her was a maze of faces, black and white, that danced about crazily before they finally settled into focus.

"I guess you're all right now, dear," Mrs. Early was saying. "But what a thing to have happen on your very first night here! I've been in Africa close to half a century, and—would you believe it?—I've never seen a python! Alive, I mean. And I didn't even get to see this one; it was so frightened of you that it got out of the hut almost as fast as you did."

40

"Will it come back?" I gasped.

"Oh, no! It's probably miles away by now," she laughed. "Like me, you may never see another big snake again. Let's all thank God that it wasn't a leopard or—or—"

She didn't finish her sentence, and I could only wonder what else might have visited me in the night.

Then, as I looked up at the faces about me, it came to me with the force of a blow that these people really did walk hand in hand with danger every day of their lives, and that they lay down at night with peril as a bedfellow.

I did not ask, and no one said as much to me, but I knew that I must get up off the friendly settee and go back into that flimsy hut and spend the rest of the night alone there. It couldn't have taken more than a minute to cover the one hundred paces between the Earlys' living room and the guest hut, and yet it might as well have been a hundred years. Every detail of that short journey is engraved on my memory, from the shape of the leaves momentarily visible beside the path to the tiny twinge of pain when a pebble turned my foot sideways with a sharp jerk.

Again Mrs. Early tucked me into bed, and looked around as though there were always some last thing she should do. My clothes were still neatly piled on the bedside chair, and my shoes still rested with their dusty soles flat on my petticoat. She could think of nothing but good advice, and she emphasized it word for word, one forefinger tapping the other smartly.

"My dear, you must never, never, never, ever again put your bare feet on the ground, or on an African floor. Jiggers, you know!"

Jiggers! The tiny, pin-point-sized insects that crawl under one's toenails to deposit their eggs. I stared at her unbelievingly, and then we both laughed.

"I guess a jigger isn't very much compared with a python. But then the snake was probably more scared of you than you were of it, and I don't suppose the jigger has ever been

41

hatched out yet that will crawl away from you. They're mean things too. Their eggs have to be picked out after they've reached a certain size, and if the sac is broken, you have an awfully sore foot for weeks and weeks."

Again we both laughed, and again she turned at the door. "But remember always to shake the snakes and scorpions out of your shoes in the morning, no matter how big a hurry you're in."

Then—such are the inconsistencies of life, even on the mission field—I fell asleep immediately and slept like one drugged until noon of the next day.

Months later, when I had learned enough of the local Hausa dialect for attempts at conversation, one of the mission *boys* reminded me of that night.

"The big snake reached from here to here," he said, carefully marking off with a jigger-scarred toe a distance my tapeline measured as twenty-one full feet.

"How do you know its exact size?" I demanded. "No one saw it but me. It had crawled off into the jungle by the time you and the other *boys* had arrived with your *pangas.*" A *panga,* used for close work, is a huge knife, something like an old-fashioned corn cutter, or a Mexican machete.

The *boy* chuckled. "The snake crawled off into the jungle, *mama.* Yes. We told you the truth when we said that. But it did not crawl far into the jungle."

"Why?"

He grinned impishly, but his eyes watched me carefully as he murmured casually, "Snake is very good—" he giggled and fell into the pidgin English usually reserved for traders—"very good chop chop, *mama.*"

I never was at all certain that first year just what mission mores demanded of me, so I pressed my lips together hard until I had overcome my desire to laugh.

"So you ate it," I said finally, with a perfectly straight face.

"Why not?" he countered. "The big white *mama* and all the

little *mamas* do not like snake. They go: 'U—u—u—u—uh!' when one mentions snake meat to them." His mimicry was delightful, and, encouraged by my appreciation, he went on. "Very well, let them leave snake meat alone. Perhaps the snake is their family fetish and it is right that they should not eat it. Nevertheless, it is very good chop chop for black men."

CHAPTER

4

THE next afternoon I plunged into my job as medical
worker for the Tani Mission.

There had been a medical doctor at Tani once—Dr. Mary,
as everyone in the Congo Territory knew her. She was an
individualist and, as a result, had trekked a good two hundred
miles north by northwest and established a station of her own
on the N'zem River, a tributary of the Tani. A great swamp
lay to the north of the N'zem which ran east and west for the
greater part of its length, and only a few miles away to the west
of the N'zem Station The Hungry Country began. During
Dr. Mary's term of service, The Hungry Country had not been
mapped; and as for exploration, Dr. Mary herself knew more
about both it and the great swamp than any other white person.

"There is life there," Dr. Mary had said, with a sweep of her
arm that included both The Hungry Country and the swamp,
"men and animals, but only God knows how they live. I know
the Pygmies, both the Batwa half-breeds and the true Pygmies,
but I keep hearing of a still smaller people who make their
nests in the trees—"

I saw Dr. Mary only twice in my life, but in my estimation
she belongs to that select inner circle of intrepid Afrophiles
composed of the Krapfs, Hannington, the Arnots, the Moffats,

the Livingstones, Stanley, and Mungo Park. Like them, she was an individualist, a humanitarian—difficult to get along with and apparently impervious to the criticism of lesser mortals. Like all great men and women, she was lonely. But she was not bullheaded. She consulted with others, and when she thought them wrong, she kept her own counsel.

Yet before I ever saw Dr. Mary, I came to hate her cordially, for there was nothing I did in those early days that Dr. Mary would not have done differently, as my colleagues told me, thereby implying that the work would also have been done a great deal better. I was never permitted to forget this fact for so much as a day; sometimes I was reminded hourly.

That first full day in Tani, for instance. No one called me, and so I slept the sleep of the exhausted until noon. If I had thought I would work into my duties gradually, that illusion was rudely dispelled at luncheon. Dr. Mary, I was informed, regardless of the exigencies of any previous day, was always up at the crack of dawn.

Lunch over, I was shown the cluster of huts that served as living quarters for the unmarried white women of the staff, including the skeleton of my future home. I carried two pertinent bits of information away with me. First, I must never use the word "hut"; it sounded too undignified to describe the living quarters of a "white." Nor must I say "kraal"; the connotation was too definitely "black." I could say "house," which obviously would not fit, or *"dukas."* But I never learned the exact meaning of *dukas*. Black men opened their eyes wide when I used it, and the Belgian officials laughed.

Secondly, the conviction was born in me that women can live too close together when the companionship is long drawn out, and they can possess too little of the world's goods for healthy social behavior. In the *dukas* that was called "The Parlor," there was a center table surrounded by a half dozen wickerwork easy chairs. Mission *boys* had made them, I was told proudly, and, quite naturally, I sat down in one of them.

45

"O Sister Ellen! That is Sister Agatha's chair!" my companion cried out in almost agonized protest.

Not knowing what else to do or what to say, I chuckled and settled more comfortably on the resilient seat.

"Here is your chair, Sister Ellen. Here. *Here!*"

I moved. I believe my companion would have pulled me out of Agatha's chair bodily if I had not done so. Then I realized that my chair, with its back to the door, the only opening in the parlor *dukas,* occupied the least preferred position. This, it was explained to me, was because I was the junior member of the staff; I would graduate to small privileges and preferments as my seniors died off or were retired. I sensed too that to move my chair out of the perfect circle described by the other, or to shift it a foot to the right or left for the sake of light and air and view, would be a *faux pas* hinging upon the immoral.

I was shown through the schools that afternoon too, and watched my sister missionaries struggle with the transplanting of our alphabet into a foreign language—a language which not only belonged to a different family from my own, but which was inflected by prefixes which were partly tonal in character. Last of all, I was led into a newly cleared space surrounding three roofless, circular walls—all that remained of Dr. Mary's hospital.

"There are always so many other things to be done—and then we didn't know what kind of thatch you'd want," Dr. Early weakly explained the dilapidation.

"I didn't know there was more than one kind of thatch," I answered.

"Dr. Mary always wanted atap leaves; but they have to be sewed and that costs money." There was a defensive air about his statement that made me wonder if we were talking about the thatch, or something more fundamental.

"Other thatch is cheaper?" It seemed obvious that the answer must be yes, but I asked because I felt words were expected of me.

46

"Wel-l-l-l, no," was the surprising answer. "If you have a grass thatch, you really ought to have a muslin fly under it to catch the dried and rotten bits that shatter off, as well as—other things."

"Pythons?" I suggested, and we both laughed.

"The truth is, we haven't anything in our budget for medical work," Dr. Early went on. "Dr. Mary had these *dukases* put up because she wanted them, and when she moved on to N'zem, we used them for storerooms for a little while. But when the roofs fell in, we didn't have them repaired because they were too far away from the other buildings to be convenient."

I wondered if it cost less to thatch buildings nearer the center of the compound, but I merely asked, "Which is really the better: atap leaves or grass?" Again my companion spun out a long, "Wel-l-l-l," and then conceded: "Atap, I guess. It costs more in the beginning—for workmen, that is—but I guess *you* can afford it."

I couldn't see that a few francs one way or another, francs that I certainly did not begrudge, made any difference, still—should I choose the cheaper roof in the interests of mission harmony?

But Dr. Early was speaking: "When I first came to Africa—more years ago than you are old—there weren't any medical missionaries, at least near us. We came here to save souls, and we preached the gospel." His tone was level, but his eyes were hard.

"Do you object to healing bodies?" I wondered if he and I read different meanings into the New Testament.

"No!" he spat out aggressively.

It was an awkward moment, and I suppose I should have said something placating, but, after all, had I not come to Africa with as good intentions as any other member of the mission staff? Was every newcomer greeted with this curious mixture of graciousness and hostility?

"I'll have the atap leaves," I said suddenly. "And while

47

the workmen are here, we'd better have the necessary furniture made."

"The atap sewers don't make furniture; our own mission *boys* do that. They're busy right now on furniture for your sleeping *dukas*. When they finish that, they have to mend the schoolroom benches, and the chapel needs going over." His voice had that curious air of one who has not finished speaking, but who has stopped to search for words.

"My furniture can wait," I suggested. "I have my camp cot to sleep on, and I can move my easy chair out of the living room *dukas*."

Dr. Early's eyes popped as wide as Sister Susanne's had done when I had unwittingly sat down in Sister Agatha's chair. "Oh, no, you couldn't do that!" he gasped.

"Do what?" I demanded defiantly. "If I choose hospital furniture instead of personal furniture, I think that is my own affair. And as for that chair in the living room *dukas*, neither I nor any other woman would spend five minutes a day in it with its back squarely to the door." I could feel my throat muscles tightening and my voice shrilling, but I went on, "I'll give just as little offense if I move it into my sleeping *dukas* as I would if I swung it around so as to get a little light and air—and so sat with my back to other people."

For ten seconds we faced each other as defiantly as a pair of cocks in a barnyard. Then two amazing things happened swiftly. I realized that missionaries, although set upon a pedestal by their church groups, are only idols of brass with feet of clay, simple human beings, every one of them. And just as suddenly, my companion endeared himself to me. "You mustn't mind us—too much, that is," he was saying. "We live so close to our work and so much alone with it that we lose our sense of perspective. I suppose that eventually we become ingrown a little—and like a person with an ingrown toenail, we yell when we're afraid something may bump up against us."

I sensed that the personal integrity of this man was pure

48

gold. What did it matter that he resented his poverty? But I have feet of clay too, and belligerently I held on to the small advantage I had gained. "Tomorrow morning I shall hold a clinic for—for the mission workers and for anyone else who cares to come," I stated didactically.

"You should have some patients," Dr. Early assured me. "But, you'll need someone to translate, and—and—"

"There's no money in the mission budget for a mission-medical translator," I finished for him. "I understand, and I am prepared to pay for the translator myself."

"No, Sister Ellen, you don't understand." His tone was as firm as any my father had ever used to me as a small child. "Missions were started by evangelists. Those who sent us out had one thing in mind: converts to our faith. I know just as well as you do that a sound body is the happiest abiding place for a healthy soul. But that is not all there is to the problem. Minds have to be freed from their servitude of fear by literacy. When you take an *assegai* out of a warrior's hand, you have to put something else worth-while in its place. This means schools and trade schools. And tools and textbooks. And the textbooks have to be written. Who are to do all these things? And how are they to be paid for? Oh, the Board back home understands the growing needs of the mission field. They want these things done, but they would rather send us three technical workers without tools than one worker equipped for efficient service. Why? Why!"

"I'm beginning to see some things," I stammered.

"You'll see more as time goes on," he added grimly. "And if you discover a solution, well—every missionary in the Congo would bow down in front of you."

Neither of us made further mention of a translator that day.

The next morning work started on the roofing of the hospital huts, and I held two clinics, one for the white workers in the guest *dukases,* and the other near the hospital huts. I had two white patients that day. One, the small daughter of the mis-

49

sionary who taught carpentry and operated a sawmill for our few neighboring planters in order to subsidize his work, had a sore throat. The membranes were red and angry-looking, and she had a bit of fever, but in those days we didn't talk of "strep infections," and penicillin had not yet been discovered. I swabbed her throat out with dilute iodine, and was about to tell her mother to give her cod-liver oil daily when I remembered the size of her income.

"Give her plenty of fruit and see that she eats a generous portion of liver, preferably fish liver, at least once a day," I advised. The child looked like a bleached-out little gnome, and I did not know whether or not I dared speak of the beneficial qualities of sunlight.

Sister Susanne had a toothache. Could I give her something to relieve the pain a little? I must not imagine that she was a dope addict—why, she didn't even drink coffee because it was a stimulant. If I gave her something, she would take it only at her most agonizing moments. She did not want to show me the tooth, but her face was swollen and I insisted. The tooth was almost entirely black, and there were three open pus ducts in the gum above it.

"I'll have to pull it," I told her.

She looked ill at the thought. I dissolved a sleeping tablet in a glass of water; at least that would take away her dread of what was to come.

"Take this and then go home and lie down," I said. "In about two hours I'll extract the tooth."

"I couldn't do that," she answered quickly. "I have classes all morning, and other work during the afternoon. Could you pull it right after twelve o'clock? I don't mind doing without my lunch."

I hesitated for a second and then I tossed a second sleeping tablet into the tumbler.

"I could wait until after you've had your lunch," she was offering.

50

"Any time you like," I answered. "Empty the glass. Every drop."

Twenty minutes later Sister Susanne found teaching on her feet too much of a chore. She sat down on a bench beside one of her small charges, blinked a time or two, and started snoring. No one could waken her, so they called me, and I went armed with a handful of cotton swabs, an iodine bottle, and a pair of forceps.

A half dozen pairs of arms carried Sister Susanne to her sleeping *dukas* and laid her gently on her bed. Then, although her co-workers were as much concerned about her as I, they left her in my care while they went back to tasks that they believed could not wait on human frailty. I pulled Sister Susanne's head over to the edge of her pillow and propped her lax jaws apart with a wad of cotton. There was no need for novocain; she had never taken a sedative before in her life, and I don't believe she would have awakened if I had cut off a leg. I prepared the tooth, picked up the forceps, looked at the festering gum, and shuddered. "You fool!" I snorted at myself. "What do you know about dentistry?" But men and women enjoying all the benefits of civilization have died as the result of lesser infections. That I knew well.

I took a deep breath, gripped the forceps—and began what was to become as habitual with me as the breath in my nostrils or the beating of my heart.

"God, our Father, please let that plagued thing come out all right. If it breaks off, I could never in the world get it out. You've got to help me, God. I'll do the best I can, and you—you—"

It was a pathetically childish prayer. And selfish, as all prayers born of fear are selfish. But it was sincere. The tooth came out as clean and sharp as a whistle on a frosty morning, and a month later Sister Susanne had gained six pounds and looked and acted like a different woman. But she never ceased to regret that one lost day of teaching.

51

Then came what I, in anticipation, had so optimistically called my first native clinic. I can't remember just what I thought might happen that afternoon. Perhaps I pictured myself in spotless white with an immaculate table of instruments on one side, and of course a long line of patients waiting for my ministrations. Nothing could have been farther removed from fact.

In the first place, there were no tables, there was no long queue of patients. There was nothing but a few bottles and rolls of gauze in a basket at my feet, three doorless, roofless huts behind me; and a half dozen old women squatting on their heels and mouthing crushed peanuts between their toothless gums. They were so obviously healthy that I wondered if they were there only because they were too old to be employed at some useful task. They stopped munching for a moment to look at me and then fell to chattering among themselves, eying me keenly all the while.

"Giving me the once-over," I snorted under my breath, and felt like a monkey in a zoo. I was helpless, and I suppose the old women knew it.

"I suppose everyone in the mission knows it," I muttered, and felt my temper rise at the thought. "Very well! I'll have this matter out with Lemuel Early right here and now, or—" I gathered up my basket and whirled about before I had fully straightened up again, thereby nearly butting N'ege off his feet.

N'ege was one of those strange creatures known only to Africa—a breathing, eating, walking, talking corpse. He achieved this dubious state as a very small child, when a witch doctor had given him up for dead. Preparations were being made to throw him to the jackals when he had begun to whimper and twitch his limbs. Everyone had been horrified, most of all his parents. The witch doctor had called him dead; therefore these signs of life could be nothing but the malicious perversions of evil spirits. No one would feed him or otherwise care

52

for him. The villagers fled beyond sound of his feeble cries and his father and mother built another hut for themselves on the opposite side of the chief's kraal.

Dr. Early had found the waif in the deserted hut and taken him home with him, but even in the mission compound N'ege's position was a curious one. The children were afraid of him and shunned him as much as permitted, while their elders treated him with the respect one shows a strange dog of impressive size. Finally, out of sheer pity, Mrs. Early had taken the child into her own home and was rearing him with her own children.

Of course I did not know all this at the time. I merely grabbed at an arm and held the urchin upright after butting him like a goat with the side of my head.

"I have a terrible wound on my leg, Sister Ellen," he murmured, in soft tones that pleaded for attention.

"Let me see this terrible wound," I whispered in anything but a brisk professional manner.

"Here it is," he answered, and twisted his body around to show me a hairline scratch on his right calf.

I would have laughed had it not been for his eyes searching my face trustingly, eyes as big and soft and round as an antelope's. "My goodness gracious, we'll have to fix that up," I assured him solemnly.

His entire face crinkled into a smile of complete happiness. I did as thorough a job on that scratch as any surgery nurse assisting in an operating theater.

"Why don't you wrap up L'ladbo's arm?" he asked, when I had finished with his leg.

"L'ladbo? Who is L'ladbo? And what's the matter with him?" I demanded. Then, without waiting for a reply, I continued bitterly: "What good would it do for me to see L'ladbo? I couldn't talk with him."

I cannot emphasize too greatly the inherent courtesy of the jungle natives of Africa—"stupid bush Niggers," I have heard

53

elegant ladies of the coastal towns call them because, having never seen fine linen and china, the untrained native does not know how to prepare such for another's use.

N'ege did not remind me that he had been speaking with me in good American English learned from the Earlys. And I was too full of my own frustrations to realize that I had found "a tongue," as many translators are called. He merely held up a slender, chocolate-colored twig of a finger and murmured, "Come."

There was even a bit of swagger in his stride as he stepped along before me. "L'ladbo works in the carpentry shop. There is a splinter of wood in his wrist. It does not pain him—it is not nearly so serious as my wound!—but there is pus about it."

In the carpentry shop I treated three patients in all: I extracted two splinters imbedded too deep in the flesh for the native's scalpel—a splinter of bamboo—and I lanced a gumboil the size and color of a wild grape. When I instructed this patient to come to my clinic on the morrow to have the diseased tooth pulled, he answered with an enigmatical, "What pleasure!"

N'ege and I went on to the gardens where I looked over a number of fat babies parked in the shade of a huge old silk-cotton tree while their mothers hoed endless rows of yams and peanuts. I was examining an ulcer on old Ndertoo's foot when Dr. Early caught up with me. Once again N'ege erupted with that face-covering grin and then scampered out of sight in a series of stiff-legged hops. I bent over Ndertoo's foot and cleansed the gray, suppurating sore as best I could. Dr. Early waited, now and then exchanging a word with one of the workmen. Finally I straightened up.

"I'll need N'ege tomorrow," I remarked in what I hoped was a casual tone. "Ndertoo must come to my clinic tomorrow afternoon and let me look at this foot again. And change the dressing."

Dr. Early spoke briefly to the workman, and the old man re-

54

plied in a half dozen guttural syllables. Without being told, I knew that tomorrow I would have at least one patient at my clinic. I gathered up my basket and started toward my *dukas*, trying not to look triumphant. Dr. Early walked along beside me.

"N'ege skipped Mrs. Early's class for the children this afternoon," he remarked finally, "after deliberately scratching himself with a thorn so he could be important."

We laughed together, although briefly.

"I'll have a linguister—a translator—at your clinic tomorrow. Of course you'll have to pay for him yourself; there's—"

"I know," I broke in, "there's no money in the mission budget to cover a translator for me."

Another moment of silence passed. Then he went on, "I'll send out word to the villages that tomorrow their sick—"

I scarcely heard the rest he was saying, for again I had visions of a queue of dusky-hued patients waiting for me.

"Of course it takes patience. Faith and patience—"

Dr. Early knew his Africa as I did not; the next day, and for many days to come, there were very few people except the same curious old women. But, gradually, these old women were joined by other crones whose faces I never saw in our chapel; therefore I knew they were "bush natives" from the surrounding villages. These women had ulcers and occasionally a bit of scabies, but for the most part they came for entertainment rather than for medical help. I talked with them through my linguister, an insufferable young man who fawned upon me and whom I suspected of browbeating "my guests," as I began calling the old women.

I chatted with these crones as best I could through a supercilious second person, and persuaded them to tell me about the younger women of their villages, and the children and the men. Then a few really sick patients were brought to me. The first was a young girl in her early teens who was an epileptic. She had rolled into the fire, and through burning, and later gangrene, had lost most of the muscles of her left hip. I cured her, but it might have been more merciful to let her die, for she lived an unmarriageable cripple. There were always three or four ulcers a day, and now and then a leper crept into the compound. At that time I didn't know about chaulmoogra oil, and I could only pity these poor wretches and pray God's mercy for them.

I had enough to do, I suppose, to justify my presence in the mission, but it was nothing like what I had anticipated. I learned African architecture by helping the workmen rebuild and refurnish my hospital. I learned to tie rafters and to sew atap leaves for the thatch. I became fairly skillful at weaving the crude wickerwork which is the basic framework of huts in our district. I learned the right proportion of dung and anthill clay to use in churning up plaster for the walls. And I helped apply it by the simple expedient of standing off a short distance and hurling great handfuls of the soft stuff against the wickerwork. I helped smooth the plaster with my own hands. Then, as whimsy seized me, I built up on one side of the central hut a bas-relief ℞, and on the other side an Hippocratian staff with twining serpents.

The workmen admired my artistry—and so did Dr. Early, I believe. But he was quick and almost vehement in his condemnation.

"Smooth 'em out! Smooth 'em out!" he commanded, and laid his own hand to the task of destruction. "Our hardest struggle here is against sorcery and black magic. These—these —pictures may be symbols of honest and honorable science to you, but our people would regard them as the same sort of things that the witch doctors rattle. They'd be your charms!"

CHAPTER
5

Sister Agatha didn't become my patient until I could no longer help her. That sainted woman suffered from what she called "a little tickling in my throat sometimes." Her furlough was not due for a couple more years, and she refused to go home before then. Give up just on account of a little "tickling"? Both Dr. and Mrs. Early had upon occasion whispered to me that she had "the lung complaint." She had a pathetic little trick of pressing the back of her wrist against her chest when a spasm of coughing racked her.

"Now and then I have a twinge of rheumatism in my arm," she explained defensively one time when she caught me watching her. Anyone could tell there was pain—but it was not in her arm.

I was amazed to learn that she was only in her middle thirties. Tall and gaunt, she looked sixty. With her unnaturally large, fever-bright eyes, she could have posed for the portrait of a medieval ascetic.

And the spirit of the ascetic was there too. "There is no need to coddle myself because of—of a little tickling in my throat." The only concession she made to her infirmity was to accept tasks that allowed her to sit while performing them.

But the morning finally came, before I had been in Africa a

full year, when Sister Agatha could not even sit up in bed, much less get out of it. There was nothing I could do except ease her pain a little, and I told the Earlys as much.

"Then we'd better send for Dr. Mary," Mrs. Early said, and it was plain to see that she was voicing the thought of the rest of the staff.

I was only a nurse, and professionally I had no right to feel indignant, still my back stiffened a little, and I heard myself saying coldly: "You are perfectly justified in taking any steps that you think right, but Sister Agatha is dying. I don't know what has kept her alive this long."

Dr. Early placed a fatherly hand on my shoulder, and cleared his throat. "Sister Ellen, Mary is the best doctor any of us has ever known. There is something about her—I don't know what it is— Well, I've seen her work miracles."

"It will take a miracle to save Sister Agatha," I muttered. "How long before Dr. Mary can get here?"

"Well, N'zem is something over two hundred miles away, and at twenty miles a day that would take ten days," Dr. Early figured aloud. "But not Mary. She'll start early, and she'll push the porters on right through the heat of midday. She'll be here in a week."

She was there in four days. Within an hour after the big drums pulsated out the message of our need she left N'zem. But she didn't come overland; she and a dozen men did what every white man in the Congo was afraid to do. She shot the rapids of the N'zem. But even so she was too late.

The morning of the third day, with no other aid but her indomitable will power, Sister Agatha rose, dressed, and went to her classroom. A few minutes later one of her pupils came running to say that she had fallen asleep with her head on her desk. It was that sleep from which there is no waking.

In the tropics we bury our dead on the day they die. I prepared the corpse, amazed at what I found. There was practically nothing left of the physical body of the woman; I could

58

span her waist with my two hands, and I lifted her as easily as I might a child.

The next day Dr. Mary arrived. Our black *boys,* their ears cocked to drumbeats almost too faint for us to detect, told us to the minute when she would reach Tani, and their eyes picked out her boat before any of us could see it. They chattered among themselves, and Dr. Early snorted in disgust.

"O Lemuel!" I heard Mrs. Early wail to her husband.

"What's the matter?" I asked, in honest but unwary sympathy.

"The woman is coming by dugout," Dr. Early hissed close to my ear.

"Well?"

"Don't you understand? She is traveling like a native. That sort of thing tears down the dignity of white people here in the tropics."

"How should she have come?" I asked.

"By *tipoye* or *shimbeck.*"

He bit off the word with such suspicious haste that I hardly needed to ask: "Does she have a *shimbeck?* For just one person?"

"She could have come overland, by *tipoye,*" he countered with almost dogged sullenness.

"But she's cut almost a week off her traveling time by coming by dugout." I felt that in some vague way they held me responsible for Sister Agatha's death because I was not "a miracle worker." My helplessness made me argumentative.

Dr. Early stared at me for a second, and again snorted, "You medical workers!"

Our mission head was a saintly man, and there is no way of estimating the good he has done. But he inherited his religion within narrow, denominational confines, just as he inherited the pattern for his social behavior, his emotional reactions, and even his phrasing in times of stress. I have never been as wise, or competent, a workman as he, but I was astute enough to in-

59

terpret his words. In those days no medical worker was on a par with the evangelist. My "boss" was simply hurling the religious caste system in my teeth. However, I was spared the childishness of a reply.

Singing, as Congoese always do when nearing a journey's end—but singing softly, chanting now for "the little white *mama,* asleep under the jungle trees"—the boatmen drove their dugout its full length up onto the sand beside the *shimbeck* landing.

I heard someone behind me suck in her breath. "Tsch! Tsch! Tsch! Short sleeves!"

And then even I shared the electric shock of the assembled whites. Clad only in a sun helmet and a bathing suit—barelegged as well as barefooted—Dr. Mary stepped out of her shallow dugout and was bending over to pick up a pair of handmade leather moccasins. She dipped her feet into them and straightened up. Her glance took in the tongue-tied group and came to rest on me.

"Jiggers! And scorpions!" Her knowing wink told me she had identified me instantly. But I wondered if, away from Tani, she was always this careful, for in the second before she had slipped into her moccasins, I had caught a glimpse of badly scarred feet, one of them with two toes missing.

I glanced sideways at Dr. Early and saw him drawing in a long breath that was a menace to his threadbare shirt. Dr. Mary saw it too.

"O Lem, don't be so stuffy about my bathing suit," she scolded in a good-natured tone. "I've been in dugouts that rolled over and it's enough of a job to fight current even in a bathing suit. I'm wet as a dishrag just from the spray." To illustrate, she turned up the short skirt of her Gibson girl costume and wrung water out of it.

I waited for the storm to burst, but instead my colleagues crowded around Dr. Mary and greeted her as cordially as they had first greeted me. Later that evening, as we sipped tea and nibbled the precious cakes again brought out of the locked tins, I realized that these people were genuinely fond of her, and that she knew it and discounted their envy and criticism as a wise mother overlooks petulance in a tired child.

Dr. Mary had very few questions to ask about Sister Agatha's illness and death. She already knew everything we could tell her, for even when the drums are silent, gossip seems to float from village to village on the African breeze. She sensed my feeling of frustration and more than once she assured me: "There wasn't anything you could do. One way or another, folks kill themselves all the time. Some think it a virtue, and others become obsessed with the importance of their picayune chores. All of them think they ought to be highly respected for their self-imposed slavery—and it does fight boredom."

I was eager for Dr. Mary to visit my "hospital." There were a thousand questions I wanted to ask her, particularly about my outstation work. Did one notify a village ahead of time that one was coming? And how? Or was word carried by the jungle grapevine? What did one do immediately upon entering a village? Was I well enough acquainted with the language now so I could dispense with the services of an interpreter? (I knew I was not.)

I had suspected on more than one occasion that my "linguister" lost the thread of my meaning in a hopeless confusion of circumlocutious courtesy that got neither me nor my patients anywhere at all. Too the *boy* was beginning to irritate me beyond measure. He was the African version of an intellectual, and he would have nothing to do with manual labor of any kind. Translating—improvising would have been a truer word —was his work and, not only had he steadfastly refused to render the smallest "hand service," but of late he had also begun to nag me for a *toto,* a small boy to perform menial tasks for him.

"Kick him out," was Dr. Mary's blunt advice. "Kick him out, but don't hold his insolence against him too much. To teach a man to read is one thing. To change his outlook on life is quite different. Literacy is power in Africa, and social power and humility of spirit do not go hand in hand in a primitive village any oftener than they do in America. And besides, when you're on your own, Ellen, you'll understand a lot more of what is said around you than you do now, because you'll have to, and then too your patients will love teaching you. They can't help you now because your 'linguister' stands in between and won't tolerate any interference."

"I wouldn't have judged, from the heat and the humidity, that this was as healthful a climate as it is," I told Dr. Mary as we walked over to the hospital the next morning. She shot me a quick glance. "The kids never have anything wrong with them but an infected toe now and then, and very minor abrasions on their arms and legs," I explained.

"These abrasions—do they look as though they had rubbed against the bark of a tree? or had fallen on gravel? But still absolutely clean?" Dr. Mary asked.

I nodded, and my white-haired companion threw back her head and laughed merrily.

"The *totos* are having an awfully good time with you," she chuckled at last. "They love bandages. They look upon them as ornaments, and wearing them makes the youngsters feel important. So they rub their arms and legs with the underside of an *eeysoe* leaf—their fathers use *eeysoe* leaves to sand down their drums and stools—and when a little blood appears, they run straight to you. They wear the bandages until they rot and drop off, don't they?"

I felt deflated, but Dr. Mary did not let me dwell on my embarrassment.

"What about your other patients—the strangers, that is— the men whom you never saw before and probably never will again? I know about the mission folk—suppurating tooth roots, bellyaches, and malnutrition. They need meat, Ellen. Africans are meat eaters, and you can't change a man's eating habits overnight without doing him harm. In their villages they hunt almost every day; here in the compound they become men of the workbench and there is no time left in which to stalk and kill the game they crave and need. Why don't you, as a doctor, do something about that, Ellen?"

I was already used to being called a doctor, but I quickly denied right to the title to Dr. Mary.

She brushed my protestations aside. "The African native draws wonderful distinctions among his own witch doctors, but so far as you and I are concerned, they see no difference between us. They'll expect as much from you as I'm able to give them. No matter what kind of case is brought in to you, pray and go to work on it."

I thought of Sister Susanne's tooth and wondered if I should tell Dr. Mary about it, but she was speaking again.

"Do you get any women among the strangers?"

No, I hadn't, and I didn't know why. "The men have badly infected sores, and terrible ulcers, and once I treated a young fellow whose arm and neck had been bitten by a leopard. He was in terrible shape before they brought him to me, Doctor, and—except for Sister Agatha, that is—he's the only patient I've lost so far."

"The strangers are always in bad shape before they come to you. Just resign yourself to that. If the witch doctor can cure them, he does. He sends his hopeless cases to us. If we cure them, well and good; if they die—well, that maintains his prestige and tears down ours."

We were both silent for a moment, and then my companion asked gently, "What about those patients who don't come to you?"

"Why *don't* they come to me?"

"Fear. Fear of you who are unknown to them. Fear of the trip from their villages, for they believe that when they leave the influence of the friendly spirits of their villages, they are exposed without protection to all the evil spirits of the jungle.

63

Fear of their relatives who may disapprove of such a bold step. Fear of the wrath of the witch doctor—unless he has sent them. Just a little advice from an old-timer to a greenhorn: make friends with the witch doctors if you can, Ellen. And if worst comes to worst, don't antagonize them any more than you have to. Remember, many of them are very intelligent, most of them are clever, and all of them have behind them centuries-old tradition. So do you, for that matter, but the witch doctor's tradition is known to his people; it's the framework on which community life is built. Your tradition is unknown to them, and sometimes when they try to adapt to it, utterly ridiculous mistakes are made. Not only in medicine, but in all walks of life.

"Did you ever hear what happened to Mrs. Early when she first came to Africa?"

I shook my head, and Dr. Mary continued.

"Well, she was going to institute what she called 'social afternoons for the native woman,' not realizing that a half day spent gabbling and guzzling tea would be looked upon by their menfolk as demoralizing. The natives couldn't understand what it was all about. A dozen or more of the women came, freshly polished with castor oil and smelling to heaven as a result, and with their best bark loincloths wound around their hips. Mrs. Early had never seen so many bare breasts in her life; she told me that she put her hands up over her face and cried from embarrassment. Then she lectured the women—through a 'linguister' of course—on immodesty. It must have been hard for a woman of Mrs. Early's generation to say the things she felt she must to the male interpreter—and heaven only knows what the linguister in turn said to the women. Anyway, the bewildered women were instructed somehow to go home and come back the next day with their breasts covered. They did, but they used the only bit of cloth they had for the purpose—their loincloths. From their waists down they were as bare as the limbs of a fig tree in January."

64

Dr. Mary eyed me sharply, but my nurse's training had knocked out of me whatever prudery my Victorian mother had instilled. We both laughed.

"And don't let that pompous husband of hers fool you, either," Dr. Mary went on. "That stuffy air of his is just a pose he puts on when he doesn't know how else to face a situation. He's had his experiences too. Once, not more than ten or fifteen years ago, he had some important visitors from back home— members of the governing board or something like that—I don't know just what. Well, Lem wanted to make an impression on them, and when they suggested that they visit a native village untouched by white man's civilization except through missionary influence, Lem had some notion of doing himself proud. He picked out a village carefully. Then he sent instructions to the men that they should come to meet the visitors, and that they should have some refreshments prepared for them. And he sent each man four or five yards of *merikani*—figured calico, you know—with instructions to wear it on the big day instead of their old, half-rotten, animal skins. But they weren't to wind the calico around themselves until the visitors were arriving; he wanted them to look unusually fresh and clean.

"Now, Ellen, that village acted in the very best faith imaginable, and this is what happened: The white men who had actually had the greatest effect on the lives of the elders of that village, and whom they remembered with the deepest respect, were the last of the Arab slave runners. These Arab slavers worked in loincloths and ponderous turbans. Consequently when the village went to meet their guests, they wore elaborate headpieces of *merikani* and nothing anywhere else except for ostrich down tied to their genitals. One dusky Beau Brummell proudly sported half a dozen sleigh bells dangling almost to his knees. They'd followed Lem's instructions to the letter; there wasn't a cowhide cape or bark G strap in evidence in the whole village.

"They had refreshments too. Wonderful refreshments! Goat

and monkey stewed together, with the eyes and ears and fingers floating around on top. And there was enough palm wine and *mealie* beer for the guests to drown themselves in if they'd wanted to. They could smell the alcohol in the palm wine and let that alone, but *mealie* beer at its ripest smells and looks like nothing else on earth than a bride's first attempt at custard. The visitors were good sports, and before Lemuel could stop them they had sampled the beer. The woman got sick right away, too sick fortunately to notice or care much what her husband was doing; he liked the stuff and got drunk as a hoot owl. He danced and sang and hugged the virgins and in general made an ass of himself. The villagers to a man loved him, and for years they begged Lemuel to try to persuade their white brother to come back and live with them. As inducement, they offered him free a harem equal to the size of their chief's."

As Dr. Mary chatted on, we rounded a bend in the path and came in view of the three huts which had once been her hospital and were now mine. I stopped and stared. The dozen, or at best two dozen, patients who would normally have greeted me were lost in a sea of mahogany-hued bodies. My companion strode forward, calling a greeting to this one and that, until she stood directly in front of the central hut. There she stopped, turned, and saw me still staring.

"Come on," she called. Then when she saw the surprise in my face she explained, "Remember, because of my age if nothing else, I'm the *Big* White Witch Doctor, and you're only the *Little* White Witch Doctor."

"Goodness," I exclaimed, "how old does one have to be to— to become as big a witch doctor as all this?"

"I'm seventy-three, Ellen," she answered simply.

My mouth fell open. Seventy-three and on the mission field? I didn't believe it. Except for her snow-white hair, she didn't look a day over forty-five.

"Well, let's get to work. That's why we're here."

First she stood up in front of the throng and harangued

them. "What were you saying?" I whispered when she had finished.

"I told them that of myself I haven't any power to heal, that it all comes from *Muungu*—the biggest God—that only he can ease pain and mend broken bodies." She paused to laugh lightly. "After all, it's the truth, and it makes Lemuel feel better—and maybe makes his work a little easier."

Preliminaries were not yet over. The oldest men were queueing up, and the first was already in front of my companion. One by one each passed in front of her. As he did, he held out his clenched fist with the thumb sticking rigidly upright. And Dr. Mary seized each thumb and gave it a smart jerk. As she did so, each man leaned forward and spit very accurately into the middle of her blouse. I don't know how many times this splattering greeting wrenched the breath out of me in what I thought was an unvoiced "Oh!" but suddenly Dr. Mary spoke up quite distinctly.

"Oh, shut up! If you can't stand a little of raw Africa, get out of the country before it's too late. Better still, try to get it through your head that our customs seem as bad or even worse to them. 'When white sisters meet, they spit in each others' mouths!' That's what they say of white women's kissing. Those who have been to the coast and have seen men kiss women look upon it as being as great a perversion as you and I consider homosexuality."

There were no *eeysoe* cases that morning. The small fry, gathered in a knot off to one side, watched every move of this famous white witch doctor of whom they had heard their elders speak with such loving respect. In the front ranks of the assembled mob were not the sick folks, but Dr. Mary's old friends. I never saw such patience and stamina as she displayed that morning. Every man and woman was remembered and greeted by name. And after the native equivalent of at least five hundred handshakes, Dr. Mary was wet from her chin to the hem of her skirt.

It seemed to me that surely all the halt, the blind, the ulcerous, of Africa passed before us that day, and when evening fell, there were as many more waiting to be treated. Sometime during the afternoon, limp with exhaustion, I burst out: "You're fooling about your age. You can't be seventy-three."

"Maybe I can't, but I am," Dr. Mary answered, without looking up from a great gray ulcer which had eaten clear through a boy's foot so that the bones showed like the spokes of a wheel. "And don't *you* begin talking about my retirement. This is my home, and these are my people, but the Board secretary in the United States has a one-track mind. Her little suburb is *home* for everyone else, and if you don't agree, you're 'a problem.' "

When Dr. Mary dismissed the last patient, she turned to me with eager eyes. "Would you mind waiting a few minutes, Ellen? I know you're awfully tired, but I'd like to see Chimbwe before I let the day go."

"Who's Chimbwe?" I asked.

"Oh. I keep forgetting that you're not too fluent in Hausa yet. A dozen people have told me about him today; he's an elephantiasis case. When word went through the villages that I had left N'zem and was coming to Tani, his wives started out with him. They arrived late this afternoon and he's been resting out there." She waved her hand vaguely toward the circle of cooking fires which were twinkling on the edge of the hospital compound.

Elephantiasis cases were common. I had seen many a man with enlarged knees, lower limbs, and a testicle the size of a goose egg or even a coconut, but I had never seen anything like Chimbwe. Few people have. He made quite an entrance. A six- or seven-foot path opened for him among those in front, then a couple of elderly women—wives Chimbwe had inherited from his father—came chattering along, making more room with all the self-importance of Oriental dragomen. Then there were two young, strong women—wives Chimbwe had bought him-

68

self. These were walking sideways, facing each other, grasping the four corners of a zebra skin on which lay what looked like a grape as big as a small washtub. Chimbwe could not stand and bear the weight of that testicle. A wife behind him grasped him under the shoulders and kept him from falling while he slid his feet out in front and sat down. At the same time, the two burden bearers in front lowered the zebra skin until it rested on his knees. Thus seated, he grinned up at Dr. Mary. He chatted for a while, there was much laughter from all sides, and then Dr. Mary folded her hands, closed her eyes, and thanked God that he had given her the power to help these people—and our workday was over.

"Chimbwe takes his affliction in good humor," I suggested as we trudged off to the unmarried women's bath *dukas*. "What were all of you laughing about?"

"I told him that if he were in the land from which I had come, he would make much money just letting people look at him."

"What did he think of that?"

"He said he doesn't need the money, that he has plenty of strong wives, that he has chickens and goats to eat and daughters coming on to a salable age, and that he wants his virility back."

"Poor thing!" I murmured.

"Why do you say 'poor thing!'?" Dr. Mary demanded.

"There isn't anything you can do except just lop his testicles off, is there?"

"Emasculate him? Good grief, Ellen, I had better kill him outright than that. African women haven't many rights, but they can demand to be sent back to their families if their husband can't give them children. He could stand the poverty—which is what wifelessness here means—but he couldn't stand the ridicule of being neither man nor woman. He'd turn his face to the wall and die. They can do that, Ellen. Don't ask me how, but I've known more than one old woman, her days of usefulness completely gone, to lie down, turn her face away from everyone, and apparently by sheer will power, cease to live."

"But—at Chimbwe's age," I stammered. "Would virility make so much difference to him?"

Dr. Mary laughed. "How old do you think the man is?"

"Why—" Then I broke off, remembering how wrong I had been in judging my companion's age. From Chimbwe's appearance he should be a hundred; but I knew my guess would be wrong. "Oh—sixty? Or sixty-five?" I ventured blindly.

"He doesn't know exactly," Dr. Mary answered. "They never keep records, but he's in his late twenties or very early thirties."

"But you spoke of salable daughters!" I thought I had her.

"Yes, his father probably gave him his first wife when he was fifteen or sixteen, and in Africa a girl is ready for marriage at puberty—'when she is ripe' they say. Puberty comes early here, sometimes at ten, or even nine, and never later than fourteen or fifteen."

The next morning Dr. Mary operated on Chimbwe and I assisted her. She gave him an injection of something that had a many-syllabled native name, and as she did so, she lectured me on the indiscriminate use of anesthetics among Africans.

"They have their own opiates," she said. "A good witch doctor has a knowledge of drugs probably greater than your own. They're all homemade, of course, but they're effective. But even if they weren't, neither you nor any other missionary could hope to alleviate all the suffering he finds. Oh, I know you have a little money, but it isn't enough—however much it is. And don't squander money on refined drugs; Africans believe that tasteless medicines have no strength. If you don't do anything but give them an aspirin, dip it in quinine first, because the nastier and more disagreeable a medicine is, the more faith they have in it. And the same principle holds for pain. To the primitive mind, all sickness is caused by devils, Ellen, and no devil leaves such a nice, comfortable abode as a human body willingly. It fights to the last against being evicted. Such a titanic struggle is bound to rip a man to pieces inside and therefore hurt him exceedingly. The bigger and stronger the devil, the worse the struggle to get him out, and consequently, the greater the pain, the prouder they are—after it's all over."

As she talked, Dr. Mary laid back the skin and began slicing off layer after layer of fatty tissue. A stone jar standing on the floor beside her was filled with the stuff, pushed out from under the mosquito netting tent under which we worked, and another shoved in to take its place. Then another and another until I actually lost count of the number of jars so filled.

"It's just as well," Dr. Mary consoled me. "Now he can boast that they were as numberless as the leaves of the silk-cotton tree and no one can contradict him."

She turned to her patient and murmured something. He only grunted, but there was a great burst of admiring laughter from the black mob outside the operating tent. I looked up quickly and met Dr. Mary's eyes.

"You didn't catch it?" she asked.

"No," I answered.

"Wait until you begin to dream in Hausa," she chuckled. "Then nothing will get past you."

A few seconds later: "Oh, I might as well tell you myself. A thing like that will get around—and Lem will be shocked to death. I meant to tease Chimbwe a little bit and accidentally paid him a very great compliment. I told him that, what with all this fat, it was just like butchering a hippopotamus, and hippopotamuses have a reputation for being great performers sexually. If I asked it of him, he would probably give me the first child born to him nine or ten months from now, he's so grateful."

"Will you ask it?"

"I shall ask that some of his sons be sent to the mission school here in Tani."

"Not that they be baptized Christian?" I pressed.

Dr. Mary straightened up from her patient and looked at me sharply. "I believe you can't *make* Christians or force Christianity upon anyone; you can *win* a few if you make your way of life more appealing than what they have been accustomed to. Or you can catch them young and bring them up to ways of love and forbearance and then let them decide for themselves."

That was as close to a sermon as I ever heard Dr. Mary deliver.

She was with me for more than two weeks. Technically, I suppose, she was the guest of the head of the mission, and she spent a part of each evening in the Early home, but her days were mine. And in those days I saw an Africa that had remained hidden to me until then.

"When I learn Hausa well enough so that I can go on itinerary intelligently, I'll find these cases, won't I?" I remarked half to myself as I wove palm-leaf splints for an arm with a month-old compound fracture which Dr. Mary was dressing.

"Then you'll learn surgery!"

The words were a challenge, and I was quick to deny pretension to qualifications I did not have.

"So, you think you're only a nurse! Is that an excuse? or a defense?" Reputation gave Dr. Mary "a tongue," but she had never spoken so sharply to me before. "Well, let me tell you, Ellen, in Africa, this far from any white man's town, you're whatever the occasion demands—or you're nothing at all!"

I knew there was no use arguing with this strong-willed woman; still I couldn't help asking, "Don't you think it would be criminal of me to pick up a knife and begin slicing away on a patient like Chimbwe?"

"That would depend on the personal attitude with which you—sliced," she answered. "How much studying are you doing, Ellen? None? I thought so. All young missionaries are like that—and most of the old missionaries too. But you, dear girl, unfortunately chose the one profession where more real technical knowledge will be demanded of you than in any

72

other. Subscribe to some medical journals, get some books; better still—better still—" Dr. Mary's voice almost died away, and she looked off into the jungle for a full minute before she completed her sentence—"come back to N'zem with me. I'll teach you everything I know, and I've got books."

"If only I might," I whispered, and I too stared off at the blank green wall of jungle while my fingers idled among the palm fronds.

"You're always welcome," she said. "More than welcome."

Perhaps I might have gone to N'zem right then if she had not amazed me with details of her work. It was not the twenty outstation clinics she often held on a week of itinerary, not the bouts of "magic" with hostile witch doctors, not the precious hours and days lost searching for some plague-ridden village that had apparently disappeared into the jungle, not the horror of having to deal with unbelievable human agony with one's stock of opiates completely exhausted—it was none of these things nor a thousand other similar ones that deterred me. It was not even consideration for what Dr. Early would have said to such a move.

I was frightened by the folk mores of my people. This sort of social hysteria, which a good many missionaries experience, comes when you find yourself uncertain of being able to adapt to a different civilization, really a different era in point of evolution of the human race. While it lasts, this fear is as limiting as the loss of one's hands. Could I preserve the inhibitions and restraints of my advanced civilization while all about me primeval communal laws were operative?

I didn't know what else to say other than a weak, "I—I could be a help to you, couldn't I?"

"Help?" There was genuine surprise in my companion's voice. "H'm! Yes. But— What are you going to do, Ellen, when—if a doctor should be sent out? The Board is always looking for doctors, you know, and when they find one, Tani is the logical place for him to come. That'll be wonderful for the

73

mission, but—you and I aren't the kind of women who can be happy at a lifetime of tying bandages, swabbing out throats, taking temperatures, and running errands for some man whose claim to domination is the fact that he wears his pants on the outside where everyone can see them. Better come to N'zem with me."

"What would the Earlys say?" I countered.

Several times during the next minute Dr. Mary opened her lips as though to speak and then closed them again without uttering a syllable. I was left to draw my own conclusions, and to decide for myself.

Basically I don't believe I'm a coward, but I stayed on at Tani. Nor did Dr. Mary again bring up the matter of my going to N'zem with her until the day she left. Then, almost the last thing before she got into her dugout, she turned to me before everyone. "Come to N'zem any time you like, Ellen," she said lightly. "You'll always be welcome there."

I thought she was letting go of my hand, but her palm merely slipped from mine to grasp my thumb and give it a quick, sharp jerk, native fashion. I had a strong impulse to lean forward and spit smack into the bosom of the scandalous bathing suit she had again donned. Many times since I've wished I hadn't smothered it.

CHAPTER

6

I WORKED hard at Tani. I can't say that I accomplished
much, but my days were full. I had anywhere from ten to
fifty dispensary patients a day, the smallest group always on
Mondays, and the number growing until on Sundays my hospital was mobbed. Dr. Early always tried to send them away,
but they wouldn't go until evening.

I was under the strictest injunction to "remember the sabbath day, to keep it holy," and I am reasonably sure that I was
watched so that any infringement of this cardinal prohibition
would be detected instantly. I could read on Sundays, and
write letters, and guzzle tea until I splashed inwardly, but sew-
ing was forbidden; nor could I walk in the jungle, since that
would necessitate the services of a *boy* to keep me from getting
lost—although not working myself, I would be putting another
to work, which would be just as sinful.

In two months' time I had exhausted all the reading material
at the mission—half a dozen tattered books ranging from
Paradise Lost to a very precious Sears, Roebuck catalogue. Because I've never been able to live in a vacuum, I was driven to
what many of us have said we always wanted to do but, most
conveniently, never find the time for: I memorized the favorite
psalms. Then I turned to the hymnal. I think I would have

75

taught myself to play the mission's cottage organ had that not fallen under the category of work and was, therefore, *verboten*.

"Disease, accidents, and human frailty don't know anything about a six-day work week," I protested on more than one occasion.

My reasoning was honest and, I thought, rather clever, but Dr. Early knew all the answers. They boiled down to two main points: I had no right to set a bad example for my African brothers, and, "Are you sure, Sister Ellen, *really sure* that you were *called* to the mission field?"

Consequently my largest number of patients waited in vain each Sunday until late afternoon and then, help not forthcoming, melted away into the jungle. Only a handful of the hardiest, or the most helpless, camped overnight or made the long trek back again on Monday. Though I felt that I had made progress and sowed confidence each week, my seventh-day behavior was unaccountable to all except those well acquainted with mission life. For six days I was kindliness personified, and then, for no apparent reason, I sat in my *dukas* and sulked while the unfortunate suffered outside my door. What report of me these people took back to their villages is anyone's guess, because the village African, like the socially diplomatic of civilized nations, will tell a superior only what he thinks one wants to hear. They were discouraged, and by the time a little confidence had been reborn, my day of hymn- and psalm-memorizing had come around again.

"My dear, Sunday is for worshiping the Lord," Mrs. Early told me primly when I complained.

I believed then, as I still do, that no one but a neurotic can spend ten, twelve, or sixteen hours in uninterrupted devotions. I went to church in the morning, but the rest of the day became, by social compulsion, that sort of vacuum which the devil so loves to fill with mischief. And—woe to us Christians! —the devil is such a canny fellow, so artful in his disguises, that we seldom recognize him until we have trodden the downward path for some distance. So it was with me. I took to letter writing until that innocuous activity became a Sabbath mania. Each Sunday afternoon I wrote detailed accounts of the Africa I was coming to know. At first I wrote of my patients—what they looked like, what they wore, the household gear they brought with them when they visited my hospital, their ailments, how they responded to treatment. After I had exhausted the subject of the sick, I turned to recounting the personal anecdotes my co-workers frequently shared at teatime.

I don't think I consciously embroidered these tales, but I did try to supply the deficiencies of personal modesty. Perhaps I fabricated just a little. And my excuse is—if an excuse is in order—that I began to feel that those of whom I wrote should be as human and lovable to my readers as they were to me.

More than one person wrote back to me, "I have shown your letters to so many people, and we think you ought to write a book about your experiences."

Finally a letter arrived from the executive secretary of the Mission Board at home. She had seen some of my letters and she wanted "stories," as she called them, like that for publication in the church school papers. "None of us knew, or even suspected, that you had this ability to get down on paper the poignant aspects of human relationships," she stated bluntly. "If you can weave these incidents about personalities together and spin them out into little tales, it will be a real contribution to mission work, perhaps as great as your medical service. I'm sure you understand our position in the matter, but of course we cannot promise publication until we see what you are able to turn out."

I laughed at the time, but I'm not sure that she wasn't right. The challenge of missionary work—to say nothing of its romance—is known to only a very few people, because, as a profession, we are pretty inarticulate. The only people who write about missionaries seem unable, or even afraid, to make their heroes or heroines anything but bigoted, or overly pious nin-

77

compoops. As a result, missionaries have become comedy material for the literary world.

Little of this was in my mind, however, when I received our secretary's letter. My reactions were just like those of anyone asked to embark upon a totally unfamiliar field of work. But I would try! Mornings and evenings, as well as Sundays, I sat up in bed and scratched my scalp sore trying to think up a "story." Finally I got something down on paper. I wasn't particularly proud of it, but it was a more or less coherent narrative of our part of Africa and it was about a real flesh-and-blood man. I never saw that man. Other people had told me about him—a word here, a joke there, a bit of description from someplace else.

When it was finished, I prepared a fresh copy and wrote out the title with a flourish: "Onege's False Teeth." But the by-line stumped me. Should I put down, "By the staff of the Tani Mission Station, a hundred native parishioners, and a half dozen chance visitors"? In the end, I omitted a by-line as I copied down the tale of an old black reprobate who did everything in the world he could to harass the missionaries near his village.

The story began with a description of the filing of front teeth, once a mark of cannibalism. The teeth were not literally filed. The witch doctor sat on a boy's chest and, with a stone chisel and wooden mallet, chipped bits of the teeth away—much as the Indians used to make arrowheads. The operation, unbearably cruel, was a test of a boy's manhood, of his general fitness to become a hardy, responsible member of his tribe.

Some of the teeth were hopelessly ruined, and when the boy reached the foppish age of young manhood, he carved others to take their place. These were sometimes amazing creations. Carved of wood or ivory, according to the wealth of the young man, they represented his accomplishments—a lion killed, or an elephant, or a leopard, or, if he had somehow acquired much wealth and therefore many wives, a phallic symbol. Some were exquisitely carved. But, beautiful or crude, these teeth were set on pins and inserted into the decayed roots in the young warrior's head.

Onege had many such teeth, some of which lampooned missionaries. Because he was something of an artist, the sarcasm intended by the ivory caricatures which protruded from the old man's repulsive mouth could not be mistaken.

Onege's best beloved son, N'Gurki, fell in with evil companions at a labor camp, and began developing traits of character that would unfit him to succeed his father as the chieftain of his tribe. No one would challenge his right to the tribal stool, as a West African throne is called; there would be no need, for the young man would simply not outlive his father by more than a few hours. And no white man would ever be able to explain the black princeling's timely death.

Onege knew this well, and since his son's ruin was being accomplished at a camp organized and officered by white men, his rancor grew until it was the consuming passion of his life. What the outcome might have been had the matter run its course, no one will ever know. But the labor overseer, recognizing the abilities of N'Gurki, and the danger to his whole camp should he continue his increasingly audacious behavior, sent the young devil to the missionaries. Under their guidance the boy proved capable of changing his antic ways, and Onege watched his son grow into a young man of poise and great wisdom. Potentially he was a budding chieftain, who could preserve the best of his people's tribal customs and yet live at peace with their white overlords.

Onege was appreciative, and he acknowledged his debt to the missionaries in his own fashion. He carved himself one more tooth, which he always wore in the presence of a white man. It protruded from his upper gum and extended over his lower lip clear to the tip of his chin. It was a beautifully proportioned, exquisitely carved ivory cross.

As I have said, it wasn't much of a story, and full of imperfections in the telling, but I sent it off and then forgot about it.

Several months later, we were waiting for mail. Word had come to us via the drums that one of the Congo boats carried a sack of mail for the Tani Mission. Dr. Early sent a couple of *boys* down the Tani River to meet the boat and in due time they returned. That evening the entire staff was invited to the Early home "for coffee." It was understood that invitations to dinner, except on state occasions, were out; family budgets did not permit much hospitality. Accordingly, we gave the Earlys plenty of time to finish their meal before we appeared; then, like good children, we stood around and drank coffee, because our mail, which Mrs. Early had sorted into separate heaps that afternoon, occupied the chairs and divan.

Mail day was like Christmas. All afternoon we worked from a sense of duty, as patiently eager as a cat watching a refrigerator—and almost as well-bred about it. But no one denied that this puerile supervision by the Earlys of our only contact with home was a strain. I saw Sister Susanne's hands tremble until she dared not lift her coffee cup for fear of spilling its contents. Quietly I maneuvered her into a corner of the room, took her cup, and poured the coffee into the middle of one of Mrs. Early's potted ferns.

"Suppose it kills it?" Sister Susanne whispered, but concern for the plant did not hide the relief in her voice.

"Suppose it does!" I muttered. "Aren't potted ferns a little silly in Africa? A few hundred feet out in the jungle she can get more any size she wants."

When every cup was empty, Mrs. Early, with a dramatic sweep of her arms, gave us permission to pick up our mail. We literally pounced upon it: letters from loved ones, messages from friends, months-old home-town papers and journals, the omnipresent advertising pieces, the enticing mail-order catalogues. Each heap was divided neatly into first- and second-class mail, and we knew that postmarks and handwriting had been carefully noted and more often than not the writer identified. Our mail in our arms, we edged toward the door, assuring our hostess that her coffee was delicious, that it was wonderful of her to have us over, and: "Good night," "Good night!"

I had one foot on the step when Mrs. Early laid a detaining hand on my arm.

"Lemuel would appreciate it so much if you could give him just a minute," she murmured.

"Of course," I answered, with what grace I could. I knew that the Earlys had read their own mail that afternoon, and I felt irritated that mine must be further postponed for one of their interminable minutes. I was not going to sit down until I realized that the atmosphere of the room had suddenly changed from one of gay hospitality to constraint. I sank into a chair with a sigh, my mail huddled in my lap, and waited for the blow to fall.

Dr. Early picked up an issue of our denominational magazine, opened the pages to a bookmarker, and held the periodical out at me. As I took it, my eyes fell instantly on some American artist's conception of a particularly hideous African tribesman. I looked up wonderingly. I had seen many such pictures—what did one more matter? And what did I have to do with it?

But Dr. Early was pointing a mandatory finger at the accompanying article, and I read:

"Onege's False Teeth

A Story

by Ellen Burton."

I was conscious of neither pride nor embarrassment—only overwhelming amazement.

"Why— Why—" I was merely articulating a nervous reaction, but Mrs. Early caught me up with, "That is just what Lemuel and I asked each other, 'Why?'"

I suppose I answered her, but I now have only a confused memory of accusations, sternly condemnatory from Dr. Early, timorously querulous from his wife. But what had I done that was wrong? I had merely tried my best to fill a request from the home office.

"Read it!" Dr. Early thundered.

Obediently I picked up our little magazine and read the story through to the last word. And the dialogue, as someone had edited it, was really not bad. As I read, I forgot where I was until I laid the magazine down and looked up into the stony faces of this good man and good woman of whom I so often seemed to run afoul.

"What do you think of it?" Dr. Early asked.

I misunderstood my superior often, but sometimes I knew exactly what was in his mind. And now, I was morally certain he didn't care a rotten coconut for my opinion of the little story which bore my by-line. Unreasoning anger surged up within me.

"I like it," I answered. "I liked Onege when all of you told me about him. That's why I wrote about him in my letters to people in the United States, and made up a story about him— when I was asked to."

Dr. and Mrs. Early looked at each other. Then one sighed and the other shook his head.

"I think more stories like it should be published," I went on, my anger continuing to rise. "Folks in the United States ought to know something of our work other than—than just figures. These people, our people, the ones we work with, are human beings before they are statistics. Inside their black skins they're as much like you and me, and the people who support us as—as —as two monkeys swinging on the same branch. Well, this story gives me an idea. I'm going to tell them about others here, people as irritating and as lovable as old Onege."

Then I stood up and my mail spilled all over the floor. Mrs. Early and I went down on our knees to collect it, bumping our heads together more than once. You can't remain mad at a woman under those circumstances, and I think I might have apologized for my temper had her husband only let me alone.

But— "Then you confess to writing this story?" he demanded.

"Yes," I answered, still scrambling for letters. "Why shouldn't I have written it? I've written countless letters home about Onege, and about a lot of other people. People like to read them—so they write me; and if they like this story, I'm going to write more."

It was a childish statement on my part, but I'm glad I made it, for it left me free to make what I do consider my most vital contribution to mission work.

Dr. Early stamped out of the room, slamming the door behind him. Still on her knees, his wife piled the last bundle of mail in my arms and then helped me to my feet. It was then that I saw tears running down her face.

"My dear! O my dear!" she sobbed. "Lemuel writes the reports for the mission. He always has, and—and—it's about the only way he has of keeping his name before the folks at home. He's very careful to mention every one of you in the reports. And now this—this story—it gives the impression that you did this work—all alone. If there hadn't been a school in Christian surroundings—for you—for the missionary who did it—to send Onege's son to—"

Suddenly she threw her arms around me and kissed me good night, and then ran through the door her husband had just slammed. And as I trudged back to my hut, I wondered bitterly if perhaps it would not have been better for me to be content to serve as my sister's handmaiden in Indiana. There I could certainly have eased very real burdens; here, try as I would, I seemed able only to add to them.

CHAPTER
7

Back in my hut, I reread my story about Onege, and, in spite of Mrs. Early's tears, I determined to try another one. I might not find anyone half so charming to write about as the old scoundrel with the amazing false teeth, but there were countless characters of whom both missionaries and mission *boys* and *girls* had told me. The boy who was imprisoned in the heart of a war drum, for instance. And N'ege, the Earlys' little adopted black son. Or the girl whose life was divided up into three periods of hoeing, each period marking a stage of spiritual evolution. The Africa I know is full of human beings, and it is still one of civilization's "far horizons"—two of the indispensable elements of romance.

I picked up the magazine again and began turning the pages, reading a paragraph here and there. Then I gasped and re-read:

"The Mission Board is very happy to announce the appointment of Dr. Charles Clyde to work in the Belgian Territory. Dr. Clyde is a graduate of Johns Hopkins Medical School . . . interned at the McGill University Hospital in Montreal . . . wife a graduate nurse with several years' hospital experience and special training in obstetrics. . . . Both speak fluent French . . . splendidly prepared young people. . . . They will leave in a few weeks to organize and head up the medical work at our Tani Station, where at present there is only a nurse."

I had known that for several years the Board had been looking for just such a couple. And when I had been sent to Tani, there had been no thought in anyone's mind, least of all mine, that I either could or should head the medical work for a thriving mission center. And yet those three modest huts on the edge of the compound had become mine after that peculiar property sense which is born of personal mental and physical labor. With ocher dug from a tribal "paint pit," I had whitewashed the walls inside and out; with my own money I had paid for the best material and best workmen to thatch each hut. With my own hands I had tacked up a muslin fly. I had directed a primitive carpenter in the building of tables, benches, shelves, even a desk. The medical unit of the mission compound was *mine*. How could I subordinate myself to some stranger? What would I do if I couldn't? Where— Dr. Mary, that wise and knowing old woman, had said, "You'll always be welcome at N'zem."

Suddenly I knew what I should do.

I think I was more cheerful the next day than at any time since I had come to Africa. I took more time dressing, and I hummed a tune that was not a hymn! I dawdled over my breakfast, telling my companions to leave whenever they liked. But we were punctilious about the small courtesies at Tani, and although everyone was sitting on the edge of her chair before I scraped up the last spoonful of porridge, no one arose until I too pushed back from the table.

"What has come over Sister Ellen?" I could read the silent query on their faces. And, "In all my four terms of service, I have never been late to class before," one murmured to another as I picked up a banana to carry to the hospital for midmorning lunch. There was no one in sight when I started for my hospital; the entire mission was at work as I strolled along, as Kipling's elephant returned aforetime, if not without a care in the world, certainly with the rebellious intention of not troubling myself unduly.

The school unit, like my hospital, was a cluster of huts, each teacher presiding in one of them. My path lay so close to Sister Susanne's hut that I could have put out my fingers and brushed the wall. As I strolled by, there was a little buzz, a pleasant, homey, comfortable sound, and I stopped to enjoy it for a moment. Prayers obviously were over, and Sister Susanne was explaining in Hausa:

"We are late this morning, children, so I shall have to tell you a shorter story than usual.

"Once upon a time there was a village where for several seasons everything went wrong. All kinds of bad luck fell on the people, through no fault of their own. The rains which should have fallen did not fall at all, not even the tiniest drop, and the land became as parched and dry as a desert. The women planted their beans and squashes as usual, but the little seeds lay in the dry earth and didn't sprout. Finally the ground mice ate them all up. So the women planted again, but the same thing happened all over. Even the streams dried up and the fish died and rotted in the mud."

"Oh, no, Sister Susanne!" I heard a tiny voice. "Our fish bury themselves in the mud and sleep and then come awake again and swim off when there is more water."

"Well, perhaps that is what these fish did too. Anyway, they disappeared. The leaves shriveled on the trees in the forests, and the game animals went far, far away to other parts of the country where there was water for them to drink and green grass and leaves for them to eat. At last the locusts came in a hungry cloud and ate the buds and even the bark off the dying trees. In the end, everyone who could not leave the village died of starvation. Among those who went away was a widow and her small son. They traveled many days until they came to a green land which did not look as though it would ever dry up and become parched.

" 'This looks as though it would do,' said the woman; and she looked about for a safe place to build her hut. She had no husband to protect her and her son from the wild animals, so she had to choose a place where it would be difficult for wild animals to come. At last she found such a spot right on the top of a small mountain whose sides were very steep and rocky. There the woman left her little boy while she planted a garden in the valley below.

" 'Now don't you ever leave the mountaintop while I'm gone,' the woman said to her son. 'Because if you do, the lions and leopards which are all about will pounce on you and eat you.'

" 'No, Mother,' said the little boy, 'I won't leave the top of the mountain.'

"The first day, while the mother was working in the valley below, a lion came to the path leading up to the top of the mountain and tried to climb it, but his clumsy feet merely pulled stones down and finally he gave up trying. So he called to the boy: 'Come on down and play with me, little fellow. We'll have such fun if you do.'

" 'No,' answered the boy. 'I must not. My mother has forbidden it. You come up here and play with me.'

" 'There isn't room up there for me to play,' the lion replied. 'One leap and I'd be over a cliff and that would be the end of me. You come down.'

"But the boy remembered what his mother had said to him, and he would not leave the top of the mountain.

"The next day a leopard came along, saw the little boy at the top of the mountain, and thought to himself, 'Ah, a fine dinner for me without my going any farther!' Then he too tried to climb the mountain—"

Standing outside the schoolroom hut, I smiled tolerantly. Would Sister Susanne, like the villager from whom she had undoubtedly heard the tale, recount the visit of animal after animal? No native leaves out the smallest detail of a story, no matter how repetitious or long-drawn-out it may become. But Sister Susanne had promised that her story would be short.

"At last a rabbit came to the foot of the hill and looked up at the little boy. 'Come on down and play with me,' he called.

" 'No,' answered the little boy. 'You come up and play with me.'

" 'I can't get up,' the rabbit answered honestly. 'The stones roll back on me. And anyway, your mountaintop is really too small; if either of us ran or jumped, we'd go over a cliff and be killed.'

"The little boy knew the rabbit was telling the truth and he liked him for it. For that reason, and because he was lonely, he lay on his stomach and looked over the edge of the cliff and talked to the rabbit for a while. Suddenly he thought to himself: 'Why shouldn't I go down and play with the rabbit? He won't eat me. Why, he's so small he couldn't hurt me if he wanted to!' So without another second's hesitation the little boy scrambled down the path and he and the rabbit had a glorious romp together. They played so hard that neither one of them heard the lion. Neither one knew that the king of the beasts was anywhere about until *simba* pounced upon the rabbit and pinned him to the earth with one of his great paws.

"The little boy was petrified with fear. He couldn't run from a great beast like *simba*. In fact, what could he do to save himself? And then, he could scarcely believe his ears.

" 'Take him. Eat the little boy,' the rabbit was screaming. 'There's more meat on his bones than on a dozen rabbits. If you will spare my life, I will even cook him for you.'

"Well, in less than five minutes the rabbit had a fire going and a pot bubbling over it; and curled up inside the pot was the little boy, simmering away like a mess of fish and wild spinach.

"The lion lay down under a tree to take a nap until his lunch

88

should be ready, and the rabbit busied himself gathering fire-wood and keeping a good hot blaze under the pot.

"Now as everyone knows, the rabbit is not a meat eater. Ordinarily he wouldn't trade a leaf of wild celery for the biggest fish or the fattest antelope in the jungle; but he was curious. He lifted the lid off the pot and looked in to see how things were going with his playmate of only a few minutes ago and the most delicious odor he had ever sniffed wafted about his nostrils.

" 'I wonder how meat tastes,' he said to himself, and stared at the little boy for a long time. Then he whispered to himself again, 'If I took just one ear, it is so tiny the lion would never miss it.' So he cut off an ear and ate it down to the last scrap and licked his paws.

" 'H'm,' he said to himself again, 'the boy looks funny with only one ear. Maybe I'd better take the other so as to balance him up.' So he cut off the other ear and ate that too.

"He was still staring into the pot when the lion woke up and came over to ask how his lunch was getting on. Then *simba* saw that the little boy's ears were gone, and he roared in anger.

" 'You sneak! You thief!' he bellowed. 'You've been nibbling at my lunch. You've eaten the boy's ears.'

" 'Oh, no!' the rabbit squeaked in terror. And then, in order to save his own skin, he lied again, 'The boy hadn't any ears.'

" 'You fool! You cheat!' the lion snorted. 'All human beings have ears.'

" 'This little fellow didn't!' the rabbit squeaked.

" 'Yes, he did!'

" 'No, he didn't!'

"Just then the little boy's mother came along, going home from her work in her garden. She stopped and stared in amazement. Surely one never saw a stranger sight than a lion and a rabbit quarreling at the top of their voices in the middle of a jungle.

" 'What's the matter?' she called.

" 'Ask her,' squeaked the rabbit in desperation. 'She will tell you that her little son had no ears.'

" 'Very well,' said the lion. 'I'll ask her. Madame, did or did not the little fellow who used to live at the top of the hill have any ears?'

"The woman knew immediately what had happened, but in order to make sure, she walked over and looked down into the cooking pot.

" 'No,' she answered slowly, after a moment of thought, 'my little son did not have ears. If he had had ears, he would have listened to his mother, and he would certainly have heard me tell him never to leave the safety of his mountaintop and come down into the valley to play with the jungle beasts—whether they be big and strong like the lion or little and timid like the rabbit. No, my son proved by his actions that he had no ears!' Then the woman picked up her hoe and trudged off to her lonely mountaintop."

I stood outside the hut a few seconds longer enjoying that almost imperceptible bustle of a schoolroom settling down to work. Then I lifted one foot and set it back down in exactly the same spot, as sudden realization hit me with all the force of a physical blow. Sister Susanne had told the story in Hausa and I had understood every word without a translator. I had ears! I had ears at last! I could go anywhere I chose now without upsetting the routine of the mission. I could go on itinerary to our neighboring villages. I could go to N'zem without being a burden to Dr. Mary. All that day I looked at each patient who passed before me and wondered how I would feel toward him and how I would treat any or all if they were my people—just mine and God's—and did not belong also to others "older, wiser, and more experienced," who figuratively at least peered over my shoulder and criticized each dose of medicine I doled out.

That morning I dismissed my linguister. "Never again!" I promised myself as I shooed him out of sight. And I was so exhilarated by the new independence that I did not hear the big drums when they began booming through the jungle like a monstrous heartbeat. But I noticed at last that my patients were listening, listening and watching me curiously.

"What is it?" I demanded of the *pickinin* for whom I had just lanced an abscess behind the left ear.

"The drums say that the *big* white witch doctor is dead," he answered.

I was stunned. True, Dr. Mary had told me that she was seventy-three, but she had been in good health only a few months ago, and there seemed to be something eternal about the woman, like the jungle in which she lived.

The drums stopped, and for a few seconds the air about me was curiously empty of depth. I stared wordlessly at my handful of patients and they stared back at me. Was it a new sense of respect I saw in their eyes? Then I realized that now I had become the *big* white witch doctor, for in Africa a witch passes on his bag of tricks as estate in exactly the same way an Indiana farmer passes on his acres.

Then the drums began again, this time so close that we felt rather than heard them. It was the mission drums speaking across the miles of jungle. I knew that in the next village men were listening, and that when our drummer should stop, one among them would take up his sticks and repeat the message exactly, beat for beat, and that this would continue in still more distant villages until the ones for whom the drums were speaking should hear with their own ears.

When there was a slight lull, I opened my mouth to ask what our message had been and to whom; but the drums boomed out again and, like my patients, I waited silently. Then it was all over, and an old man spoke up.

"The drums spoke with two voices," he began.

So there were two different messages.

"With the first voice, they told the people of N'zem to go back into the *big* white witch doctor's *dukas* and to take care of

her. The-Round-Little-Man-Who-Talks-Often-to-*Muungu*"—
in other words Dr. Early, the one who prays often in public—
"assured them that her spirit is not evil and that, even should
she die, no harm would come to them from her naked spirit.
Then he threatened them with the vengeance of the white men
with guns"—the civil administrators—"if they let her suffer
from neglect.

"The second voice spoke to the people of the *big* white witch
doctor's own home village, wherever their kraals may stand."
That is, a telegram was being relayed to Léopoldville for trans-
mission to the United States. "It said that her years are too
many, and that the unseen ones of the jungle now beckon to her
spirit."

I knew that the old man had translated the messages of the
drums exactly; still, if it were true that Dr. Mary was dead,
what he had said did not make too much sense. I smiled
grimly; only a few short hours ago I had been so certain that
now I had ears. But I had forgotten that the children of the
Dark Continent speak with as many different voices as their
lighter-skinned brothers. Hurriedly, I did what I could to
relieve those of my patients who were suffering and sent all of
them away. Then I almost ran to the Early home.

When I got there, preparations for a long safari were already
well under way. At least fifty *boys* were squatting on the grass
before the living room *dukas;* there were porters with bundles
of food, cooking utensils, tent, and camping supplies; twelve
men were grouped around Dr. Early's *tipoye*. Three sets of
carriers for this combination hammock-sedan chair! Dr. Early
meant to travel fast. Inside the *dukas,* I tried to ask questions,
but no one had time to stop and explain all that was going on. I
turned to a luggage roll Mrs. Early always kept packed for
emergency trips and helped her check over her husband's kit: a
change of nightshirts, Stick-tite for his false teeth, soap, first-aid
kit—everything was in perfect order. Finally we saw Dr. Early
and his retinue of mission *boys,* at least half of them only one

generation or less removed from cannibalism, row across the river and trot off into the jungle on a long trek that would have tried the stamina of a young fellow in the prime of life.

Then Mrs. Early explained to me: "We don't know just how bad off Dr. Mary is. Oh, I know the message said she was dead, but that just means they expect her to die. And when they say it of a person—particularly one of their own people—that person usually does die. But Mary may be alive when Lemuel gets there; she's not young any more, but she's strong, and she—she—"

Words failed Mrs. Early until something in my face prodded her on again.

"Oh! Of course, I keep forgetting you don't know as much about Africa as the rest of us. You see, natives, before they become Christian, believe that the spirit is probably a malignant thing, and they don't like to take chances with it. When they think a person is stricken mortally, they leave that person alone until after death—unless, of course, it is a chief or someone like that. They hope the spirit will be away or in a pleasant frame of mind when they come back to the hut to remove the body. Then they burn the hut so that the spirit will not try to live among them any more. And in order to make sure of that, they build the spirit a tiny hut off somewhere in the jungle and put the dead man's or woman's most prized possessions in it, after breaking them so no vandal will carry them away."

"If Dr. Mary is as sick as the natives think she is, why didn't I go instead of Dr. Early?"

"Why-y-y-y-y! Lemuel is the head of the mission; it's his *duty* to go."

"But if she is alive, can he treat her? or take care of her?" I protested.

The familiar frustrated, yet stubborn, look crept into Mrs. Early's eyes and her voice was hard as she countered, "If Sister Mary is dead, could you give her Christian burial?"

I stared at this good woman, wishing that I had the gift of

words—words that would not arouse anger but would compel people to listen and win them to my way of thinking. I felt forlornly that, no matter what I said, this woman—I repeat, this good woman—would immediately take issue with it. Surely she believed, as I did, that one Dr. Mary alive was worth a hundred, or a thousand, Dr. Marys with six feet of jungle mold and a little wooden cross above her head.

"What—will the—Board say?" I managed to get out.

It was capitulation to the mores of mission life. Mrs. Early recognized it, and I watched the lines of her face soften as she went on. "They'll tell Lemuel to send her home. They always do when he mentions her age in a monthly or quarterly report. This time, now that she is really sick, I—hope they say to drag her out of there by the hair of her head if necessary. It's—it's indecent, her working away off up there all by herself."

"Not—indecent!"

"Well, why doesn't she go home to her people and behave as an old woman ought to!"

It wasn't a question, but I tried to answer nevertheless. "Maybe she feels that this is home, and that she is among her people."

"Nonsense!"

A reply came from the Mission Board that afternoon. It might take us from six weeks to three months to get our mail, but we were never more than an hour from the nearest cable office. Down in Léopoldville the cable operator, using a mission code book, translated the crazy alphabet that had come over the wires into words that the jungle telegraph in turn boomed to us through the reaches of primeval forest.

"SEND MARY EVANS HOME."

"Drag her out of N'zem by the hair of her head," I murmured sarcastically when Mrs. Early transferred the message to old T'oomi, our mission drummer.

"Yes, *bwana*," he murmured to each of us in turn and flung his head upward to signify that he understood perfectly.

94

A month later Dr. Early and Dr. Mary were back at Tani. Dr. Mary was scarcely more than skin and bones, and I suppose for the first time in her life she really looked her years, but her eyes were clear and she was almost spry. She was with us for a little better than a week, waiting until boat connections were available at Léopoldville. During those days she went with me to my hospital every day, and sat or lay in a palm fiber hammock and gave sage, and on occasion even gay, advice while I ministered to my patients.

It was a trivial thing to have irked me, I know, but once I asked her point-blank, "What do you think about medical work on Sunday?"

"Ellen, there were doctors before there were Christians, and down through the Christian Era doctors have continued to take the original pagan oath of service. I have never felt there was any incongruity in this. You came from a farm, and you understand why it is that a farmer must work on the Sabbath —six-day cows haven't been invented, and livestock don't lose their appetite one day a week. Disease is like that; it strikes regardless of the calendar. And accidents happen as unpredictably as summer storms. I took my medical oath seriously, and when suffering humanity needs my services, I give them— and I'm none the worse Christian for it."

Another time we were discussing her recent illness.

"It was blackwater fever, Ellen," she said. "Women seldom get it, but I did. It was my own fault; I was careless. I had run out of quinine and I knew I was rotten with malaria. Then one day there was blood in my urine and I knew I was in for it. I'll tell you what you must do, Ellen. When you go—well, when the time comes that you're in some outstation, quite on your own—you must take a case of champagne along. It's the only thing I know of that will pull you through a bad bout of blackwater. I left some at N'zem, but not enough; you'll need more —wherever you finally locate. You may never need to take it, but off all by yourself that way you see so much suffering around

95

you it seems wicked to take or to hold back medicine just as a preventative.

"What would Lemuel say? And all the other 'Lemuels' on the Board? Dear Ellen, sooner or later they snoop into every niche and locked recess of your soul, but you can—and you should!—keep their prying denominational fingers out of your medical kit. And a specific, whether or not it comes by the case, is medicine. Have a trader bring it in for you. There's a fine fellow, John—L'loni we called him in N'zem—who comes through about once a year. Address your bank in Léopoldville and they'll find him for you."

A week after Dr. Mary left Tani, she boarded a coastwise steamer. Two days after that, she was dead. They buried her at sea, near a bay where slavers used to throw their chained live freight overboard when capture by an English man-of-war seemed imminent. It was fitting. I like to think of her sleeping there among her people.

CHAPTER
8

DURING my residence at Tani, I was to see mission *boy* after mission *boy* enticed away from us by some white hunter's promise of all the fresh meat he could eat and the luxury of a spoonful of salt to lap up from the palm of his hand each evening when the day's work was done. We could have had "salt Christians" without number if we had had the money to buy guns, a game license, and a few sacks of salt.

I watched this sort of thing for many months and then, taking my courage in my hands, I sat down and wrote Monsieur l'Administrateur a letter in my almost nonexistent French. I did my poor best to explain the need of our mission people for meat and the harm the lack of it did our work. I told him that the necessary license and equipment were within my financial reach, but that aside from a little rabbit, squirrel, and quail hunting with my brother in Indiana, I knew nothing about guns or game. Was there anyone who could teach me the things I should know?"

Then, fearful lest I should change my mind, I sent the letter off immediately—by two *boys,* as the post still travels over a large part of the interior of Africa. The letter carrier proper bore a cleft stick in which the letter was inserted in such a way that the address was clearly visible. The second man was honor guard to the first. Neither man could read; letter carriers seldom can. But they are guided by "the jungle grapevine," and they travel as directly as geography will permit until they are near the addressee. Then they stop every white man they meet, show him the letter, and ask if he is "the one for whom the paper will talk." If he is not, he passes on any information he may have concerning the whereabouts of the addressee.

Such a system may seem incredibly cumbersome, but our postmen were back in less than two weeks with a reply from Monsieur l'Administrateur. It was a rather cryptic letter. Did not missionaries enjoy a short rest period each season? he asked. He and Madame would be delighted if I would spend my next vacation with them. If that fell within such and such a date, they would be at L'tere, near an outstation of our mission.

I know it is believed by governing boards in the United States that missionaries do take vacations or rest periods regularly. Those who teach "have the summer"; the medical and evangelistic workers "move about—new faces, new localities, you know." Conditions are somewhat better now, but then, almost three decades ago, the only thing approximating a vacation that any member of our station had enjoyed for some time was a two-day "policy conference," attended by the "older" workers—that is, those who were at least in their second six-year term of service. Obviously, I could not take a vacation without some very good reason.

Still, how could I refuse Monsieur l'Administrateur's invitation? There was nothing to do except go to Dr. Early and make a clean breast of the whole affair. I was embarrassed, but he surprised me.

"You have to go," he told me calmly. "An invitation from the king's representative is almost as much of a command performance as one from His Majesty himself." Then he peered at me speculatively. "So you're going to be our 'white hunter' now, eh? I used to hunt as a boy, in Kansas. Jack rabbits, now and then a coyote, and, once in a great while, a wolf. I was a pretty good shot too."

Perhaps it was the boyish grin of pleasure that spread over his face at the memory that loosened my tongue. "Dr. Early, couldn't I—I'd really love to—"

"Buy me a license? And gun?" he interrupted.

"Yes. It would give me so much pleasure to share what I have."

He leaned forward slightly, an outspread hand on each knee, and for a long minute he seemed to be inspecting each finger with scrupulous care. Then he surprised me again by chuckling aloud.

"*Bwana n'du tembo!* Remember, I called you that first. That, or something very similar, will be your name in the native kraals when you return with a gun over your shoulder. *Bwana n'du tembo,* Little Sister of the Elephants."

I laughed with him, but the sound sobered him. "We've changed a lot in the last thousand years, we Christians," he burst out suddenly. "During the Dark Ages the professional religious took an oath of poverty. He wore sackcloth, tied a rope around his waist, went barefoot; sometimes he even tried to live on roots and water and in a cave like an animal. We don't do that sort of thing any more—oh, no! The preacher or the missionary is expected to maintain the social amenities, to set a high cultural level for his parishioners. And how do we do it? Why, we have almost as much to live on, to educate our children with as—as the poorest, illiterate, roustabout laborer."

My intentions had been of the best, but I could have bitten my tongue out anyway. He must have sensed this, for he broke off and leaned still farther forward to pat me on the shoulder.

"Don't mind me," he said. "Don't mind any of us. We don't blame you for the privileges you enjoy, not really, in our hearts."

So it happened that I, the newcomer on the staff, the one who least needed it, took a vacation. Twenty-one mission *boys*

99

left their gardens and workbenches to row me down the Tani to the small Government post where Monsieur and his many-petticoated wife's safari of inspection was camped.

I spent almost a full month with Madame and Monsieur, and it was one of the most delightful vacations of my entire life. I learned a good deal of French, and more about our Hausa natives than my months at the mission had taught me. Monsieur had me sit beside him hour after hour as he held court; he asked my advice on how he might secure more wholehearted co-operation from his black and white underlings; he complained pleasantly, but sincerely nevertheless, of the disadvantages of his position.

"It's hard to get the truth from anyone," he grumbled. "Everyone is trying to make a good impression on me—or make me suspect the worst of the next fellow."

Madame showed me how to make onion soup and to stuff a fowl with the mushrooms that went to waste about us all the time. She taught me to spin, using a curious instrument that looked like an overgrown top with spines; she prattled of her home on the north slopes of the Pyrenees, and extracted a promise from me to visit her parents there sometime on my way to America.

But best of all was Jacques.

Jacques was neither French nor Hausa, but there was much of Africa and a little of Gascony in his veins. He was a mountain of a man, tattooed and scarred "beautifully," any African would have said.

"He has the slave marks of a dozen West African tribes on his face and chest," Monsieur l'Administrateur told me once. "And he has worn chains on his wrists and ankles."

"Meaning what?" I asked.

"That he has served time in Cayenne or in some other prison camp."

"Aren't you afraid to have him about?" the query burst out in spite of me.

"Afraid?" Monsieur laughed, but there was no merriment in the tone. "Is Africa a land for cowards?"

The answer was so obvious that it did not need words. Still I asked, "Do you think it's quite safe for me to go out hunting with such a person?"

Monsieur looked at me in astonishment. Then he guffawed until the flimsy walls of the Government camp hut shook. "How many of the men who rowed you down the Tani had pointed teeth? Or no teeth at all above, in front?"

"Why, only a few of them really had teeth," I answered. "There were—" Quickly I counted in my mind. "Eight of them had pointed teeth left in front. The rest may have had filed teeth once, but they are rotted away now."

"You know what the filed teeth mean?"

"Yes. That the men came from villages that once were cannibal." Suddenly I peered at him doubtfully. "I suppose that the trappings of cannibalism linger on after the practice itself is uprooted from a village?"

Monsieur took his time about answering me. But the impact of his words could not have been blunter. "There was not a man in your boat who could not estimate to the fraction of an ounce the amount of good, lean, red meat on your bones."

"Oh, no!" I might have said more, but Monsieur did not give me time.

"Why do you suppose Madame and I have made the trip up here and settled down prepared to stay as long as necessary?"

"Your periodic tours of inspection—" I broke off momentarily because he seemed on the point of laughing at me again. "You must judge disputes that have been taken out of the hands of native elders, and cases that involve white men—"

"I could finish with these petty disputes in a day or two," Monsieur interrupted. "But an outbreak of cannibalism is a different matter. It used to be a simple village custom, but since it has been prohibited by law, it hides itself in the deepest jungle and cloaks itself in sorcery. Its devotees are more frightened of their witch doctors than they are of the severest punishment I can administer. Ferreting out the guilty men is no easy task; nor can it be accomplished in impatient haste."

I remembered that Monsieur sat under the canopy of palm leaves day after day and listened while a small jury of local chieftains tried to make sense out of the interminable orations of people setting forth their grievances.

Monsieur had told me about some of the trials, all argued with gusto, all deadly serious to the principals, all of a slightly comic nature to the Occidental mind.

"One morning before you arrived, I heard the complaint of a husband asking damages from the elders of his village. He was very young, and as yet had but one wife. But he was a son of a rich and powerful man, so he had been given one of the daughters of the local chief." Monsieur paused, gave me a quick look, and then went on: "As you probably know by now, there is no restraint on the sex life of the daughters of a ruling chief until they are married, and then each one takes the social status of her husband and must conform to the tribal mores. Either this woman found it difficult to settle down or else she was bored with her very youthful husband. Whatever the case, she was taken in adultery. The guilty man fled and was never heard of again, which probably means one of three things: He was seized and sold into slavery back in The Hungry Country, beyond the reaches of white man's laws, or he was killed by wild animals, or—" Monsieur looked at me keenly.

"He was killed and eaten by men?" I asked slowly.

"Only possibly, I say," Monsieur answered.

"And the woman?" I went on.

"Dead," he answered. "She fell into a pool and was seized by a crocodile—that is the story as it came to me."

"Do you believe it?"

"No," he answered simply, "but I have no proof to the contrary."

"And therefore no case against the village," I only half questioned.

"None," he agreed.

"Suppose you did," I went on, "what sort of decision would you hand down in such a case?"

"I never hand down a decision in cases that do not infringe upon the restrictions His Majesty's Government has seen fit to impose on this territory. If at all possible, I uphold the decision of the native elders. I sometimes make a suggestion, or ask a question that is taken as a suggestion," he added quickly. "Murder is another matter; we cannot permit that. But when it isn't proved—well, I'm not here to sit in a tribal court of domestic relations."

We were both silent for a moment. I was full of admiration for the wisdom and tact required of a man who could occupy Monsieur l'Administrateur's position to the profit of his Government and at the same time command the respect of primitive tribesmen whose social mores were widely divergent from his own.

Monsieur's thoughts were revealed by the question he asked me abruptly. "Have you heard, Ma'amselle, that a lion, once having tasted human flesh, never ceases to be a man eater thereafter?"

"Why, that's common knowledge," I answered, surprised by his change of tone as well as subject matter.

"Is it?" he demanded.

"They say so." I felt defensive.

"Did you know that 'they' also say that a man who has acquired a taste for human flesh doesn't give up the habit easily?"

I felt the skin on the back of my neck begin to prickle. But Monsieur was laughing. "I didn't mean to scare you to death. Cannibalism is pretty well stamped out, but now and then there are sporadic outbreaks of cannibalistic cults. The leopard men are one such. More often, some individual, usually an old man —somewhat like the old lion no longer able to kill his buck— becomes a ghoul. Oh, yes, just that. He digs up corpses and devours them. Since the only natives really given burial are chieftains or otherwise important men, such an individual is seldom driven out of the tribe when discovered. Instead, he immediately falls under the protection of the witch doctor, probably because they believe the spirit of the dead man enters the body of the ghoul. But I don't really know, since one way a native has of protecting his private beliefs is to agree pleasantly with whatever you suggest to him by questions. Anyway, his friends and neighbors, even his own family, become afraid of him—too terrified, in fact, to report him to the white authorities. But word does come to us, one way or another."

"And that is why you are here? Now?" I gasped. "You suspect an outbreak of cannibalism?"

Monsieur nodded. " 'Suspect' is hardly the word. I feel reasonably sure, but I must have proof. That is why I sit day after day, listening to the trials of petty thieves and loose ladies."

"But the cannibal? How do you find him if everyone is too afraid of him to report him?" I asked.

"Fear seldom prevents boasting. Sometimes it even promotes the habit. It was the boasting around a dozen campfires that brought me up here prepared to stay until I get the guilty man—or men. How? I have among my safari *boys* a half dozen trained detectives. They listen. They egg a man on to talk more than is wise. When he hesitates, they match tall tale with tall tale. Then, when such a *boy* pours my wine, or lays out my clothes, or comes to me for his daily ration of *posho*, he drops a name in my ear—as I measure out the corn meal."

"Then you have the guilty person arrested?" I asked.

"Oh, no, Ma'amselle! At home, among white men, we say one must fight fire with fire. Here my magic must be bigger and stronger than that of the local witch doctor. I wait until I am absolutely certain of my facts; and then one day, right in the middle of the hottest part of debate over some woman, I begin to sniff; then I arise and point an accusing finger at the culprit or culprits. Thus 'smelled out,' they never deny their guilt; so my soldiers bind them and drag them off. Shortly thereafter, I leave the native grand jury under the direction of a subofficer and continue my tour of inspection or go back to headquarters."

"Then you try them?" I asked.

"Try them?" Monsieur was amused at my words. "Ma'am-selle, here I am the judge of the last court of appeal. My investigators have listened to the witnesses, including the men themselves. I am careful not to act hastily and therefore make no mistakes; and when confronted with such powers of 'smell-ing out' as I possess, the culprit gives up. When I point my finger at him, he knows, and his people know, that I am passing sentence."

"Is he—hanged? or shot?" I could not bring myself to ask if Monsieur l'Administrateur, like the labor supervisor, had men beaten to death by *kiboko,* the native cat-o'-nine-tails, made of dried rhinoceros hide with the tips of its lashes hard as nails and sharp as knives.

"Now and then there is a man who boasts of having stolen a living young woman or a few children for his lonely midnight feasts. Him, of course, we must execute," Monsieur admitted. "But what charge can I bring against the usual present-day cannibal other than the desecration of a few graves?"

I had no answer, and he went on. "There are those who think I am unjustifiably harsh when I sentence such a ghoul to lifetime hard labor at one of the mines. But what can I do? When a man will rob a grave for flesh, I think he has become incurable, like the old, man-eating lion."

I had heard terrible accounts of the atrocities committed upon native workmen in the Belgian mines; still I could not help voicing the obvious, "At least he will eat no more human flesh at Kilo, or Katanga."

"Exactly!"

Suddenly Monsieur threw back his head and laughed. "Now Jacques. Does he seem so bad after all? I admit that in other days he might have been an ebony-hued pirate, or a runner for the Arab slavers—but what might you and I not have been in other times and in other circumstances? In many ways he is the best servant I ever had—lusty and adventuresome—but not an evil man. He is not native to these parts, but came from the far north. I think there is Arab blood in his veins. Who knows? Perhaps he peeped at a sheik's daughter while she was bathing, or cast covetous eyes at a fine camel and attempted to ride away upon it one dark night. Put your mind at rest, Ma'am-selle; I would not give him to you if I did not consider him the best. There are many natives who could track and locate game for you, but Jacques understands the animal's mind. He shoots like an Arab, and he respects a gun and cares for it—as only a man who has loved soldiering ever does."

"The Foreign Legion perhaps?" I queried lightly.

Again Monsieur's eyebrow shot skyward. "I have a nephew who attended the Military Institute in Paris. He has served a couple of years as a lieutenant with the Legionnaires. I shall have to ask him sometime if he has ever known a soldier named Jacques."

"An ebony-hued Jacques," I reminded him.

We both laughed, and that was as much of the history as I ever knew of one of the best teachers I ever had.

In a little over three weeks' time Jacques taught me how to take any type of shoulder firearm apart, clean it perfectly, adjust it, and even make minor repairs. He impressed upon me, as thoroughly as a drill sergeant might have, that a dirty or a faulty gun is worse than no gun at all. Then I stood with him for hours at a time, in all kinds of light and shadow, learning how to shoot at both stationary and moving targets. I never reached his perfection, of course. I have seen him bend over a tall sapling, tie a clod of dirt to its tip with a length of rawhide, and then walk away. At fifty paces he would shout to the *boy* holding the tip of the sapling to let go. Then he would whirl about and with one shot burst the clod into a thousand fragments as it sped through the air.

I said "with one shot," and Jacques explained laconically one day: "You start with a full clip of ammunition, yes—four or five shots. But *simba* does not know or care when he charges."

"But I'm not going to hunt lions, Jacques," I protested. "I only want to be able to bring down meat for the mission folk and for my porters when I am on safari. Guinea fowl, geese, bustards, and a buck now and then."

"If you hunt at all, you will go where *simba* hunts, *mama*, for man and *simba* eat the same meat. And what will you do if *simba* argues a kill with you?"

"If *simba* wants whatever I kill, I will walk away and let him have it," I said finally.

Every tooth in Jacques's head gleamed as he grinned, but he pressed on. "But suppose the king of the beasts refuses to be put off with a fat buck or a zebra? And he is not the only one with whom you may have to deal. What will you do when *tembo* flings his trumpet into the air and screams that you must not shoot in his domain?"

I felt fear in the pit of my stomach, and wondered if after all I were not being silly about guns and hunting. What would I do if I met an elephant and it were not disposed to turn and slip noiselessly into the jungle? Or if I met a rhinoceros on the open plain, where the only possible protection from its mad charge might be an anthill or a wisp of thornbush? Worst of all, what if I disturbed a herd of buffalo, that most dangerous and wily of animals, and found myself being stalked by a wary old bull which could double on its tracks so skillfully that not even the keenest-eyed tracker could detect the ruse? Neither

107

tembo nor *simba* fear the buffalo, any native will tell you, but both respect it and make no attempt to interfere either with a herd or with individuals.

The upshot of the matter was that I embarked upon a highly intensive study of the anatomy and the psychology of the bigger animals, the beasts of prey, and those with reputations for bad tempers. Jacques did not use these learned terms in his instruction, of course, but he was thorough nevertheless. He drew diagrams in the sand to illustrate the thickness of *tembo's* skull and the futility of trying to stop an avalanche of flesh by pouring bullets into its frontal armor plate. He told me that he had seen *simba* charge twenty-five, fifty, seventy-five, and on one occasion two hundred, feet with a bullet through his heart. Why should I kill a rhinoceros? Only the vultures and jackals would eat its flesh. No, nick it at the base of its frontal horn with a bullet and this antediluvian relic would turn and thunder off to nurse its sore nose in solitude.

My vacation sped by. When Monsieur had finally smelled out his ghoul, and the mission *shimbeck* had been summoned via the jungle grapevine to carry me back to Tani, I was suddenly frightened. Would Monsieur not lend me Jacques for just a little while? six weeks? or a month? There were so many things I still needed to learn.

"Non, non, non, Ma'amselle, it would never do. Jacques, he is—he is not—" Monsieur broke off to look at me sharply.

"Jacques isn't Christian?" I supplied for him. "We have *boys* at the mission who are not Christian, Monsieur. Of course, we hope they will become Christian. Jacques is very amenable, and perhaps if you told him—"

"If I told him to behave himself, he would," Monsieur took up the thread. "And after all, there is so little I know about the man, why—he might even be able to sing hymns with you."

There was more raillery, but in the end I got Jacques— "Jackie," I promptly christened him—"for keeps." I suppose he had his faults, but I don't remember what they were. I do remember that he was more than a good and faithful servant; he was a true friend.

As a missionary, I made a strange spectacle returning to Tani, armed with a personal servant who looked like a pirate; with a general game license, a special permit for big game, a shotgun, two rifles, one heavy and one light; and with as much dread for what I had mapped out as one small woman can conveniently carry in her heart.

CHAPTER

9

The morning after my return I shot a lesser bustard—the African wild turkey—and perhaps a hundred guinea fowl. The latter live in such immense flocks in the Congo jungles that all I had to do to bring down a dozen or so was merely flush the birds, point my shotgun in their general direction, and pull the trigger. That night guinea fowl simmered in every cooking pot in the native compound, while all the whites contributed delicacies from their precious hordes and dined on bustard with the Earlys. Even Dr. Early donned an apron and whipped up his specialty—the pulp of green coconut, whose kernel is still in the milky stage, mashed smooth and beaten to a creamy consistency. It was better than either custard or ice cream.

There were jokes at my expense, of course, some of which were undoubtedly barbed, but for the most part it was a thoroughly enjoyable evening. Certainly there was no comparison between our fat, juicy wild fowl and the stringy, undersized chickens we ordinarily bought from native women.

"We ought to do this oftener," someone at the dinner table said, but in that tone of regret which implies that too much carefree camaraderie might be demoralizing.

"I do wish—I feel silly to say it—but, really, I do wish—"

Mrs. Early broke off in confusion, blushing at her temerity. "I do wish that Ellen would shoot us a—a—hippopotamus. There now!"

A shout of laughter followed her words, but everyone turned to me.

"Well, you've got all this expensive equipment—why not put it to good use?" It was Dr. Early speaking. I thought they were spoofing me and I tried to laugh it off, but it was no use.

"Why not?" was in every pair of eyes and on most lips.

I turned to Mrs. Early, and for the first time I believe I understood how very timid the woman really was. She was not now "standing up" for her husband, and apparently it was impossible for her to put forth the same effort for herself. As I looked at her, her eyes filled and the lines of her mouth sagged.

"Why, of course, I'll try to shoot you a hippo. Jacques didn't take me out after any of them while I was—while I was in training," I tried to make a joke of my vacation trip. "So I don't know how successful I'll be. After all, a hippo seems awfully big to be killed by anything as tiny as a bullet, but— What in the world do you want a hippopotamus for?"

"The fat! It renders down like lard. Like real Kansas farm lard. I can sift and sift and sift the native flour and get it as fine as I can and make some pies, and oh! lots of things for Lemuel —and all of you—"

She babbled on. Pies, tarts, doughnuts, cakes. I had never seen her so animated. She was really a pretty woman, a good and thoughtful wife, a wise and loving mother. It was a new and likable Mrs. Early I was seeing for the first time. I vowed that I would get her a hippopotamus if I had to wade in, chase it ashore, and club it to death.

When we left the table, Dr. Early put on his hat and went to the native quarters to make arrangements for the hippo hunt.

The next morning I learned that the prospect of meat was

infinitely more engaging to my patients than bandages and pills. There was no one waiting for me except two *pickinins*, who were playing hooky from school with the intention of going along on the hunt written all over their small faces, and a superannuated mission *boy*, who in his senility had become a bone of contention in more than one mission staff meeting. He had to be kept away from worship meetings, for he was as apt as not to rise in the middle of a sermon and demand palm wine or banana beer.

"How can one pay homage to *Muungu*, the great and fearful overgod of the jungle, if one does not pour libations into Mother Earth and one's own thirsty gullet?" he would shout, until a scandalized brother on either side picked him up by the elbows and carried him out. He usually visited my clinic once or twice a week to demand that I help him secure a young wife, someone big and plump, to lie behind his back and keep him warm.

I gave each urchin a light spank and ordered them to return to Sister Susanne, and I told the whimpering old man I would see if I could get him another blanket. His wails followed me as I went back to my *dukas* to change into rough clothing and to get my biggest gun.

The hunting party consisted of Dr. Early who, in spite of his conscience, took a morning off and went along purely for sport; myself; Jackie, of course; and about twenty porters.

"They are to carry the meat," Dr. Early explained, as I eyed the small army.

"They—and you—have more faith in my marksmanship that I have myself," I assured him.

He hesitated a moment and then turned appealing eyes full upon me. "Sister Ellen, we've just got to get a hippopotamus," he said.

I agreed that we must if we could, and silently I prayed that we might.

We walked about five miles cross-country, over trails perceptible to native eyes but invisible to mine. At that time I wasn't used to trekking and my legs were on the point of giving out when we reached a sharp bend in the Tani, where the river was in the process of cutting a new channel and leaving the old bed to become an oxbow lake.

"Aren't there any hippos nearer the mission?" I demanded between puffs more than once, and the answer was always the same.

"Yes, *mama*," a dozen voices assured me promptly, "but we are taking you to the best place."

"Why is one place better than another?" I panted a little later. "After all a hippo is a—just a hippo."

"But *mama,* meat that the hands cannot reach is no comfort to the belly," a chorus replied quite logically, although I was too winded to ask just what they meant.

But I was not too tired to grumble. "Are you sure there are hippos where you are taking us?"

"Oh, yes, *mama.*"

The barely literate showed off their knowledge by counting for me. "There are a hundred, hundred, hundred, *mama,*" in crescendo voices. The frankly unlearned held up both hands, fingers rigidly extended, and fluttered their wrists to indicate that, at the end of our trail, hippopotamuses were as numerous as the leaves on an old silk-cotton tree.

Then we pushed through a curtain of lianas and came out on the banks of what looked like a beautiful bayou, and for a full minute all I could do was stare. I tried to count them and finally gave up. Surely there were "a hundred, hundred, hundred!" of the huge monsters in the water before me. Some that were standing in the shallows moved leisurely into deep water; those on the far bank merely turned gargantuan heads in our direction and some yawned prodigiously. In the middle of the stream, everywhere I looked, noses as broad and blunt as washtubs pointed at me, and protuberant eyes, which looked like blinking warts, stared.

"Shoot, *mama*."

"Shoot!"

"Shoot now!"

"Much meat!"

"Good meat!"

"Shoot! Shoot! Shoot!"

The porters' words buzzed in my ears, like a gnats' chorus, and I contemplated the great horde helplessly. Which one should I shoot? And where should I aim? Jackie had explained at great length about elephants, but I couldn't remember that he had so much as whispered a word about hippos.

"In the eye, *mama*," a voice came over my shoulder. "The socket goes clear through to the brain." Jackie too again calling me *mama!* I remember only my pleasure in this evidence of respect in my gunbearer's words. Perhaps I was too inexperienced, or just plain stupid, to realize that an eye is an awfully small target. I tried to estimate the distance, adjusted my sights, and lifted the heavy gun. It shook in my hands like a young bamboo in the wind.

"Steady, Ellen," I heard Dr. Early whisper under his breath.

Jackie solved my problem. Before I knew what he was about, he had slid in front of me on all fours, plugged his ears with his index fingers, and offered his buttocks for a gun rest.

I went down on one knee and aimed with painstaking care; then, trying to remember everything I had learned about guns, pressed the trigger firmly.

There is nothing in the world quite like the complete absence of sound for a few seconds following a gunshot, or the extreme confusion of noises that accompany the rebirth of sound. A moment of stagnation—then the porters shouted, Dr. Early grunted, birds in the trees above us screamed, squawked, and flapped their wings, and there was an undertone of countless scurrying footsteps through the leaves and vines at our feet. Out on the river before us there were big and little splashes, followed by big and little ripples, widening until they died in the rotting sedge at our feet. Then absolutely nothing.

I looked at Dr. Early. "I thought I hit it." I was distinctly surprised, maybe even a little petulant.

"I thought you did too." There was as much confusion in his tone as there was on his face.

But the porters lifted their voices in a joyful chorus.

"Meat!"

"Meat!"

"Chop chop!"

"Chop chop chop!"

Then my gunbearer rolled back onto his haunches from his knees, clapped his hands together softly, and spat lightly on the ground between my feet. In a second every other *boy* surrounding us was gazing at me with big, black, softly rapturous eyes and gently clapping his hands.

"They are honoring you as a mighty hunter of hippopotamuses," Dr. Early exclaimed in amazement.

"It would be more to the point if I'd aimed better," I said bitterly, and stared at the placid water as though it had done me an injury. As I gazed, a pair of wide-set eyes and then nostrils broke the surface. Then another and another until it seemed that again there were "a hundred, hundred, hundred" hippos all staring solemnly at me.

"Well, I can try again," I said doggedly, and at my words the porters sucked their teeth rapturously. Jackie rocked forward onto all fours again, and once more I sighted across his broad back.

Within the next hour I emptied five clips of ammunition into that herd of hippopotamuses and not a single animal squealed or roared or kicked or writhed in mortal agony, or turned over onto its side, or floated on the top of the water. Finally I refused to make a fool of myself any longer and turned my face toward home. Dr. Early trudged along behind me while the porters, some in front and some trailing us, broke into an unaccountable song of fulsome praise detailing my prowess as a huntress. After exhausting that theme, and since a woman's sole function in a native village is to work and bear children, they switched to such details of my probable ability as a mother as would ordinarily have made me blush and certainly would have called forth a sharp rebuke from Dr. Early. Now, however, we merely stalked along in silent misery. When we reached the edge of the mission clearing, I turned to my companion.

"I'm sorry," I said, "just as sorry as can be. I did the best I could."

"I know," he answered. "And—I'm sorry too." His tone implied that for some obscure reason he was as much to blame for my failure as I myself.

Mrs. Early came to meet us, her face aglow with the happiness of a dreaming homemaker. Looking at her and listening to her as she babbled along took physical strength as well as courage. Finally I could stand it no longer, and blurted out the whole miserable truth, while her husband stirred the grass with a restless toe like an embarrassed schoolboy. To our amazement, she laughed merrily.

"Oh, you two," she chided gently. "I'm not taken in by your little joke. Lemuel is going to have a fresh coconut pie tomorrow—all of you are, in fact. And then—doughnuts!" She clicked her tongue at us as though we were babies she was tempting with a tidbit, and I wanted to cry.

I didn't eat lunch that day. I wasn't hungry. Instead I walked over to the hospital so that I could be alone with my wretched sense of failure. But the senile old graybeard was waiting for me.

"You *are* a woman," he exclaimed in amazement. "You really are *female*." Then he clucked like an old rooster scolding his hens.

"Of course I'm a woman," I retorted. "Don't be so silly."

"In my day," he went on in a tone of wonder, "a woman was nothing but a pair of hands and stupid as a hen. And now they tell me that you have killed these many of the great river pigs." He held up eight fingers. "A pair of hands! A mere pair of hands!"

I left him muttering to himself and went into my dispensary, pulling the door shut behind me. But grandpa was not to be denied. At first a crack, wide enough for only one eye, then a hand's breadth, and finally half ajar he pushed the door. And the rest of that afternoon he was never more than a dozen feet away, staring at me, his rheumy old eyes bright with senile amazement.

"Eight hippos! Eight! And I would have been satisfied with one, and that a small one!" I moaned wordlessly.

About ten o'clock that evening, an hour after I had gone to bed in an attempt to get away from myself as much as anyone else, I was awakened by an uproar in the compound. Someone—it sounded like Dr. Early but it couldn't be—was trying to yodel outside my sleeping *dukas*. Then two fists began hammering upon my door and so vigorously that the thatch over my head rustled and I could hear it shedding fine particles down on the muslin fly.

"Come out! Wake up and come on up to the mission house, Ellen. They're bringing in the first of the meat!"

I sprang off my cot and flung open the door. There was my boss behaving like a young buck at a village dance.

"Have you gone crazy?" I demanded sternly.

He seized me by my shoulders and swung me around three or four times before he replied: "By heaven, Ellen, they say there are seven dead hippos piled up on a sandbar about two miles below that bend in the river where we were this morning! They say you killed eight, but that maybe one was swung out into midstream by some eddy and has gone on past."

"Stick out your tongue," I commanded. "Are you feverish?"

"I've not taken leave of my senses, and I'm not sick. I'm telling you the truth. The *boys* are bringing in the meat. Come and see for yourself!"

I slipped into moccasins and a kimono, and for the next few hours sat on the Earlys' steps, receiving such homage and viewing such quantities of raw, dripping meat as I hope never to have to encounter again.

During the next few days tribesmen from the surrounding jungle gathered by the hundreds, and so huge is one of these river pigs that there was meat for all. It was a month before the stench of rotting blood and flesh, which the natives ate in any stage of decay, blew away or sank into the soft jungle mold underfoot. And the following weeks were simply wonderful. Invitations came by the dozens for me to visit this village or that, many of them formerly cold, if not hostile, to mission work. Some definitely specified that I was not to come with my Bible and medical kit, but with my gun, if you please.

In desperation I asked Dr. Early what I should do, and he told me to accept as many of the invitations as possible. And, by way of persuasion, he told me the story of a pigheaded missionary like myself—only he didn't describe her quite that way. She had loved the beauty of Africa from the first day she had stepped ashore at Tani, and before a week had passed she was uprooting jungle vines and shrubs and planting them around her personal *dukas*.

"We warned her," Dr. Early said, "that the shrubs would make an excellent hiding place for snakes and centipedes and scorpions, that the vines on her roof would hasten the rotting of the thatch, and that when it and the mud walls had to be renewed, her work would have to be destroyed. She replied that we had blinded ourselves to the beauty all about us. Well, Mother Nature is a wonderful teacher. We let her have her way, and I must say that in a matter of weeks her *dukas* became one of the prettiest sights I ever looked at. Here and there she had stuck orchid bulbs which blossomed into all colors of the rainbow: flamboyant purples, pure white, and right above where she sat to sew on an afternoon, an almost unbelievable green flower with frilled and fluted petals and dark-brown hairy polka dots down its throat.

"One day she was sitting there and two strange, stark-naked little *pickinins* came along. They sat down on her step and began to jabber. It was wonderful language practice for her. They never mentioned the flowers, and she was so intent on language and eventually saving their souls that she hadn't any thought for the orchids above her head either. They stayed until the sun went down, and bright and early the next morning they were back again. One or the other or both of them sat on her step continuously for the next six weeks.

"Then one day a delegation appeared before her door—mamma, papa, brothers, sisters, aunts, in-laws—the whole tribe. They were polite, but they had work to do. Carefully they pushed her back off her own porch, spread a loosely woven mat of fine bamboo fibers where she had been in the habit of sitting. Then papa got his blowgun, inserted a splinter the size of a small darning needle, and took careful aim. About two seconds later the biggest, ugliest, green-and-brown spider you could ever hope to see was sprawling on the mat, hopelessly entangling its horrible furry legs in the bamboo fiber. It died in a few minutes, with that poison dart through its middle.

"Then the good sister learned that it wasn't her fascinating personality—or religion—that had kept the urchins on her doorstep continuously for six weeks, but an orchid spider. The boy's father had made his son a marimba, and the best marimbas, with fine, high-pitched tones, always have sounding drums made from the skin of the egg sac of orchid spiders. Having found such a spider, the youngsters had stood guard until the egg sac was just the right size.

"After that terrifying experience, our missionary didn't object at all when we cut down the vines and cleared back the brush and put a new thatch on her *dukas* roof too. The old one smelled like a grave, and great, slimy chunks of it had been dropping onto her bed and table and her for some days.

"All the time repairs were going on, there was no sight or sound of the two urchins; apparently they'd just melted back into the jungle. She didn't talk about them, and we felt kind of sorry for her, so we didn't mention them either.

"Then one day she came into my office with a strange look on her face. The boy had come back, she said, and since he felt grateful to her for having the finest marimba in his village now, he wanted to play for her and her people. And he wanted to play where we always have music—in church. He didn't know any Christian tunes, he said, but he could play all the Hausa tribal melodies. What in the world should we do with him?

" 'Bring him to prayer meeting, marimba and all,' I told her. 'I'll throw the sermon I've prepared out of the window and preach on: "Make a joyful noise unto the Lord . . ." For a long time we called that youngster our Spider Christian—just among ourselves, you understand. He quickly learned to play our hymns, and—"

"Jonas!" I burst out.

"Uh-huh, Jonas Gaavanehaa," Dr. Early answered, naming the youngest deacon in our church. "Marimba or organ, he's a fine musician, isn't he? Did you know that he's been invited to play at parties at Government House in both Elisabethtown and Léopoldville? And that once an American company sent technicians and equipment here to the Congo Territory for the sole purpose of making recordings of his Hausa tunes? And where would you find a finer, better Christian in Africa—or America—than the man who as a boy followed a spider's egg sac to the altar?"

I didn't know what to answer, and while I searched for words, Dr. Early went on again.

"Visit all the villages you can. Take your guns—if you can afford the ammunition. Jesus made his Galilean disciples fishers of men; that was only a local pattern, and it will bear variation to fit geography. The Salvation Army calls a crowd together with a drum and trumpet; you take your guns. After all, hungry men listen with their stomachs; you fill their stomachs, and then they'll listen with their minds and hearts."

So in the next few months I went on itinerary and learned to trek over all sorts of terrain. I learned to judge the temper of a village even before I entered it—friendly, curious, or hostile. I came to recognize the signs of something untoward in the air— a vague, intangible something which invariably went underground at my approach. I accustomed myself to variations in dialect, lisps, grunts, and guttural clicks. I could tell, from the flowers among the vegetables in the native gardens, which villages had known the services of a missionary even in the remote past. I learned to take care of myself, alone with a handful of black men, in the depths of the jungle or on the sun-baked veld.

And I wrote Monsieur l'Administrateur a long letter telling him exactly what had happened on my first hippo hunt. There was no limit on hippos at that time; still I knew, jungle gossip being what it is, that twenty-four hours had probably not passed after the first shot was fired before he knew everything, and I didn't want him to take me for a gun-crazy fool.

Monsieur, as always, was the perfect gentleman. He was lavish in his praise of my marksmanship. Then he went on to say that he was granting me permission to shoot as many rogue elephants as devastated the shambas, as the native gardens are called, of my parishioners—and of course I knew that in such a case one tusk belonged to me as a bounty and the other to the Belgian Government. And at that time the value of a good tusk equaled a missionary's yearly salary.

Truly all things must work for good, however false a front circumstance draws over them at first appearance. For no sooner had my feeling of self-sufficiency returned and my sense of independence reasserted itself than word came that Dr. Charles Clyde and his nurse wife were on their way to Tani. There was no suggestion in the letter from the Board that I should move on to a new field, but I knew that the time had come. Consequently I was not surprised when Dr. Early asked me if I would like to take Dr. Mary's place at N'zem.

"Of course I'll go," I answered. "But I can't take her place. No one ever could."

"No," he agreed. "But then, no one ever takes another person's place, not really. We just make a place for ourselves, and sometimes it's easier where others have been before us."

"When shall I go?" I asked.

"Whenever you like. Before or after Dr. Charles comes—it doesn't make much difference either way."

CHAPTER
10

I WAITED for the new doctor. It seemed only right to divide up instruments and other equipment with him if he should be short of supplies. And, besides, I wanted to see the newcomers too.

It was fortunate that I did wait, for in that way I met John —L'loni, as we always called him, since most West Coast natives find "J" a difficult letter to enunciate. He was the trader Dr. Mary had told me about, and arrangements were made for me to travel to N'zem with him.

When Dr. Charles came, I laughed at his mountainous luggage, forgetting that I had been guilty of exactly the same thing. Among other odds and ends, he brought a galvanized iron bath tub, which we all looked at with wondering eyes, hoping desperately that sometime, somehow, we should be invited to bathe in it. Just to sit down in that tub and feel soft, warm, perhaps even perfumed, water lapping about our tummies suddenly seemed the most enticing experience imaginable. We never knew that luxury, however. Only a few days after Dr. Charles set up the tub in his bathing *dukas*—with a most ingenious arrangement of plumbing contrived from joints of bamboo—his wife found a snake coiled up in the bottom of it one morning, and in her efforts to kill it with a club, she knocked apart every seam in the tub.

Madame Doctor—as Monsieur l'Administrateur first called her and then we all took it up—was a beautiful woman, tall, slender, with big brown eyes and long copper-colored hair. Not only was she an excellent nurse, with specialized training in obstetrics; she was something of a linguist too, and took to Hausa like a honey bird to a bee tree.

Dr. Charles brought an operating table with him, and as I helped him wheel it into the largest hut, I was suddenly and overwhelmingly embarrassed at the size of my hospital huts and the poverty of my appointments. Dr. Charles, however, made me feel that I had done wonders in less than two years' time. I really had, but he couldn't know that; it was nothing but innate grace of personality on his part. He told me he was sorry I was leaving and I found myself wishing that Dr. Early and I had not been so definite in our arrangements about N'zem.

When John, or L'loni, reached Tani, I was packed and ready to leave with him. He and his bearers knew the way to N'zem perfectly; they had been welcomed in every intervening village numberless times. He would carry responsibility for me and my porters on this trip and vouch for me to the headman in N'zem.

I had felt silly at the thought of travel in a *tipoye,* and had told Dr. Early quite definitely that I did not want one. The idea of a grown woman lolling in a hammock chair carried by four men—nonsense! But L'loni insisted that I have not only a *tipoye,* but a bush car as well. A bush car is an adult's tricycle, with a chair for a seat. It is light, fairly speedy—for the Dark Continent, that is—narrow enough for the game trails which usually serve as paths, and sturdy enough to take the stones and branches and other debris underfoot as no bicycle could. In the years ahead, bush car and *tipoye* proved invaluable as savers of time and energy, but together they set me back almost a year's salary. Small wonder most missionaries trek on their own two feet!

The first day in the *tipoye* my helplessly dangling feet annoyed me. That evening I complained, and the next morning L'loni fixed a bamboo footrest that was a great comfort. L'loni was like that; not a ladies' man, but thoughtful as one's own brother. I asked him if he had a wife, and he gave me that quick, startled look of a bachelor at a leap-year party.

"I'm not a designing female," I assured him. "It's just that I think you'd make some woman an awfully good husband."

"Why have you never married?" he countered.

"Oh, I was too busy helping to bring up my brothers and sisters, I guess."

"Now, spiritually at least, you're going to wash and comb the heathen?" he queried lightly.

I ignored the gentle mockery.

"I guess I came to Africa because I'm one of those people who has to work for others," I defended myself. "Back in the United States there's nothing I could do that a thousand others can't do, perhaps better than I. Here the need is so great that a thousand workers are only a drop in the bucket."

He didn't needle me about my profession, but I know he felt slightly contemptuous of the men, and women too, in mission stations. It came out in little ways, like the time we were discussing native polygamy.

"A tribeswoman, if she is a first wife, from the day of her marriage begins insisting that her husband take a second wife. Not only is a sister wife company, but she halves the labor of the kraal. If the man is too poor to buy a second woman, his wife will work like a dog to earn her sister wife for him. You white missionaries would be amazed to know how often you're pitied. You, for instance. As long as you're in Africa your black neighbors will wonder why your parents couldn't dispose of you to some man. Their gossip will center around two possibilities: either as a girl you displayed such temper that no man thought he could beat you into submission or you have some hidden disease or deformity."

L'loni's stock in trade as a traveling merchant was composed almost entirely of Africa's greatest necessity: salt. No ten-cent-store trash. No liquor. When I questioned him about this, he parried with, "You don't approve of the traveling saloons, do you?"

He traded his salt for groundnuts, kola nuts, ivory, and strips of the cloth which the men of the villages weave, using their big toes as weights and boom. All this in turn he sold to the Government agents on the coast. He made a good profit; even I could see that.

"How much?" I demanded one day, when he had just concluded a bargain with a village chief.

He answered without a second's hesitation, "Around eight hundred per cent." For a moment he looked embarrassed and then added: "But after all, you see I like old M'fooloo. He and I have been friends for a long time. He used to be a gunbearer of mine before his father died and he was called back to his village to become chief."

"Eight hundred per cent!" I gasped.

"I normally aim at somewhere between twelve and sixteen hundred," he went on casually.

"You robber!" I burst out.

"How many times have you edged up toward a sermon on polygamy?" he accused, his eyes twinkling. "I'm a more effective missionary than you are. I just take the old boys' merchandise and they haven't anything left with which to buy more women."

"L'loni, you're quibbling. You're—you're making a mockery of religion," I chided.

The mirth died out of his eyes and he gave me a long and searching glance before he leaned over and laid a hand on my arm.

"Listen, Ellen," he began. "I grew up in a good home. Family prayers, Sunday school, I was confirmed, and all that. Until I came to Africa I was just an ordinary Christian. Gave a little to the Church—not enough, but a little.

"Twice in my life I have felt the need of spiritual guidance from another human being. Each time I went to preachers to whom I felt I had a right to go. Both men listened to me; I'll say at least that much for them. One had nothing to give; he was learned, but not intelligent—and spiritually poverty-stricken. The other? I don't know; he was just evasive and—and platitudinous. I think that financially and socially he felt insecure and it irritated him. Ordinarily he covered it up with an exaggerated camaraderie, but it was always there, just underneath the skin. And when someone who had all the things he lacked asked help of him, it broke through. Most laymen have experiences like these, and it embitters a lot of them and drives them away from the Church. I felt some of that too. I was young and I had still to learn— Well, the Hausas have an old proverb that puts it in a nutshell: 'You can take your troubles to others, but you can't leave them there.' "

We both laughed shortly and for no reason, the way people do when they are embarrassed by life in general.

Under L'loni's guidance, I saw another Africa which up until that time had been hidden from me. Any newcomer to the Dark Continent is amazed at the size and profusion of the flowers which are rare and costly in the florists' shops at home —or completely unknown there. L'loni showed me lilies eighteen inches to two feet across, lobelias twenty feet high, tree-sized heather, and other giants too numerous to mention, and he called my attention to other extremes—blossoms so tiny that in the distance they merely looked like colored dust beside the path or a fungus growth on the bark of the trees. He showed me plants that thrust grayish-green spars through the leaf mold and burst into bloom as I sat and looked at them.

"That's all there is to the plant above ground," he said. "By nightfall they will have withered."

127

One day while on the march he came back to my *tipoye* and asked me to come to the head of the line with him. There was something he wanted to show me, and as we passed the porters, some of them called out questioning remarks about what sounded like "butterfly trees." Still, I was not prepared for what burst upon me when we reached a little glade. There, on the banks of a tiny, sluggish stream were a half dozen trees of some gray-barked, fine-leafed variety. One of them was completely covered with blossoms of every conceivable hue. Two others seemed just beginning to blossom.

"Some bouquet, eh?" L'loni remarked. Then to his gun-bearer, "Mpika, go over and give a branch a couple of shakes."

The boy grinned and did as commanded. The blossoms shattered off, but instead of falling, they fluttered off to another little gray tree.

"Butterflies!" I exclaimed. "I never saw so many. Why do they settle on just those little gray trees?"

"I don't know," L'loni answered. "A couple of scientists came out here a few years ago just to study butterflies, and even they couldn't tell why the butterflies choose this particular kind of tree for a roost. At first they thought the butterfly drank the sap, but they couldn't find any scars on the bark of the tree, and the tree is never injured unless a small limb cracks or breaks off entirely from the weight."

"Broken down by butterflies," I laughed. I've seen such trees many times since and I never cease to wonder about them.

We had a stretch of about fifty miles of grassland to cover before reaching N'zem, and in the last village before starting across it, we picked up a boy with a purely African profession —a dew drier, Y'Ro by name. I had never heard of such an occupation, but then I had never seen the great grasslands before. I had supposed that crossing these would be the simplest and perhaps pleasantest part of our journey. It turned out to be the most difficult, and utterly monotonous. For four days of steady slogging along, we forced our way through elephant grass which towered from six to ten feet above our heads, and the growth was as rank as that of any canebrake. We followed a combination human path and game trail, and on more than one occasion I was desperately certain we had lost it as we passed through a green tunnel no wider than a man's breadth. At night we simply wrapped ourselves in our blankets and lay down where we had been standing—and I, at least, prayed that no elephant or rhinoceros would blunder along upon us. No hot water, no fire, no cooked food.

"Thank heaven the grass is still green and growing," L'loni told me once. "When it is dry, fires spring up and very few of the creatures caught on the game trails escape."

"It must be terrible," I ventured. "And no way of fighting it."

"Fighting it!" my companion laughed. "The natives set the fires. If this forest of dead giant grass weren't removed, the new shoots springing up would be lost. As it is, they burn it, and the whole plain lies scorched and black until the first rain. Then, within a week, this is the prettiest meadow in the world, with game crowding each other, shoulder to shoulder."

"When will the rains come?" I asked.

"Oh, two and a half to three months." L'loni shot a quick glance at me. "We're in no danger—of fire. I wouldn't have taken this short cut had we been."

Mornings we arose with the false dawn; crossing these grasslands was the only place we hurried. Even so, we traveled the last day without water. Thirst is always difficult to endure; those last few hours, tramping along steadily through absolutely still air, were torture.

But in one way there was water, too much for the first hour or two of trekking; that is why the men themselves hired Y'Ro. In the early dawn the elephant grass was wet with dew, which showered off at the slightest touch, drenching and chilling whatever passed along the trail. It was Y'Ro's job to go ahead of the porters, and to fling out his arms and feet, beating and kicking every stalk of grass so there would be little or none of the icy dew left to fall on the porters. The child himself was drenched in ten seconds, and for the next hour and a half he endured that icy shower bath. I protested to L'loni that it was cruelty, and torture, to a child.

L'loni laughed at me. "Don't let Y'Ro hear you call him a child. He's been through the tribal initiation rites, and he, and his people, look upon him as a man now. Anyway, he took the job so he could earn enough money to buy his first wife."

"Heavens!" I gasped. "How old is he? He doesn't look a day over twelve."

L'loni shrugged. What tribesman knows his age? Or thinks such a detail important? "There are boys in his village younger than he who already have women in their kraals. But they are sons of men of substance. Y'Ro has to earn the purchase price of his first woman himself. His first wife will be an old woman, past her childbearing days, the discard from some rich man's herd. She in turn will earn him a second wife—that is, if he ever gets the first wife." And again L'loni laughed.

Poor Y'Ro! The porters paid him well, and he was a good workman, but he was an inveterate gambler. Each evening the porters paid him for that day's services, and nightly, before he wrapped himself in the blanket that L'loni lent him for the trip, he produced a set of monkey's knuckles and proceeded to lose every sou back to his erstwhile employers.

I tried to take the child to task, but he merely grinned at me, and spat into the fire.

"He's an idiot," I exclaimed impatiently.

"He doesn't understand what you're saying," L'loni answered.

"He's not deaf," I protested, "and my Hausa—it may not be perfect, but it's passed before."

"He doesn't speak Hausa," L'loni explained.

"What!"

As I stared at my companion, I remembered that for days he

had been using pidgin English, and that I too was picking up the bastard polyglot tongue. And at the same time I had continued to feel comfortable about my Hausa; I had been told that it was the lingua franca of the native population of the West Coast.

"You're well beyond coastal territory now," L'loni remarked as though reading my mind.

"What language do they speak at N'zem?"

"Luobolanga."

I thought of the months at Tani when I had tried to diagnose and treat patients intelligently in spite of the drawback of an interpreter. Now again I had no tongue, no ears.

"You'll get along," L'loni assured me. "I'll get you a teacher. Learning the language will slow you up a little, but in the end you may make more haste by a little less speed in the beginning."

I laughed, but I had no illusions about the brutally difficult labor ahead of me.

The last night before we reached N'zem, L'loni asked me to marry him. Perhaps if I had been younger I would have reacted a good deal differently.

"For heaven's sake!" was all I could get out at first.

He was sitting across the campfire from me and he grinned, but his tone was gentle.

"No, Ellen, for your and for my sake."

"But why me, of all people?"

The grin never left his face. "Not 'of all people,' Ellen, but of all the women I've really had a chance to know."

Several times I opened my mouth, but words simply did not come.

"I can give you as nice a house as there is in Léopoldville, and everything that goes with it," he went on. "And security. I'm not too young, and neither are you, and I'm not pretending I get hot and cold when I look at you, but—Africa can be an awfully lonely place, Ellen, if one doesn't have someone to come back to after trips into the bush. And I'd be good to you. You don't seem to mind having me around on this trip; maybe, sharing a house with me, part of the time anyway, wouldn't be so bad either."

"But, L'loni, I—I'm a missionary, a professional Christian worker," I finally burst out.

"Isn't homemaking Christian work?" he answered. "For my part, I think we'd have a better world if we had more Christian wives. And if you wanted to, there is no reason why you couldn't work in the villages surrounding Léopoldville, or even in the native quarter there."

"But L'loni, I—I—" For an ordinarily glib woman to be suddenly struck tongue-tied is a curious experience. "I never thought of loving you," I finally got out, with all the finesse of an elephant in a rose garden.

"I never brought the subject up before, did I?" he answered, and we both laughed.

"Love for people our age, Ellen, isn't what it is for young folks. Friendship and respect are what count now. Young love has to boil down to that anyway if it is to last a lifetime. And— I'm clean and decent. I don't drink or gamble or dissipate. I've never bought a black woman. I've never carried booze in my trade goods. I make a good profit, but what I sell doesn't hurt or degrade any purchaser. I stick by my bargains—"

"L'loni," I broke in suddenly, "how old are you?"

"Thirty-five."

"I'm old enough to be your mother," I remarked sententiously.

"Native or missionary standards?" he queried slyly. Again we laughed.

"I couldn't bear you children, L'loni," I said.

"If I don't marry, I'll never have any," he replied.

"You'll find some nice girl nearer your own age," I encouraged. "There's Sister Susanne, for instance."

"Let me pick out my wife, Ellen," he chided.

132

L'loni didn't say much more about the matter, either then or in the future, but it was a standing offer. Any time I might have wished, for the next two decades, I could have moved into Léopoldville and taken my place with the townswomen there as wife of one of the richest, most respected men in the territory.

The next day we reached N'zem, and as we entered the village, L'loni swore softly, "Well, I'll be damned."

"What is it?" I asked.

"Dr. Mary's kraal," he answered, pointing out a small clump of huts to me. "There's her house, and her hospital, and her dispensary."

The three *dukases* were exactly like all the other huts in the village with one exception: dangling in the doorway of each was a little figurine of crudely carved wood and straw.

"Well?" Even with the figurines, nothing about the huts seemed strange enough to me to have called forth the expletive from this calm man.

"Don't you see? They didn't burn her huts!" he went on. "They believe that when a person is born, two spirits struggle for ascendency in him—Leza, who is good, and Mifwa, who is evil. Sometimes they can tell from a man's, or woman's, life that Mifwa entered his body at birth. They can't always be sure of Leza, however, because evil tries to disguise itself as good. Consequently, when a man or woman dies, they build him a little hut out near the swamp into which they throw the body, and they hang an effigy of the person in the doorway of the tiny hut so the spirit will know that that is to be its home from then on. And to make sure that no evil spirit comes back to live in the village, they burn the hut it used while alive. They must be so certain that Dr. Mary's soul was very, very good that they left her huts standing for her spirit's home. It's the first time I ever saw this happen."

"Maybe she died so far away that they think there is no chance of her soul's coming back," I suggested.

"Maybe so," he agreed. "But in that case, why would they hang the little figurines in the doorways?"

I had no answer to that, but suddenly the thought occurred to me: "Aren't they Christian? After all, Dr. Mary spent half a lifetime with them! Then, why this—this pagan custom?"

L'loni gave me a sharp look before replying, "Don't you know, Ellen, that Christianity is just as apt to be a veneer here in Africa as—as it is in Middletown, U.S.A.?"

I felt shocked and hurt, and must have showed it, but L'loni did not give any theological ground.

"With more reason here, Ellen. Back home in a Christian country, all you have to struggle with is innate human cussedness, which ought to be a preacher's meat; here you have to uproot one religion before you can plant another. And the roots of the old belief are deep and strong and very much alive."

The villagers had known for days that we were coming, and as we entered N'zem, a feast was in preparation. "For you as Dr. Mary's successor," L'loni told me.

But I wondered if it were not equally for him as Dr. Mary's friend—or possibly just because he was himself. He denied this vigorously.

There was not a great variety of food, but plenty of it, and the quantities consumed were a thing to marvel at. The men and women swelled visibly as they gorged themselves, and, once the feast had begun, no one but L'loni and I stopped eating until every scrap had been consumed.

"In a day or two you may notice that they, particularly the women, have put on weight behind," L'loni told me. "A curious thing about these people is that in times of plenty they seem able to store up food in their gluteal muscles in the same way a camel stores up food and water in its humps."

"Can they go without eating?" I asked.

"Well, they do weather some pretty bad famines, particularly in locust years," he answered.

Then, "How did you like the feast?" he asked suddenly.

"All right," I answered, but sensed there was more behind his words than the simple question. "Why?"

"That little dark-brown cake you ate several pieces of—you liked it?"

"Uh-huh. What was it? Millet cake?"

L'loni only looked at me.

"Well, what was it?" I demanded.

"Shall I really tell you?" It was evident that he was enjoying some huge joke.

"Of course!" I was very positive.

"It was midge cake."

"What?"

"Midge cake. Tiny gnats, you know. They sometimes come out of the swamps in swarms so thick that you can't breathe without a cloth over your face. The natives rake them out of the air by the basketful, press them into cakes, and dry them. Then, when they want them, they toast them a little to take any mold off. They're considered great delicacies."

"L'loni," I said calmly, "you're a beast. I turned you down last night, but you're acting like a husband anyway."

Then I stood up and wobbled around behind a hut. Firmly I clutched my forehead in one hand, leaned over, and held my skirts back with the other. Nothing happened. I straightened up and found myself surrounded by a mob of bright-eyed, curious women and children. There was nothing to do but to turn and go back to the fire. L'loni met me with a grin.

"The python and the monkey were delicious," I announced, without knowing why I said such a thing.

His grin faded and he stared like any popeyed child. "You really knew what you were eating, and you ate it anyway? I have to hand it to you, Ellen—you're some woman!"

I hadn't known until that instant, but I wouldn't have told him so for anything in the world. The rest of that evening I caught him staring at me more than once, surprised admiration lighting up his eyes. And that look, the glow on his face, filled me with a strange happiness. It was the last thing I remembered after I had lain down to sleep, but in the middle of the

135

night I sat bolt upright on my cot and said to myself in amazement: "You fool! You utter fool! Are you, at your age, falling in love? And with a—a—a—bushwhacking kid?"

I decided that next day I would have to be abrupt with him, to drive any notions he might have completely out of his mind. Then I lay down to sleep again, glowing with a happiness new and strange to me, and thoroughly delightful.

CHAPTER
11

THE next morning L'loni brought around an old man who was to be my language teacher. He was wealthy, L'loni told me. He had many women in his kraal who had borne him many daughters, and these he had sold and was still selling to good advantage. Naturally, only a man of such standing merited the importance of being my teacher. Besides, he knew more pidgin English than any of his tribesmen. L'loni armed me with a few phrases in the local dialect, such as, "What is your name?" "What do you call this?" and, "I am hungry. I am thirsty." These I memorized like nonsense syllables.

"I'll have to move on before noon," he told me, "but I'll be back to say good-by." Then he left me with the old man in what had been Dr. Mary's bedroom and living room *dukas*. Armed with a pencil and paper, I faced my teacher with the intention of learning as much Luobolanga as possible that morning, and every morning thereafter.

"What do you call this?" I asked, leveling my forefinger at a small table against the wall.

"N'lembo," came the answer very promptly.

"N—lem—bo," I parroted, writing the sounds down as carefully as my scant knowledge of the international phonetic alphabet permitted.

"*N'lembo, N'lembo, N'lembo,*" I mumbled, staring at the table. I had no illusions about the task ahead of me. The first weeks would be a brutal memory grind, and after that would come the intricacies of the grammar of an agglutinate language: that is, a language that inflected by a system of variable prefixes as well as affixes and was not above knotting an entire sentence up into one word.

"Table—*N'lembo,*" I was still mumbling when I turned back to the old man.

"What is this?" I asked, pointing at a chair.

"*N'lembo,*" he answered promptly.

I turned to my pad. "Chair," I wrote, "*N'lembo.*"

The old man grinned companionably and never took his beady eyes off me for a second. I pointed at the table again. "What do you call this?"

"*N'lembo.*"

"What do you call this?" I turned my finger to the chair.

"*N'lembo.*"

"This?" pointing at the floor.

"*N'lembo.*"

I stared at the old man in perplexity and he continued grinning. Perhaps I wasn't pronouncing my question correctly. I took a deep breath, walked over, and tapped the edge of the table with my index finger. Slowly and carefully I put the question: "What—do—you—call—this?"

"*N'lembo.*"

I flinched at the already too familiar syllables.

I tapped the back of the chair, waited a minute, then tried a different attack.

"*N'lembo?*" I shouted at him quite suddenly.

He arose from his heels, walked over facing me, and shook a finger under my nose and shouted in return: "*N'lembo, bwana! N'lembo! N'lembo! N'lembo!*"

I don't know what I would have done had not L'loni come in at that moment.

"How are you making out?" he asked.

"Someone in this hut is crazy," I answered. "And your guess is as good as mine which of us it is."

"What seems to be the trouble?"

"*N'lembo*," I answered.

He lifted his hands, and looked at them. "What's wrong with my finger?" he asked.

"Your finger!" I exclaimed.

"Well, your finger then. Or grandpop's?"

"Now you're crazy too," I assured him.

"What's the matter, Ellen?" he demanded in that tone which requires an explanation. "Begin at the beginning."

"Everything is *N'lembo*," I told him.

My teacher held up a finger for our inspection. "*N'lembo*," he put in triumphantly, without losing a wrinkle of his grin.

L'loni stared at me for a moment and then threw back his head and laughed, great guffaws of masculine superiority.

"Go ahead, chortle," I told him a trifle bitterly. "The work is mine here at N'zem, to develop as I see need. Right now a good insane asylum would about fit the bill."

He patted me on the shoulder. "Never mind, Ellen, it's really my fault," he assured me generously. "I should have told you that these people never point with their fingers. They point with their lower lips. See? Like this!"

And as naturally as I would lift a hand, L'loni's nether lip shot out in a peak toward the table and he asked, "What do you call this?"

"*L'terfi*," was the prompt answer.

"What do you call this?" His lower lip indicated the chair. "*O'lamboo*."

"You see, it's as easy as all that," he assured me.

"Heaven help me," I moaned. "I'll never be able to point at anything with my lip."

"Sure you will," L'loni consoled. "I'll explain to grandpop so he'll be patient with you while you learn."

Guttural syllables flew back and forth between the two men, words spiced with much laughter. Then L'loni turned back to me with his eyes dancing. "Grandpop thinks the men who speak your language would be awfully poor people to go hunting with," he said. "He wants to know how they could manage a bow and arrow or spear if they had to wave their hands about in order to make themselves understood."

The whole village must have laughed at me that evening, and for days thereafter, whenever I appeared, the small fry danced about me, holding up rigid forefingers and dinning into my ears: *"N'lembo, mama. N'lembo. N'lembo."*

That afternoon L'loni went on, leaving me and Jackie, my gunbearer, behind in N'zem. He also left behind about two hundred and fifty pounds of salt.

"I'll bring you some every time I come through," he told me. "Your money is practically no good here, but salt will buy you anything. A little bit, remember—measure it out by the spoonful. A spoonful for a bunch of bananas, or three or four chickens, or a basket of mealies. A handful for a goat. Make it last until I come back, even if you have to be hard to do so. Your own health, maybe even your life, may depend on it."

"A spoonful of salt for a basket of mealies!" I exclaimed in amazement. A fraction of a cent's worth of salt for a dollar's worth of corn. No wonder L'loni could afford to be generous with his black customers and still make at least eight hundred per cent profit!

The fourth morning after L'loni had left, I heard a gentle cough outside my door as I stretched and yawned preparatory to getting up. A moment later, there was another discreet cough and the door opened slowly to admit what had very evidently been Dr. Mary's tea tray. The tray was followed by a tall, handsome youth in a white *kanzu*.

My eyes sleepily took in this Mother Hubbard type of garment, which looks something like a square-tailed nightshirt and is much affected by the natives of the East Coast. Slowly my gaze traveled from the gaping neck placket to the side-dipping hem. Then I sat upright and stared in amazement, for the fellow's feet were stuck into heelless slippers, in which he walked as lightly, and much more gracefully, than I did in my brogues. He was the only shod native I ever saw outside Léopoldville and the coastal cities.

"Good morning, *mama*," he greeted me in English with a broad Scottish accent. "I am Achmed. I will have your bath ready in five minutes."

While I stared at this apparition, he plumped up the pillows behind my back, placed the tray across my knees, picked up my garments of the day before and went out with them. On the tray was a little stack of freshly baked mealie cakes, fruit, and a glass of milk. Five minutes later, punctually, Achmed appeared with two jars of hot water.

"This waters is for your face and hands and foots, *mama*," he explained. "And this waters is for your elsewheres."

He picked up the empty tray, cast careful eye about, and almost backed out of my presence. I arose and bathed—face, hands, foots, and elsewheres. When I stepped outside the hut, yesterday's garments already fluttered on a line Achmed had stretched between the trunks of two mango trees. Half of N'zem was lined up staring at them in admiring wonder. Achmed lolled against the trunk of one of the mangoes, obviously standing guard.

I was as curious as the villagers. "Where did you come from?" I demanded. "And who in the world are you?"

The *kanzu*-clad stranger snapped to attention, folded his arms across his breast, and bowed from the waist. "I am Achmed, *mama*. I am your houseboy. I will be a good servant, *mama*, never fear." I thought I detected a note of anxiety in his voice. "The Bwana L'loni sent me. He told me he will wring my neck and break my back and stake me out in the midday sun on a red anthill if I do not take good care of you, and the Bwana L'loni always keeps his word. He said you would pay me sixteen francs a month."

So far as I know, that was the only lie Achmed ever told me. L'loni had set the price at twelve francs, but with the franc exchanging at twenty to the dollar, sixteen francs was not an exhorbitant wage for a boy who before the week was out ran the domestic side of my ménage as perfectly as an English butler.

Achmed never told me much of anything about himself, true or false. Even when I asked him where he came from, he would wave his hand and say, "Over there," vaguely indicating the East. It was not until L'loni came through again half a year later that I learned his story. He was from Kenya Colony, a Kavirondo with some Arab in his blood, who had been sent to a mission school in Kisumu. Academically he had done well there, almost too well for his country and time, for his keen mind had quickly overleaped the barriers of fetish-ridden tribal customs. When he returned to his village, the missionaries regarded him as a child, and his people looked upon him as a still uninitiated man. In his adolescent arrogance, he had flouted the mummery of that ceremony, and had treated the unwed girls with the same easy familiarity he had always shown his female companions at the mission school.

"No one will ever know whether or not the kid actually did anything he shouldn't have," L'loni told me. "Anyway, the witch doctor blew his nonsense up into a major crime and demanded his mutilation. Being a mission boy, he didn't just tamely give up to the witch doctor, but fled, and he was smart enough to put the width of the continent between himself and his people."

Aside from the fact that Achmed overcharged me four francs per month, he was a perfect servant. And during his entire time with me, he never once asked for a raise in salary. I gave him several, which he received gratefully, but he never asked.

He was perfect—not that he did so much himself, but he saw that the necessary work was done, and done correctly. He trained one *boy* to cook for me, another to clean the huts, a third to wash, a fourth to bring in a plentiful supply of wood and to keep the fires going. He ran my ménage like a well-oiled machine and I was scarcely conscious of the machinery. He was with me the rest of that first term of service; and when I returned to the United States on my first furlough, he accompanied me to Léopoldville where I found him a position in a French household.

N'zem remembered Dr. Mary with love and complete confidence in her powers of healing. And now that she was gone, they came to me, the Little White Witch Doctor, with such helpless appeal in their faces and trust in my abilities that I quite honestly believe I healed by faith alone. Dr. Mary, that wise old woman, had known all along that I would go to N'zem, and had left her medical books and journals there for me, all carefully wrapped in oiled cloth against the ravages of mold, and stored in a galvanized iron trunk to protect them from the white ants. I read late into the night, every night, until I knew those few books almost by heart, and, crude as it sounds, I taught myself what surgery I know by working on living, usually unanesthetized, human beings. I am not a sadist; I have never been cruel in any degree. But I simply could not look at a shattered limb with fragments of bone protruding through the flesh and shake my head with the sententious excuse that I was a nurse and not a doctor. I tackled the hopelessly impossible because I believed then, and I believe now, that God was with me.

It was natural that I should pray with a scalpel in my hand. And the prayer was no less sincere when the intensity of the task before me broke coherent thought down into a rote: "God, help me! Help me! Help me!" Not many of my surgery patients died; perhaps no larger a percentage than die on the operating tables of America's proudest hospitals. And I don't believe I ever maimed a single patient. There is more to the maintenance of life than starched uniforms and college degrees. I worked seven days a week—and it was as surely God's work as the oratory of any preacher in his pulpit.

I worked seven days a week, ten, twelve, even sixteen hours a day. How I kept up, I don't know, but it is a curious thing that breakdowns occur usually only in modern, progressive, so-called civilized countries. The missionary who collapses does so, not on the field, but at home on furlough. I don't know what keeps one going, unless it is the very real, if old-fashioned, saving power of faith in God.

I never felt isolated or lonely at N'zem. I was surrounded almost every waking hour by people who, although I could not converse with them for several months, communicated with me nevertheless, and who needed me. Before her illness, Dr. Mary had told them about the Little White Witch Doctor who would come after her, and be their *mama*. They took me in with simple faith that I could ease all pain and cure all physical ills, and at the same time would not make too much trouble for them with their own big black witch doctors.

They came to me from far and near, sometimes simply to gaze at me because they were wretched and the only white people they had ever known had given them kindness and understanding and help when it was possible—L'loni and Dr. Mary and now me. Matters were not going well with some of them. There had been locusts the year before and the second crop of mealies they had planted had been stunted. This year there had been too much rain and the precious seeds had rotted in the soggy earth. Obesity is a mark of feminine beauty in many African tribes, and there were few belles in my section of the country that season.

At least twice a week I took my gun and Jackie and, with perhaps a half dozen men tagging along, went out after game. We could go east or south into the jungle, or west toward the great plains beyond which stretched The Hungry Country; but

144

we could not go to the north. In that direction, across the little N'zem, tributary of the Tani River, stretched mile upon mile of an apparently endless swamp.

Dr. Mary had gone into that swamp. The Pygmies lived there, the true "little men"—not the Batwa hybrids, who are merely five-foot half-breeds living on the edge of the great swamp. The Pygmies had been Dr. Mary's friends, as all human beings were, and she had snorted scornfully at the fabulous tales concerning them.

"They're shy. Just shy," had been her explanation. "That's why some fools are quick to say they're half monkey and live in trees, or that they're subnormal in intelligence. They're smart enough; they've got to make up with cunning what they lack in size and strength—and sometimes a show of knowledge isn't the smartest behavior."

I did treat the Batwa Pygmies. One of them, whom I always called Job because of his extreme patience, became a house servant of mine. I took him in because he came to me to have his body straightened. Some animal he had been trailing—I guessed from his description that it must have been an elephant, although the idea of anybody as small and weak as Job hunting elephants seemed ridiculous—had ambushed him and kicked and stamped him and left him with his back and both legs broken. Somehow he had lived and his bones had knit together, but from his shoulders down he was as angular and awkward-looking as a gorilla. He became an excellent laundryman, and with his fingers alone would smooth the lace on my underwear until it dried as crisp as any French laundress could have ironed it.

I wondered at such care until he told me one day: "It is beautiful, *mama,* like the ferns of the jungle, only all life is bleached out of it and it is dead. Why do you not wear ferns, *mama?* When they die, you could throw them away and they would not have to be washed."

I hunted twice a week. There was always fowl for my table

and usually zebra for my villagers. I don't like zebra meat; it is sweetish and high-flavored and when a native has eaten much of it, a distinct zebraish odor is discernible. The fat, tried out and clarified, is something like vegetable margarine, and I have used it for butter more than once.

I would never kill monkeys for my people, and they could not understand why.

"Shoot, *mama,* shoot! The meat is good," they would plead when some curious band trailed us, swinging along for miles in the treetops overheard. "We will stew the hands with ground-nuts and kola oil and bring them all to you," they would promise, hoping to tempt me with this offer of what they considered tidbits.

Even on the days when I hunted, I often ministered to as many as a hundred sick people. In Tani I had kept an orderly file of my patients. At the end of the first fortnight at N'zem, I burned what records I had jotted down, and used the time and energy they would have consumed in establishing a ward of sorts in a hut next to my dispensary. I could have filled that hut ten times over the first day. And when a man or woman or child enters the "sick kraal" of a white witch doctor, he does not come alone; his relatives bring him. They throw up rude shelters as near the "sick kraal" as the white witch doctor will allow, and care for the physical needs of the patient, cooking his food and feeding him, bathing or rubbing him with castor oil, and taking him home when released—or spiriting him away when treatments are distrusted or disapproved. This custom saved me endless hours of toil.

Nevertheless, I knew immediately that I would need nurses, and at dinner one night I asked Achmed's advice concerning suitable women he might know of in N'zem. He pitied my ignorance quite frankly.

"In hospitals that I have known, *mama,* the nurses were all men," he told me.

"Why men?" I asked.

He was very patient. "Because, *mama,* when a girl is big and strong enough for the work you require, she is old enough for a husband and a hoe and babies," he explained.

"How about the older women?" I questioned. "Those who are beyond their childbearing years?"

"Those dirty bitches? Would you have them about?"

"Achmed! Where did you ever learn to call women such names as that?" I demanded.

He stared at me in wide-eyed injured innocence. "Why, *mama,* that is what the white overseers at the Kilo and Katanga mines always call black women, particularly old women."

"There are wicked white men as well as wicked black men, Achmed, and you are old enough and experienced enough to know that," I scolded.

"I may know it, but I may not say it, *mama,*" he answered me simply. The matter ended there, but I couldn't help asking myself how a black *boy* was to know which of his white masters to emulate when frequently the evil man was the one of greatest worldly preferment among his own people.

A befogging sense of futility settled over me as I approached my work the next morning. And it seemed to me there were more people waiting outside my door than ever before. Each one of the miserable wretches wanted to talk to me and none of them could. My back began to ache before the day was half over, and finally a thousand little devils, each with a knife in its hand, perched themselves on my shoulder blades and began hacking away at the base of my brain—or at least that's the way it felt. It was my first attack of malaria, and, thank heaven, it was an exceedingly light one.

Stupidly enough, I did not diagnose my own symptoms. I only knew it became excruciating agony for me to wait while each patient mouthed the nonsense syllables that seemed so necessary to his peace of mind before he moved on to make room for the next ailing person.

147

"No wonder Dr. Mary killed herself here," I muttered bitterly, forgetting that my predecessor had lived to a ripe old age.

The shadows were long when my last patient hobbled away. I turned back into my dispensary and sank into a chair, too tired to sterilize my instruments and put away my bandages and drugs, too exhausted to walk the fifty feet between the dispensary and my hut where I knew the ever watchful Achmed was already preparing a hot bath for me.

If it had been Achmed coming to call me, I would have heard his step; he was always careful that I should. But there was no sound whatsoever until someone behind me coughed. I didn't move, and the cough was repeated, softly but insistently.

"Go away and come back tomorrow," I exclaimed petulantly. "After all there's a limit to what I can do."

There were a few seconds of silence and again that cough. Then I remembered that only Achmed of all the souls in N'zem could understand my English; only Job and Jackie, my Hausa; and only God, my French. I felt thoroughly beaten. Perhaps I would have burst into womanly tears, had not a vagrant breeze wafted in to my nostrils such a stench as I hope never to have to smell again. I whirled about, full of temper and quite enough energy to deal with this new problem. Facing me stood the tallest, gauntest, most wrinkled old woman I have ever seen, stark-naked except for a goatskin slung over her back and knotted across one shoulder.

I looked her over from head to foot and could not find a single blemish on her; rather, I was impressed with her air of health and physical strength. Then I came back to her face and gazed into eyes that were feverish with—what was it? Terror? But she did not drop her eyes; instead she stared back at me until I, forgetting my ignorance of the local language, waved her permission to speak.

Then I gasped in amazement, for she said to me slowly, laboriously, but still in perfect English and with an Oxford accent, "Mistress, I wish to be a mother."

148

CHAPTER
12

MORE astonishing than the old woman's English was the term of respect she had used. I had grown so used to the ubiquitous *mama,* which implies not only respect and affection, but some claim on the white woman's charity, that I wondered just what she meant. She read the inquiry in my eyes and spoke again, her voice low and supplicating, "Mistress, I wish to be a mother."

At this she seized an edge of the goatskin and slid it around until a pouch formed by the broad part of the pelt rested directly on her hip. Almost as a tabby cat would pick up a kitten with her mouth, the woman's clawlike fingers closed around the back of an infant and held it out to me.

At first I thought it was newborn, then I saw that the navel cord, which had received no more attention than the cord of a zebra colt newly foaled on the veld, was dried up hard as a twig and ready to drop off of itself. The infant had never been cleaned from birth, and its lower body was so completely plastered with its own filth that it was impossible even to tell what sex it was.

Then the baby whimpered, and the woman took a cautious step forward, dropped it into my lap, and leaped back like a child or pet that has learned to expect blows instead of caresses.

Involuntarily I shut my nostrils against the stench and held my breath as well as I could.

As I did so, all the cumulative weariness of the past months of unremitting toil engulfed me and I lashed out at the woman with a storm of unreasoning words. Under my outburst, the hag shrank into a corner until she was crouched near the doorway, but she did not go away. She watched me, keen-eyed, until I wore myself out; then she opened her lips and slowly, a syllable at a time, repeated her message: "Miss-tress-I-wish-to-be-a-moth-er."

Perfect English, but the only words she knew in the language.

My temper tantrum over, momentarily, I sighed and turned my attention to the repulsive bit of humanity on my lap. There was no doubt that it needed immediate attention.

It took me the better part of two days to clean the infant thoroughly. At the time, I picked off some of the dirt with my fingernails, but most of it I had to loosen with repeated applications of oil before I dared to peel or scale it off. I hadn't enough of the usual medical unguents and I had to use what the natives express from the castor bean for the purpose of anointing their own bodies.

As I worked, night fell and I lighted a lamp. And then Achmed came to scold me for working too long. I showed him the child, but when I turned to point out the old woman, she was nowhere to be seen. Nowhere! Neither inside the dispensary nor within sight outside of it, although I circled the hut myself and shouted.

Back in the dispensary, I turned to Achmed. "What shall I do with it?" I indicated the tiny bundle of oil-soaked cotton wool.

It was only a rhetorical query, but my houseboy took it in good faith and gave what he considered sound advice. "Throw it into the bushes for the jackals, *mama*. It is nothing. It is not big and strong enough for Leza and Mifwa to fight over. It will only cost you worry as long as it suckles and bleats."

I carried the child back to my living *dukas* and laid it on a chair. In a few minutes Achmed came in bearing a calabash neatly sawed in two. Deftly, but disdainfully, he transferred my new charge to its odd but excellent cradle.

"I would not like you to forget and sit on the little worm," he told me. "The wash *boy* would never be able to get its filth out of your skirts."

Achmed maintained that attitude toward the child, but he helped me keep it alive. For my part, I shall never again look upon a newborn child as something delicate; the tenacity with which that bit of abused flesh clung to life was amazing.

I had two goats which supplied milk for my table, and Achmed, although such labor was normally below his dignity as major-domo to the white *mama,* caught one of the nannies and tied her to my doorjamb. He milked me a spoonful while I warmed a little sweetened water over my lamp; then with an eye dropper, I gave the child its first taste of food since birth. It was so shrunken that its tiny lips could not have mouthed a human nipple. I held its lips apart with thumb and forefinger and watched its tongue. Would it swallow? Or was it too weak? The drop of warm, weak food disappeared, but I could not tell where—into its lungs, its throat, or merely through the membranes into its dehydrated body. Slowly I placed another tiny drop on its tongue.

That first feeding took upward of an hour, and Achmed stood beside me the whole time, cupping the glass that held the milk and water in his hands, in order to keep it warm, and holding it over the lamp whenever I looked at him. It was an intense and exhausting hour, but before it was over, the tiny tongue was moving, sucking at the tip of the medicine dropper. Then the little head lolled sideways on its fragile stem of a neck and there was the faintest breath of a snore.

151

Achmed and I straightened up and looked at each other, triumph in every line of our faces. I think I would have giggled or cried from the hysteria of sheer relief had not my houseboy called my attention back to the child with an expressive gesture.

"See! Mata Kwan sleeps," he announced.

I pulled a dab of oily cotton a little farther over the child's scaly forehead and felt to see if the ear on which it was resting lay back against its head as it should.

"Mata Kwan." I rolled the soft syllables over my tongue. "Mata Kwan. I like the sound of the name you have given the child, but what do the words mean?"

"Mata Kwan, the Son-of-a-Goat," he answered.

African names no longer surprised me, but I opened my eyes wide at this one. Achmed shrugged his shoulders while he pointed to the nanny tied to my doorjamb. "There stands his mother," he laughed. "You and I are only the midwives." Still laughing, he turned away, but called over his shoulder in a tone that admitted of no argument, "You must come now and have your own supper, *mama*."

"Achmed," I asked him as I sat enjoying one of his delicious custards of beaten green coconut meat, "how do you know that the child is a boy? We may have to call her Chibwa Kwan, the Daughter-of-a-Goat."

Achmed clicked a thumbnail against his strong white teeth in a gesture of extreme contempt. "A daughter, *mama*? Pffflt! A female would have died long ago. Only a male creature could be strong enough to survive such abuse."

I laughed at his reasoning but, unaccountably, hoped he was right.

Supper over, I went back to my sleeping *dukas,* and stopped in the doorway to stare. There was the strange old woman, squatting on the floor beside the chair on which Mata Kwan's absurd cradle rested. The goat tried to enter with me, and I drove the creature out with a slap on the nose. At the sound the old woman looked up. Without a word or even a change of expression, she arose, walked to the door, and milked a few spoonfuls from nanny into the glass Achmed had used. Again I warmed water over the lamp with which to dilute the milk and fed Mata Kwan, who must have downed all of two tablespoonfuls. I made no move that escaped the woman's scrutiny. Although she had disappeared from the dispensary upon Achmed's arrival, there had probably been no instant when I and the baby had not been under closest surveillance.

Knowing what was ahead of me that night, I wondered if it were worth-while to go to bed at all, but finally I undressed, set the alarm clock to go off in a half hour, turned down the light, and unrolled a straw mat on the floor. Then I motioned to the woman that she too should get what rest she could. But she did not understand about alarm clocks, and she took no chances on oversleeping. I was groggy from the malaria and exhaustion, but before I fell asleep I saw her wrap the straw mat about her shoulders. Then she squatted beside the chair, staring at the calabash cradle with all the intensity of a hen that has just discovered a bright pebble.

Stark terror and determination to defend the baby at any cost were written all over her face when next I saw it—a few seconds after my alarm went off. She was standing erect beside the baby's chair, the calabash clutched tightly in her arms. I shut off the alarm, laughing a little as I did so, for I could imagine this primitive woman, in the future, surrounded by her village sisters all agape at a tale of a white witch doctor who with a mere pat of her hand silenced the screaming devils imprisoned in a box.

Tumbling out of bed, I picked up the glass, and held it out to her. Without a second's hesitation she put Mata Kwan down, aroused nanny with a good kick, and milked me a spoonful. This time it was she who held the infant's lips apart so I could see its tongue. The youngster drank greedily, and I heard the old woman sigh ever so lightly. I looked up and we smiled briefly into each other's eyes.

Every half hour during that entire night, I awoke and fed and otherwise cared for the baby. The next morning when I woke up at the usual time for my breakfast, the woman was again nowhere to be seen. I leaped to my feet and ran to the calabash, my heart almost in my mouth. But Mata Kwan was sleeping peacefully, as he sucked spasmodically at the tips of two of his fingers. I heaved a sigh of relief, realizing that this baby in one troubled night had already woven itself into the fabric of my life.

Achmed brought me my breakfast tray and I asked him about the old woman.

"That one!" he murmured disdainfully. "No, I don't know who she is. No, I don't know where she came from. But I know she was here." He sniffed with exaggerated emphasis as much as to say: "Why, I can even smell her presence!"

So could I.

I carried Mata Kwan to the dispensary that morning, Achmed trailing behind with nanny on a string. He came to fetch me—and the goat—when lunch was ready, and took us back after a short siesta. The baby created quite a furor among my patients, and his name was a source of as much astonishment as humor.

"How do you know that the goat is not the family fetish of his people?" one old woman asked me.

"If nanny is his totem, she is doing pretty well by him," I answered in substance.

The old beldam drew back in horror at this flaunting of tribal law, and I hastened to reinstate myself in her respect. "If the goat or her milk were harmful to the child in any way, he would be dead by now, wouldn't he?"

"That surely is so," she agreed, and sighed loudly in relief that the spite of none of the malicious spirits of the jungle had been ignorantly aroused.

154

"What do you usually feed your newborn orphans?" I asked her, and again she drew back as though I had struck her. "And what do you do when a mother's milk fails?" I went on. "Does another woman act as wet nurse?" I had to explain the term to my interpreter, who took some time to get the idea across to the old woman.

I could see her stiffening as understanding dawned. "Are we women to starve our own children?" she muttered angrily and stalked away.

I was too busy to ponder long on her words. More often I thought of the strange old woman's absence when other people were about, and of her immediate appearance when I was alone. Everyone in the village of N'zem knew she was about, yet no one ever saw her but me. During the daylight hours she hid herself like a furtive animal.

At the end of two days I had Mata Kwan's body completely clean, and Achmed had been right—the baby was a boy. He had a beautiful little body, perfect in every way, unscarred in spite of the neglect he had suffered. He shed his little dried up twig of a navel cord like a calf in a barnyard.

Achmed was triumphant, but at the same time he cautioned me, "His wiving will cost you much good money, *mama*."

"His what?" I asked.

"His wiving. When the time comes that you must buy him women," he explained. Achmed was always very patient with me where my stupidity of tribal affairs was concerned.

"But he isn't *my* son," I protested.

"Neither is he hers," Achmed argued.

I recalled the only words the old woman had ever spoken to me in her carefully clipped English. Obviously she knew what she was saying. But if she were not the child's mother, how had she come by it?

I tried to question her in English, French, and what little I knew of the N'zem dialect. Carefully, a syllable at a time. She understood my gestures and that was all. But these she understood well. By the end of a week she was caring for Mata Kwan, not as a tribal sister would have done, but as though he were a white baby—diapers, daily bath, regular feedings, and naps.

I met my Waterloo when it came to devising a nipple, and the old woman was no help at all because I could not make her understand what I wanted. Achmed saved the day for us. He too apparently had never seen a nipple, but I drew pictures for him and explained its use by the women of my tribe far across the jungle and ocean and he produced a length of bamboo scraped thin, over which he had tied a tiny pouch of perforated gut. I sterilized it as best I could and it worked like a charm.

Mata Kwan had goat's milk, weak broth, and a little fruit juice, and he thrived like a plant in spring sunshine after a warm rain. He never had *posho,* the half-cooked corn mush which is a staple of native diet all over Africa. It is rolled into pellets and rammed down the throats of even the tiniest infants by determined maternal forefingers. *Posho*-fed children are pot-bellied in the extreme, and most of them are sway-backed from the weight of the huge stomachs they must carry.

In two weeks Mata Kwan more than doubled his weight. It took ten eggs to balance him on the rude pair of scales I had made out of bamboo fiber and banana leaves. When he had first arrived, his weight only balanced slightly more than four eggs. And when he wanted fresh diapers, or food, he made his desires known in squawks that would have done credit to any other child of his age.

Therefore my protests were not completely wholehearted when Jackie, my gunbearer, came to me with the statement, *"Mama,* it is more than half a moon now since the people of N'zem have had fresh food and they hunger for it."

"You mean," I corrected him, "that you would like some meat, and a chance to stretch your muscles in the jungle. You're getting fat sitting around the palaver hut all day long."

Jackie, like most African servants, did only the work for

which he was hired. One or two days a week he was an incomparable tracker, a steady gunbearer, and an expert butcher. The rest of the time he dozed or gossiped wherever the greatest comfort and the best stories were to be had. Needless to say, he had picked up the language of the N'zemi, grammar and idioms, while I was still struggling with the scantiest of substantive vocabularies. But as long as he remained with me, he never addressed me in any language but Hausa. It was so now, as he ignored my thrust and argued, "Even you cannot keep up your strength, *mama,* without flesh food."

I laughed at him. My attack of malaria was over, and I had never felt better in my life. "It must be the baby," I murmured to myself. "I've been so busy with it that I haven't had time to—collapse."

"But I think about you, *mama;* many times during the day my thoughts turn to you," Jackie answered to my surprise. I hadn't supposed he heard me. "I think of you and I am very much concerned. You need fat on your bones, *mama;* and it is flesh food that—"

"All right, Jackie, tomorrow we'll go hunting," I answered. "The old woman can take care of Mata Kwan as well as I. And—"

Again I was thinking aloud, and before the day was over there was proof that although the old woman might not be in my sight when others were around, I was constantly in hers—and in this case in her hearing as well.

"*Mama,*" she said to me that evening, "you can leave the child with me while you kill flesh food for the village cooking pots."

I don't know which surprised me more, that she had called me *mama* instead of mistress, or that she had spoken to me in stumbling Hausa! Had I only known it, I could have talked with her two weeks before when she had brought me the filth-encrusted Mata Kwan.

We talked a long time that night, two lone women there

in a hut on the edge of a great jungle swamp. Aganza—I soon learned her name—was as naturally garrulous as all her African sisters, but life had bred caution in her, and, try as I would, she guided the conversation. We talked mostly of Mata Kwan—what a perfectly formed body he had, how beautiful he was, his chances of attaining manhood in spite of the malicious spirits that surround every child at birth. Then we talked of my work, and the great need for others like me who had healing in their finger tips and love for things African in their hearts.

I questioned Aganza about herself, at first with some skill, I thought, and then with brutal directness, but the woman was clever, even brilliant. She parried every query with questions of her own. But she stumbled at length and, once I had a hold on her, I did not let go, although it took weeks to get the whole story.

She had picked up my hand and was turning it this way and that, prodding the palm and joints with her fingers. "It would never do for the hoe," she told me at length. "The skin and the flesh underneath are soft, like those of a newborn child. Your shadow would not shorten a hand's breadth in the morning sun before that skin would hang in wisps like rotting grass. Then devils would creep into the raw flesh and it, too, would fall away in evil-smelling chunks. My hands—" She dropped my palm and spread out her own fingers before her eyes. "My hands were meant for shaping pots and pounding grain and wielding the hoe. They could never seize torn flesh and fasten it together again before the spirit escaped through the rent in the body."

"Nonsense!" I started to say but the word died on my lips as my heart leaped at the thought that had just occurred to me.

"Aganza!" I grasped her knee in my excitement. "Why don't you stay with me and learn how to care for sick people? Together we could do so much more. And you would learn quickly, very quickly—I know it. Will you stay, Aganza? Can you? Will those who own you—" I was pleading, fearful of ties or tribal law that would take her away from me.

Gently the old woman answered: "I must stay with you. I will not go back without Mata Kwan, and if I took him back, they would kill him."

CHAPTER
13

Long after Mata Kwan had outgrown his calabash cradle, Aganza still slept beside him, squatting on her heels as he lay in a crib contrived from a segment of discarded tribal drum. Before I crawled into bed, I would tell Aganza about my patients of that day. At first her questions were naïve, but her mind was keen and her questions and comments quickly took on a searching quality that sent me more and more often to Dr. Mary's medical books for answers. And as I instructed her, I gradually picked up fragments of my pupil's life.

I don't know where she was born, but it was surely in Hausa territory, for that was the half-forgotten language of her childhood. And, as nearly as I can estimate, she was about my own age, somewhere in her forties. Her father had been neither wealthy nor prominent, and by African standards she had not been strikingly beautiful; therefore her first marriage had been a simple sale to a neighbor, several times her age, who already had a half dozen wives and a score of children. After her first three children had died at birth, her husband had palmed her off on an unsuspecting stranger. With her second husband, Aganza's wandering had begun, and she could no more list for me all the villages she had lived in than she could number her husbands or count her children. This man had sold her in anger because he did not like the way she cooked his mealies; that one, in order to raise money with which to pay his hut tax; another, because his first wife was jealous of Aganza and he wanted peace in his kraal—the reasons were legion. She had worked in the shambas, the gardens, of each man who possessed her like a farm animal, and apparently had calved as regularly. But Aganza never spoke of the children she had borne as hers. Both sons and daughters were chattel property— *cattle* is the word she used—and they were never included in the sale when she passed from one owner to another.

When she could bear no more children, a labor recruit, on his way home from a term of compulsory service on the Government highways, had bought her for a song. He was a young man who should have had a younger woman, but he had lost some of his earnings at knucklebones and spent some of them for rum, and he would not have been welcomed home without gifts for his father and uncles and something for his chief. Aganza was the best he could do for himself—a sorry best, for she could only cook his mealies by day and warm his back by night. He beat her unmercifully because she was not younger —and Aganza harbored no ill will in her heart, for that is normal conduct for men. She would work hard and earn the money for a younger sister wife and so perhaps, if no gullible stranger passed through the village, and if the jungle spirits were willing, she might purchase for herself a few years of peace.

But the spirits of the jungle had not been willing that there should be peace for Aganza. In the village of N'Titierte, her new home on the Oogau River, there was a man by the name of U'boli who was markedly different from his relatives and neighbors. U'boli's father owed his life to the quick thinking, courage, and skill of a white man when the two of them had been charged by a wounded buffalo. And when the black man had asked the white man how he could discharge the debt he owed him, the white man had answered, "Give me one of your sons."

The white man had gone on to explain why he wanted the child, but his words had little meaning to the tribesman. Nevertheless, U'boli's father had placed his son's small hand in the white man's big one and had watched the two of them walk away together, wondering all the while whether the white man hungered for human flesh meat. His father had never expected to see U'boli again, but in a half dozen years the boy returned, his body grown to manhood and his head full of such foolishness as the village of N'Titierte had never heard before.

He had with him curious things he called "books," by means of which he said dead men talked to him, or men separated from him by greater mountains, jungles, and bodies of water than a tribesman could cross in many a season of hard trekking. His attitude toward women and marriage was beyond comprehension. When he chose his first and only wife from among the village girls, he insisted that the marriage fee be called a gift instead of a price. And since U'boli had returned to his people a rich man and the gifts he sent were numerous and impressive, the bride's father was not inclined to quarrel over a matter of terms. Then U'boli had insisted that the girl herself be asked if she were willing to marry him.

The girl had answered, "Yes," very promptly. Why not? U'boli was young, handsome, and rich, and there would be many gifts for her as well as many sister wives to share the labor of kraal and shamba. She had been right—except that U'boli would never take other wives. Whatever she asked of him, he gave her—so quickly and easily that even she knew he was a fool. And when she found that he did not beat her, she treated him with open contempt before the entire village.

"Do you think the girl was right or wrong in her behavior, Aganza?" I asked.

The old woman looked quietly into the distance for a long moment as though strange thoughts were slowly shaping in her mind. But when she answered, it was still the primitive woman speaking. "A female at best is but a pair of hands and stupid as a hen. It is not right that a man should fetch and carry for her or bow his head silently under the weight of her angry words. Still—" Aganza hesitated and looked as though she expected a rebuke—"still—gifts are very pleasant. When I was much younger, one husband gave me a length of copper wire, and the village blacksmith wound it about my left ankle and fastened it there. I liked to hear it jingle as I walked past other women or worked with them in the shambas. I worked hard for that husband, and soon he bought another wife whose hips were broad and whose breasts were high; even I could see that she was very beautiful. The night his friends dragged her into his kraal he took the copper wire off of my ankle and had the blacksmith fasten it on hers. Soon afterward he sold me to another man, but—sometimes—I look down at my ankle and wish the copper wire were still there."

U'boli's wife had only to express a wish for an ornament and it was hers, but, plead or storm as she would, there were no sister wives. Instead, when she argued that the labor of hut and garden was too much for one wife, he had pounded the mealies himself and would have gone to the gardens with her had she not forbidden it.

Sometime later when I spoke to Dr. Early about U'boli, he explained the man quite simply. "It was a case of not yet knowing how 'to render to Caesar the things that are Caesar's.' When it happens back home, we merely say that the person is well intentioned but socially unadjusted. Here, well, what did they do to U'boli? Kill him? Sell him into slavery? Or—"

"They found him guilty of witchcraft and responsible for his wife's death. They took him out onto the veld and broke the bones of his arms and legs and left him there to the vultures and jackals," I replied.

"A whole family wiped out because a man tried to do the right thing!" Dr. Early exclaimed.

"No, Mata Kwan is his son," I answered.

The young wife's pregnancy had apparently been normal,

but labor had been difficult. Aganza, as one of the old women of the village, had tried to help her.

"I placed my heels against the bulge in her stomach and my shoulders against the side of the hut and pushed with all my strength, until the sweat ran off my body and splashed on the floor. But, at the end of two days, all we could see was the heel of one foot."

"A breech baby," I murmured.

Aganza hesitated and then explained, as she always did when my words had no meaning for her: "No, *mama,* the baby was right side up instead of upside down in its mother's body. The women with me ran out of the hut shrieking that it was witchcraft, but I had seen babies born feet first in other villages. So I pushed the opening wider with my two hands and seized the baby by his feet and pulled him out."

"You are a natural-born nurse, Aganza," I exclaimed. "That was all any medical man, no matter how well trained, could have done."

If the old woman sensed the warm commendation in my words, she did not show it. Instead she wrinkled up her nose with the intensity of her thought. "Why is it that what is witchcraft in one village is all right in another village only a day's journey distant?"

I did not try to answer because I knew Aganza would reason these things out for herself. And besides I did not want to divert her from her story.

"The child cried out, but the mother never spoke again. Presently the women returned and bound the living child to the dead woman's breast and wrapped the two of them in palm fiber matting. Then they each picked up some small thing in payment for their services, and went away again. Because I had worked harder than any of the others, I had the right to a bigger fee. As I looked about for what I might take, I heard the baby stir under its matting, although it was bound ever so tightly.

"I am not a thief, *mama*. But many thoughts came into my head when I heard the child stir. I remembered that I had borne many children, and those who lived had been taken from me by men as completely as death had taken the others. I remembered too other villages where babies born by the heels had not killed their mothers. And—*mama*, I undid the matting and looked at the child. I picked it up in my arms and held it. That—that is a very pleasant thing to do, *mama*."

The old woman's face was tremulous with pleading that I might not blame her.

I nodded understanding. "It is what I would have done, Aganza," I told her. "But why did the women bind the child onto its dead mother's breast? Why didn't one of them take it?"

"How could a village woman feed it unless she had a baby of her own?" Aganza demanded in surprise. "And having a child of her own, what woman would rob it of food for a stranger that would be taken away from her as soon as it no longer needed her?"

"But to bind a child onto its dead mother's breast and cast it, perhaps still living, into the slime of a swamp or to the beaks of vultures or fangs of jackals!" I exclaimed. "That is needless cruelty."

"Have you ever heard the wails of a hungry child, *mama*? Of a very hungry child? That is hard for a woman to hear, hard for a man to listen to also, *mama*. Since the child must die anyway, it is better that it die quickly."

"But Mata Kwan didn't die! He lived without food and care for—how many days were you on the trail coming to me?"

"I slipped away that night, and six times the sun rose and set before I reached you," she answered.

N'Titierte was, roughly, two hundred and fifty miles away, west by southwest. The old woman had covered at least forty miles at each spell of walking, and she had done the bravest thing an African ever attempts—she had traveled by night when the most fearsome beasts of prey are feeding.

"What gave you the courage!" I exclaimed in wonder. The old woman only stared at me. Perhaps she did not understand such a term as "courage" when applied to a mere pair of hands.

U'boli had entered the hut as she cradled the child in her arms, Aganza told me. That was further evidence of his peculiarity, for an ordinary tribesman would have gone to the palaver hut and, although he did not feel like talking himself, would have smiled at the jokes of others and have listened politely to the gossip of the old men. Instead, the lone Christian in N'Titierte had squatted on the floor beside his dead wife and had stroked her face with his hands, and tears had splashed on the matting Aganza had disarranged.

Finally the child had whimpered, and he had seemed aware of it for the first time. He stared at his son and touched its head with a finger that trembled, but when he spoke to Aganza, his voice, although low, was very firm. He told her she must bring the child to me. He told her what trails to follow in order to reach N'zem, and what she must say upon arrival. He made her repeat the words many, many, many times.

"At first I was not of a mind to do what he commanded, *mama*," Aganza told me. "But suddenly the thought occurred to me that if I did, and if, as he said, your magic was great enough to keep the child alive, and if—" the old woman broke off and looked at me sharply for a moment—"and if, *mama*, I could manage so that no man searching for runaway *cattle* might ever see me—then no one could take this child away from me!"

Armed with this thought, Aganza had helped U'boli roll a small pelt into the size and shape of a newborn infant, place it on the mother's breast, and rearrange the matting shroud. Then U'boli had made Aganza repeat again and yet again the words she must say to me. When he felt sure of her memory, he had gone out into the village street, wailing loudly and indecorously until every man, woman, and child in N'Titierte had followed him to the palaver hut in amazement. And when

166

all eyes and ears were turned elsewhere, Aganza had slipped out of the hut and hurried off into the night. For six nights, stopping only to drink and to hide by day from the possible eyes of strangers who might report her whereabouts, she had fled on the feet of a hunted animal until, on the afternoon of the seventh day, she had stood in the door of my dispensary, repeated U'boli's nonsense syllables, and dropped the filth-encrusted Mata Kwan into my lap.

And I—because I had been a little sick, and tired, and was feeling very sorry for myself that afternoon—had turned upon her in temper. I have thanked God many times since that I failed to speak in Hausa at that moment.

"So that is why you hide away by day and will help me only at night," I exclaimed. "You are afraid for men to see you lest they take you back."

Her only answer was a silent, watchful half-smile.

Suddenly a great idea seized me. "Aganza, you love Mata Kwan, don't you!" It was not a question, merely preparation for what I meant to say.

"Love?" The word seemed strange to her.

But I hurried on. "No one but U'boli knows you have the child—do they? No one else knows he's alive!"

She flung up her head and clicked her thumbnail against her teeth in emphatic denial.

"Then if you belonged to me, everything would be all right, wouldn't it? You need not live in fear. Mata Kwan would be yours for good. You could help me in my work—" I broke off, hardly daring to ask the next question, but Aganza waited silently.

"The man in N'Titierte, your husband, would he sell you to me, do you think?"

"Pfft!" I have never heard a sound so scornful as the old woman's snort of disgust. "A goat he paid for me, mangy and old, and two hens and a scrawny rooster—and the men in the palaver hut laughed at him for a fool."

167

"Then if I offered him, say, two young and healthy goats—"
I began.

"*Mama!* You do not know how to bargain!" For a moment
Aganza was a village woman, shrewd and keen and determined
upon every sou of value. That she herself was the object of
barter did not seem to occur to her.

The next day I hunted, with twice the number of porters
I needed to take back the meat, in the direction of N'Titierte.
Luck was with me; early in the day I shot a reedbuck, a
kongoni, and two zebras. I left half the porters to cut up the
meat and carry it back to N'zem, but Jackie, the other men,
and I headed west by southwest.

It took me eight days traveling with porters to cover what
Aganza had made in six nights alone. I liked the country surrounding N'Titierte as soon as I saw it. More than once I
paused on a rise of ground to survey the countryside, and in my
mind's eye I could imagine fat flocks and lush fields of grain
and little groups of white buildings where now there were
swales, savannas, and groves of centuries-old trees.

N'Titierte stood on the east bank of the Oogau River, on a
little spur of the hills. As I climbed the spur to approach the
village I looked over the flat bench of knoll backed by a wide
band of towering pencil cedars. "What an ideal location for a
mission station! Hospital here, schools there, mission homes on
the bluff overlooking the river!"

I stood lost in dreams until my *boys* called my attention to a
procession coming to meet us. They were used to L'loni's visits
and supposed that I too was a trader. What did I have to offer
for their ivory? Their kola nuts? The groundnut crop had not
been good. I desired none of these things? But my porters
carried head loads; what was in them if not trade goods?

Within me the question seethed: Who was Aganza's husband? She had not told me, and an African woman seldom uses
the name of her husband. Full of the importance of my mission,
I had very stupidly not asked her. Yet I must deal with him.

168

It took some doing on my part to get the information I wanted without arousing suspicion or antagonism. I held a clinic as I always did when visiting any village; I traded a little although I had not intended to; I gossiped a lot. I heard, for instance, what a worthless hag old Aganza was, and the list of atrocities that would be meted out to her were she ever caught still makes me shudder. Of course, there was always a possibility that the stupid hen had been killed by a leopard or pulled under the river by a crocodile. There was no mention of Mata Kwan. His father and Aganza had done their work well; in the minds of the villagers he had been cast out with his dead mother and had ceased to exist.

When I started back to N'zem, on the morning of the third day, Aganza was my slave. I had paid a few handfuls of salt, a couple of yards of *merikani,* and two empty tomato tins for her. Less than two dollars' value in all—yet I never spent two dollars, or two thousand dollars, to better advantage.

I make no apology here for the ethics involved in the transaction. In becoming a slaveowner, I merely adopted the only possible solution to the problem. In that section of the country women from birth until death are property, as certainly as a cow or horse is property in my part of Indiana. The father or his nearest surviving male relative owns a woman until she is married. Then she is a chattel of her husband, or his nearest surviving male relative—sometimes her own son—and frequently in old age the out-and-out slave of some rich man. To have set Aganza free without passing her on to someone else would have been like trying to tear down the walls of a house without disturbing the roof.

Achmed was indignant beyond measure upon my return to N'zem. "To spend so much for so worthless a creature!" he exclaimed, and spat scornfully in her direction. I promptly boxed his ears and asked him what he would have had me do? Let her husband discover her whereabouts, as he surely would have sooner or later?

Achmed side-stepped neatly by telling me that I could have purchased for my salt and empty tomato cans a much younger female, whom I could have turned over to him for a wife.

"I have long been of an age for a wife, *mama*," he told me plaintively.

"I pay you well. Why haven't you bought yourself one?" I demanded. "I will even give you time off so you can go to Tani and make arrangements there with the parents of some nice Christian girl."

"But, *mama,* I have no money. I am in disfavor with N'roolroo." This was a name of which I was never quite certain. It meant the spirit that governed games of chance.

I wanted to laugh, but I felt I must be severe. "And you a mission *boy!*" I began with all the scorn I could muster in my voice.

Achmed might be lacking in skill with the knucklebones, but he was a past master at the art of evasion. His words dripped condescension even as they sought pity for his wifeless state.

"Even a mission *boy* desires the comfort of a woman. And he makes a better counselor in the palaver hut if he has a female on whom he may vent the irritations of his day when night falls."

"Well, I won't buy you a wife," I answered. "As long as you gamble your own money away, I won't buy you anything."

But to return to Aganza—I won't say that everything began to go right as soon as we built her and Mata Kwan a *dukas* beside my own and she became my mainstay. I do believe, however, that through the relationship I acquired a sense of direction in my work. For the first time since coming to Africa, I was at peace with myself and those about me. I know that Aganza would have been nothing without me, or someone like me, and I know equally well that much my colleagues give me credit for is really Aganza's doing.

At first I thought I might train her to help me so that I could have leisure for what I called "more intensive study and proper care of myself," but at the end of a few months Aganza and I were sharing responsibilities almost as equals. I never saw anyone absorb knowledge with greater facility or apply it more naturally. I have a reasonably good mind myself, but beside Aganza I'm a dolt.

Work in the dispensary went so well that we expanded. Together we built a real hospital—nothing pretentious, just a few simple *dukases*. As soon as they were finished, serious cases, usually the victims of tribal witch doctors, filled them completely. Once again I began to keep a card file of the hospital cases. And, since Aganza was immediately curious about the file and I thought it might be helpful to her, I kept it in a phonetic version of Hausa. I am not conscious of ever having done more than murmur the names on the cards aloud as I ran through them and, perhaps, follow the legend with a forefinger as we discussed a case. Yet one day Aganza went to the file, picked out a card, and read to me what I had written there. I thought it was a case of memory, and tried her with another card. Then another. We went through every card in the file, and she read every one of them back to me.

"But, *mama*, the bits of paper speak to you. Why shouldn't they speak to me?" she protested in the face of my amazement. "I am your *boy*." Only she didn't say *boy*; rather, she used the term meaning an apprentice to a witch doctor.

I chuckled inwardly and turned back to the cards. It could be a phenomenal memory, I told myself again, still unable to believe the implication of her performance. So I took a blank card, searched about in my mind for something suitable to write on it, then filled it out for Chimbwe, the man on whom I had watched Dr. Mary operate in Tani.

Aganza studied the card carefully, and, with no hesitation in her voice, handed it back to me. "This card lies, *mama*. We have never had a patient of that name. But this evil spirit you call 'elephantiasis'—it is common enough in the bush." There was no question about it. By the grace of God, and with less

171

help than any other pupil I have ever known, Aganza had learned to read.

I tried to convey to her something of the wonder of her accomplishment, but when I had finished, she only said: "My magic is very little, *mama*. Only these bits of paper speak to me." She ran a forefinger along the card file as she spoke. Then she leaned over slightly and rested her hand on one of Dr. Mary's medical journals. "This bundle of paper won't say anything at all to me. Perhaps it is because it is big magic and for white people only, while this—" picking up a card—"this is little magic and for black people too."

"You—you have tried to read these books!" I stammered in amazement.

"Was it wrong, *mama?* I meant no wrong. Yes, I picked them all up, every one of them and held them in my hands. I crooned to them and caressed them and offered them bits of food and sips of palm wine, but they would not speak to me, *mama,* not so much as a faint grunt from a single one of them."

Of course not! They were in print, not script, and English, not Hausa. I started to explain this and then stopped as sudden inspiration hit me. When I did speak, it was merely to say, "Come to my *dukas* after you have eaten this evening, Aganza; then, if you want it badly enough, I will make these big bundles of paper speak to you too."

Her eyes gleamed and she questioned almost wistfully: "They are very stubborn spirits, *mama.* Are you sure you can make them obey you?"

I drew a long breath. "They will obey me, Aganza, unless they can discourage you first. But if you do exactly what I tell you, and do not give up, I can make them speak to you."

CHAPTER
14

WHEN I told Aganza to come to my *dukas* of an evening,
I had thought that I would teach her to write; then I
would read the medical journals to her and she could make
copies for herself in Hausa. She picked up writing as easily as
she might have hoed the weeds out of a row of beans, and we
started the translating and transcribing. As we worked, I grew
increasingly impatient with the prolixity of scientific men who
seemed childishly fearful that credit might not be given them
for every scrap of work done. I took to abbreviating mercilessly until sometimes the gist of a ten-page article would be
compressed into ten sentences in Aganza's notes. Later, when
Aganza could read English, she looked up from a journal one
night to say, "These witch doctors of your country, *mama*, for
all their great knowledge, are as proud and jealous as a very
young African witch doctor who is not yet quite sure of his
charms and fetishes."

Before very long I knew that I must teach Aganza English,
for if her study was to be confined only to what I could translate, intellectually she would be like a blind man who has never
learned to walk alone. That task really scared me, but, like
most things that frighten one, the task was accomplished while
I was waiting for the terror to materialize. Aganza had never

spoken English other than her stilted declaration at our first meeting, but before my first furlough came along—she had been with me scarcely more than two years by then—she read and wrote both English and Hausa with complete ease, and used an English dictionary to help her with the medical terms.

As she learned, we became partners in the truest sense of the word. And why not? She was my intellectual equal and the same sources of information that Dr. Mary had opened up to me were open to her. True, she probably could never have passed a formal intelligence test. Also true, I had had three years in a hospital at formal nurses' training. But scrubbing floors and carrying bedpans are not particularly instructive activities.

As my clinical safaris into the bush increased in length and frequency, I found, curiously, that it was oftentimes not *my* fame that had spread.

"Do you come from Mother Aganza?" more than one headman asked me. Then he would go on: "My oldest son by my third wife suffered from a hunting wound that did not heal. He went to this black witch doctor in whose kraal you live, white woman, and she took a knife and cut away the jagged edges of flesh in which the devils festered. Now my son's body is clean and whole like that of a newborn infant."

Our hospital grew too, hut by hut, until when Dr. Early visited us, we had a little colony of eight *dukases*. My superior had made the trip to N'zem ostensibly as a pastoral call, but I secretly believed he came to see for himself if the work at N'zem had developed sufficiently to merit a substitute while I was on furlough. I made no attempt to repress the pride I felt as I showed him my ménage. He hesitated a moment when I led him past Aganza's hut next to my own, and I tensed myself for the criticism I anticipated—whites living next door to blacks—tsch! tsch! tsch!

When he spoke, it was to say, "When I first came to Africa,

174

my hut was built so close to that of the headman's that rain from our roofs dripped into the same mud puddle."

"Well?" I demanded almost belligerently. "Did you do better or worse work?"

He laughed comfortably. "You can't always measure life by that yardstick, Ellen. I was young, inexperienced, and I had no help whatsoever in learning the language—or anything else; but nobody crept into my hut and drove a spear through me while I slept. That's something."

I felt humbled, and I wanted to ask him about those early years when a missionary had to protect his own life, to wring sustenance from a hostile land, and to preach the gospel all at the same time. I didn't, however. He would have felt that the tale of his heroism was boasting.

Aganza was not in the hospital when I showed him through the dispensary and the sleeping *dukases* provided for our patients, but I talked a lot about her, as there were evidences of her handiwork everywhere. I was showing him a contraption she had devised for an intravenous injection—a gourd for a tank, tapering lengths of bamboo for the glass conduit, and finally a scrap of rattan through which the solution trickled in just about the right quantity to prevent shock—when he burst out: "Where is this wonderful Aganza? Or is she like good children, merely to be heard of and not seen?"

A moment later I pointed Aganza out, bending over a little fire in front of her hut, cooking her *posho*. She must have looked to him like any other woman preparing the evening meal for her family, but his first reaction surprised me.

"For heaven's sake, Ellen, why haven't you put a dress on her?"

The human mind plays curious tricks. I can honestly say that, although I resented Aganza's nakedness the day she first appeared, after I was drawn heart and soul into the battle for Mata Kwan's life I never again thought of clothes in connection with her. I don't know when she discarded the rotting

175

goatskin she had worn then; now she had on a strip of bark cloth of native manufacture. It was scrupulously clean, but it barely covered her from her navel to her thighs.

"Why should she strive to be different from her people except in the ways that are really constructive?" I defended.

Dr. Early laughed at me. "It is the formal thing for a Christian convert."

"But—but—" How could I confess to my superior that my mainstay in my work was still pagan? "But she—she—is not—Lemuel, she is a Christian who has not yet confessed Christianity," I hedged.

His eyes danced, but all I heard was, "H'm!" and then, "Do you remember old What's-her-name's Spider Christian?"

So there wasn't to be any pompous reprimand. I could have hugged him in my relief.

"What's her reason for holding off?" he asked, but went on before I could answer. "Religion is a curious thing, Ellen. With most people, religious decisions come from the heart. Then there is a phase when it is entirely logical. But if it is to be constructive and to endure, it must be mind and heart working together. Faith and logic tempered with mercy."

He looked at me inquiringly, so I tried to explain. "Apparently she has skipped the first phase. Who can blame a woman of her experience for not being emotional? But she is terribly, almost childishly, logical about everything. She says she can see that my medical practices are superior to those of the ordinary witch doctor. Fewer of my patients die, fewer of those who live are deformed, all of them suffer less from my treatments, and—it is pleasant *not* to be afraid of me. These things she is certain of because she can see them. But, Lem, she can't see God or heaven. What can I say to persuade her?"

"Nothing. A mind like that has to convince itself," he answered.

I looked at him in some surprise. "But what can I do in the meantime?"

"Continue your normal work. And wait. Time is on the side of truth, Ellen. Always."

He was not so comforting when it came to determining the future of my station at N'zem. "I'm afraid we'll have to give it up," he told me.

I bridled instantly, but he held up a hand to shut off my protests.

"Now, now! Dr. Mary knew we'd have to give it up eventually, but she always said, 'Not in my lifetime!' The swamp across the river is moving in—you can see that for yourself. When Dr. Mary first came to N'zem, you could trek for two or three days beyond the river before you came to the swamp. Everything was dry land around here, and it looked like a good site for a permanent outstation. But the swamp has moved in steadily ever since. Whether the ground is sinking or the water level is rising I'm not geologist enough to know, but in another five years you probably would have to go around in boots and bed your patients down in mud."

I can't say that I had seen the swamp rise, but I had heard my people complain, and more than once I had wondered what we should do when the slimy green monster began to swallow us.

"What would Dr. Mary think of my deserting?" I demanded. "Her lifework that she built up—"

"Dr. Mary is dead, and her lifework is ended," he answered me. "It is now you and your lifework."

Again I knew he was right, but how could I give up my lovely hospital? It was as though he read my thoughts.

"Your hospital isn't so much, Ellen. A dozen or so mud and wattle huts. You can do as much elsewhere in half, in a tenth, the time it took here—both the buildings and the winning of human confidence. Have you, during your itinerant work, come upon another place that would make a good site for an outstation?"

Then I told him about N'Titierte. Everything was in its

177

favor, it seemed to me: the hills, the river, the number of villages in the surrounding countryside. I even spoke of the beauty of the location. Dr. Early kept nodding his head, and when I paused for breath, he took up the theme.

"I know the place. 'Big Bush,' the natives call it from the appearance of the coral trees that were in bloom when you saw it. N'Titierte means 'Big Bush,' you know."

We were both silent for a little while. When Dr. Early spoke again, it was as though he were taking me into his confidence for the first time. "Did you know that right across the Oogau River from Big Bush there is an extensive deposit of copper?"

"No. How could I have known such a fact?"

"The Belgian Government has known about it for some time."

"Well?"

"The world is changing here in Africa, just as it is elsewhere. Though our people are backward and underprivileged now, they may not always be so. Also, the type and quality of backwardness and lack of privilege will change, and we've got to meet those changes too. When the Government starts work on that copper deposit across from Big Bush, what is going to happen to the village of N'Titierte? and to all the other villages nearby?"

He peered at me speculatively. "If we're firmly intrenched there with a good strong mission station, when that mine opens—" He paused as though the rest were obvious—and entirely up to me.

"Good heavens, Lem, I'm not a social worker," I burst out.

"Eh? No? What are you, Ellen?"

I glared at him for a moment, but it was I who gave in. "What about Dr. Mary's Pygmies?" I demanded, with what I thought was sudden inspiration.

"What about them?" he countered.

"She once told me—well, she was always making trips into the great swamp. She hoped—hoped that—"

"Uh-huh, she hoped. She made a lot of trips into the great swamp, and she never got anywhere with the Pygmies—from a missionary point of view, that is. All of us have had our failures, Ellen. Even Dr. Mary. She came to know more about the Pygmies than any other white person, I grant you, but she never sent us one Pygmy child for the school and she never reported one Pygmy convert."

"That's no reason why I should let down the work she started."

My subterfuge elicited a frankly derisive grin. "I was always keenly interested in Mary's trips into the swamp. How many times have *you* been there, Ellen? Tell me about them."

"Well, I—I—"

"You never sent in any reports of such trips, and you should have, you know. You haven't got around to it yet? But of course you're going?"

"Of course!"

"When?"

"Just as soon—" I ranged about desperately in my mind for some planned work on which to hinge a date.

"Just as soon is the same as never," he crowed.

Again I glared at him, and he attacked me from a different angle.

"How many Pygmies do you know? Name them off for me. You don't know any, do you!"

"Job!" I spit out.

"Yes, Job," Dr. Early agreed pleasantly, and the deviltry died out of his face. Both our minds were full of Job the cripple, a twisted gnome of a man, in all probability cast out by his people, and at best only a Pygmy half-breed.

"I'm not going to put off my trip into the swamp any longer," I said finally, but without rancor.

"I wish you wouldn't," he answered with equal calm. "You should go, Ellen, by all means, at least once. And let me know about it, won't you? I'm honestly interested."

He started back to Tani that afternoon. Before he went, he said: "Mother and I are leaving on our furlough very soon now. Dr. Charles will be in charge during my absence. He's a good fellow, Sister Ellen; you can take your problems to him. He's young, but then you outgrow youth faster in Africa than in a lot of other places.

"Mother and I will be gone—oh, fourteen, fifteen, sixteen months. When we come back, you go on your furlough, and by the time you return, we'll know what to do about N'zem."

A few weeks later I left Aganza in charge of the hospital and made my first trip into the great swamp. The Pygmies, I knew, spoke neither Hausa nor the language of my N'zemi. Some traders say that they don't have a language at all, that they merely grunt to express elemental reactions, but of course that is absurd. I heard a small group of men chatter away among themselves with ease, and there were several people in N'zem who said they could speak the Pygmies' language. One of these latter I took along into the swamp as a porter.

I also took my rifle, thinking that if I could shoot some game and supply the Pygmies with meat, it would help win their friendship. I forgot that the true Pygmies, among the cleverest hunters in the world, are the only African tribe that is able to subsist almost entirely on meat of its own procuring. As it turned out, my porters and I, none of us swamp-bred, made so much noise that the only sort of game I saw on that trip was a few snakes.

I took along half of the salt L'loni had left me. Dr. Mary had said that when she went on a search for Pygmies she acted as though they were the farthest thing from her mind, but that when she broke camp in the morning, she left little heaps of salt in conspicuous places. I did the same thing; then I doubled back later to see if the salt was gone. It always was. The elusive little men were with me but, true to their reputation, always out of sight. At the end of two weeks my salt was gone, the other stores exceedingly low, and my porters uneasy and discontented at the lack of fresh meat, so I had to return to N'zem.

But every step of the way back I could see Dr. Early's mocking face. I made up conversations with him as I trudged along and I always had the better of these one-sided arguments. At first that was some small comfort. But, like all false victories, the rosy glow of triumph melted under a blast of logic. If I did not find the Pygmies and establish work among them, what reasons could I give for continuing at N'zem?

The arguments were all against me, and so I tried to meet the situation with anger. Back at N'zem, I had a hot bath and a good night's rest, rounded up a new group of porters, and prepared to invade the great swamp once again with the remainder of my trading salt.

The first trip had been difficult, but there are no words with which to describe the second. The first time we had entered the swamp at an angle and had described an arc in our wandering. This time I insisted on striking directly toward the heart of the swamp in a straight line. All my *boys* objected, argued vociferously, and in the end obeyed me. I know now that only an exaggerated sense of loyalty kept them from deserting me, for I led them directly into a dry swamp.

Compared with all the monstrosities of which Africa is guilty, in my opinion nothing equals or even approaches the horror of a dry swamp. So far as I know, it is a purely African phenomenon. No scientist has ever given me its geological causes, so I've had to fall back on my own imagination for an explanation. I think it is probably due to a combination of an extraordinarily high subsurface water table and the undeviating heat of a tropical atmosphere. Overhead there is a green twilight in the tangle of gigantic jungle trees, many of them blanketed with a thick layer of lianas. Underfoot there is anywhere from six to eighteen inches of rotting vegetable glue, covered over with a half inch or so of dried mud that breaks into jagged fragments with every step, scratching one's ankles and calves like pottery shards. The air is thick, day and night, with stinging, biting, voracious, bloodsucking insects. There was no place to pitch a tent or build a fire, so for two days we ate cold food and for two nights we kept on our feet.

The third morning my porters either avoided my eyes or looked at me strangely. Their attitude could mean anything, and I was so numb with suffering that I wondered vaguely if they were going to desert me, or if I were collapsing or going insane. Nothing could be worse than the predicament we were in—or so I thought. And then we ran into a colony of land crabs. Thousands upon thousands of the repulsive things! Everything from babies only a fraction of an inch in diameter to bearded grandfathers four or five inches across. If we relaxed our vigilance for a second, they were all over us with the persistence of ants. We slogged forward doggedly, slapping and slashing frantically at the crabs with sticks and leafy branches. Whenever we crushed one, its shell and pincers seemed perfectly empty. Yet a worse stench arose than I have ever caught, even from the leeward side of a guano island.

Then, just as suddenly, we were on dry land, if any portion of that bit of jungle can be called dry land. At least the dry swamp and its loathsome crabs were behind us. It was then that I understood the peculiar looks of my porters. In an effort to save our lives they had abandoned their loads during the night. At first I was too weary to care, but after I had rested for an hour, I realized that it would take from two to three years of my salary to replace my camping equipment. And my salt! My precious salt for the Pygmies was gone, every last grain of it.

"Why couldn't you have saved just a little?" I moaned. "Just one load!"

Only Jackie, that black pearl among his dusky brethren, had held onto my gun.

My headman sat down on his upturned heels directly in front of me and explained that the salt was nothing—we were without food and weapons, and in unknown, forbidding territory. Suddenly the headman, still squatting in front of me, began to sway and dance crazily. The rest of that day, and most of the following night were a prolonged nightmare. After that I was conscious only of being shaken and rolled about. Days later, when I was back in N'zem and resting in my own bed, the headman and others of my porters told me what had happened.

"The hours passed and you fell silent. Too silent. You did not ask us questions or tell us what we should do," said one.

"Then you chattered like an angry monkey in the treetops," another put in. "And your words were all about people and villages strange to us."

"You wept and you laughed and you wept again, and when we spoke to you and you did not reply to us, we—we—" That porter faltered, but another took up his words.

"We knew that the spirits of the Great Mother Forest were calling to you, and we debated among ourselves as to whether or not we should break open your skull and set your spirit free so that it might answer them."

"Then the jungle on one side of us parted and a band of 'the little men' slipped into our midst," my headman went on before I could recover from the shock of his companion's words. "They spread a length of game net on the ground and laid you on it beside a long pole. They wound the net around both you and the pole, and then several of them picked up each end of the pole. That is the way they carried you home. To us they gave a few pieces of fat for food and many pipefuls of tobacco for courage, and thus fortified, we followed along behind."

So I had found the Pygmies—or rather they had found me —I mused bitterly, and still I had not enjoyed a glimpse of them. Should I go back into the forest after them again? and make an even bigger fool of myself? Or should I acknowledge defeat and use my energies in laying plans for moving my out-station to a more suitable location?

The problem was solved the first day I got out of bed and sat outside my *dukas* for a bit of the late afternoon sun. I had no more than got settled when eight Pygmies, none of them over four and a half feet tall, and all staggering under the biggest elephant tusk I had ever seen, came down the path, mounted the steps, and laid the ivory at my feet.

I grinned and they jabbered. When I called for someone who could understand them, they jabbered harder than ever. The translator, grinning wider and broader than any of us, explained to me that ivory is the most precious possession of the Pygmies. As they never sell any of it, the individual to whom they give a tusk can look upon himself as having won blood brothership with every member of the tribe. The commonest use for ivory is for purchasing brides, and, although my skin was a loathsome ashen color and I had habits strange beyond belief, the chief was desirous of adding me to his harem.

The Pygmies had watched every step of my excursions into the jungle. They had even seen me enter the dry swamp and come through on the other side. Such a woman has—he used the Pygmy equivalent for "guts." She would mother children who would undoubtedly face triumphantly that moist green hell in which they make their home. My *boy* replied in long phrases and, if gestures are any criterion, with beautiful oratorical effects. The Pygmies grinned again, and turned and trotted out of sight.

"What did you say to them?" I asked.

"I told them that white women are not like our females. That they do not know men and do not bear children. I said everything they have comes out of tin cans, and that this is undoubtedly the case with their young. That—"

"Why, that's not so. We do marry and we bear children," I burst out.

"I have never seen a white woman who had a husband or children, or a white man who had a white wife," he answered simply.

That was true. The only white women he had ever known were Dr. Mary and me. So far as I know, Mrs. Early never visited N'zem. The only white men were a handful of itinerant traders. How could I explain?

"The—the—Pygmies left their ivory behind them," I stammered finally.

"It is tribute to a woman who they think should be a chieftain's wife. It is a pledge of their friendship from now on," my *boy* answered.

My diminutive suitor never pressed his hand upon me again, but I have often wondered what he looked like. And if it would be humanly possible for a white woman to adjust herself to the scarcely more than animal existence that the little nomad men enjoy in their perpetually twilit home.

CHAPTER
15

THE weather furnished the final argument in favor of moving my station while Dr. and Mrs. Early were on furlough. The wet season, of course, takes the place of winter in tropical Africa. Then it rains for two or three hours every day, beginning in the early afternoon, with sometimes a shower in the morning too. The sun may shine between times, but it is a sickly, wan-looking sun that makes only a halfhearted attempt at drying off the land. At other times, the heavens open and it pours for days on end without a break. The first rains of the season sink into the earth; then the water forms in little rivulets which run off into the river, cutting individual beds that become ditches in an hour and ten-foot gullies overnight. In the year of which I am writing, the rainy season was a prolonged one, and the river rose until it was on a level with the land and the whole earth seemed one great, swirling yellow pond.

"Next year it will be the same," Job said to me one day. "And the year following that, it will also be the same. The river has drunk too much, *mama,* and cannot swallow any more. It is best that we go away."

Aganza told me, with gentle complaint in her tone, "I have never before lived in a swamp village, *mama.*" She showed me her feet and the callouses were spongy as though she had soaked them too long in a hot bath. I wore English boots, but even so my own feet became tender. Most of the patients who came to me coughed miserably, and were racked with pains in swollen joints. There wasn't much I could do about it. Aspirin? Bromides? I could have spent my entire capital for such and still not have had enough to go around. And what trader would have made the trip in with supplies for us? When what we had on hand was gone, we had to go without. And that went for everything else as well as medicine.

In times of disaster the number of births seems to multiply, at least in African villages. Almost every woman in N'zem gave birth to a child that winter, and, when I slogged through the liquid plain to other villages, it was the same. But all the babies born that wet season died. Perhaps a half dozen out of hundreds were still alive at the end of a month or six weeks, but in the end all of them died of pneumonia or hunger before the rains stopped. I saw more than one tiny corpse floating past on the river, bobbing up and down, or swirling dizzily in an eddy. There were too many for the crocodiles, and the jackals and vultures had long since fled the rains.

We were all hungry. Every hut had a little food stored away, but who knew when the rain would break and the land dry out and the river shrink back within its banks once more? What food we had must last until the wild asparagus and spinach and celery and bamboo sprouts shot up through the hot earth and the game came back again. We could get along then until the women furrowed up their shambas and the carefully treasured seed sprouted. Many a night I lay on my bed wondering what would happen to my N'zemi, and the dozens of other villages up and down the river when the food was gone. I knew, but I was afraid to admit the truth to myself. One by one the old people would turn their faces to the wall and cease to breathe. The children? If *Muungu* willed that there be breath in their nostrils when the famine was past, well and good. If not—few African tribes have any word like the Arabic "kismet," but they all accept fate with unquestioning stoicism. The women would feed the precious seed almost grain by grain to their husbands, for the men must be strong enough to hunt when game came back; they must be alive to father other children.

One night I lay awake torturing myself thus when I heard a strange sound. My bed, a variation of the typical N'zemi cot, was woven of rattan and hung on discarded drums which raised it about a foot from the ground. The rattan was as resilient as springs, and quite comfortable. I should have been asleep, but hunger and fear make poor bedfellows, and I tossed about instead of resting. Every time I moved, the rattan creaked. I sighed and tried to relax—but the creaking continued. Fainter, of course, much fainter, more like the rustle of dead leaves than good, well-seasoned rattan, but a distinct ghostly crackle. I held my breath and listened. The noise still continued.

I sat up, reached out to the bedside stool, and picked up the box of matches lying there. My blood still runs cold when I think of the way I bounced about and the time I consumed. I pried off the tin lid with my thumbnail, and struck a match across its rough surface, but in spite of the protection I had tried to give the matches, they were sodden. The head flared briefly, sputtered, and went out. I struck at least a half dozen before I got a steady flame with which I could light my lamp. Still deliberate, I secured the chimney on the lamp, closed the match box, and then turned.

At first I didn't see anything. Apparently my visitor had stopped to watch me, but as I sat quiet, he moved again. Then I saw him—and started up a shrieking such as only the spirits of the unhappy and malicious dead in a jungle storm can equal. I was looking straight into the beady eyes of a deadly puff adder, half of whose length was already sprawling across the end of my bed.

It seemed a lifetime before Aganza, and I don't know how many others behind her, stood in my doorway. Her gaze followed my staring eyes, and even she gasped, but she did not hesitate. Seizing a spear from one of the men, she used it as a club, and with one smashing blow she crushed the adder a few inches behind its head. A man leaped forward, grabbed the ugly, writhing thing by its tail, snapped it like a whip, and carried it away.

Aganza shoved the others out. I had desperate need of her, for the blow that had killed the snake had broken one of the bones in my right leg just above the ankle. We had to set the break, and make a cast and splints for the leg. It was a nuisance, of course, but I didn't anticipate any great difficulty. It was a clean break, and, working together, Aganza and I pushed the edges of the bone back into alignment. I held them in place while Aganza went to the dispensary for bandages, plaster of Paris, and the bamboo splints we always kept ready.

When we opened the plaster of Paris tin, we found it filled with a neat little rock. At first one by one, and then carrying our entire supply in a blanket, Aganza brought all the plaster of Paris to my bedside, and all we had for our pains was a stack of beautiful, perfectly shaped little stone blocks. The lids, designed to keep out insects and dust, were far from proof against the wet air of a jungle rainy season.

As I sat there doubled up in bed, clutching my ankle with both hands, I tried to recall what Dr. Mary had said she used when she ran out of plaster of Paris. It was a sort of papier-mâché made of salt, maize flour, and the pith of a trailing ground vine. What was the name of that vine? I leaned over and stared at the floor of my hut as though that would help me remember. Then I knew why the adder had sought my bed, why it had clung over the edge instead of dropping to the floor and slithering away as I fussed with my lamp. Aganza was standing in at least two inches of water.

"We're— The village is flooded?" I gasped.

"Yes, *mama*," she answered.

My mind raced this way and that, frantically gathering in just what this catastrophe meant to the people of N'zem.

"In some huts where the ground is low, the water is up to here," Aganza was murmuring and at the same time measuring against her leg.

"Even the beds are flooded!"

"Yes, *mama*."

"The hospital, Aganza! We must take care of the people there no matter what happens." Without thinking, I let go of my ankle and moved both legs as though to swing them over the edge of the bed. I heard the two ends of bone grate as they slid apart, and the pain of a red-hot spear shot clear to my thigh. Whatever care was given my patients would have to be by other hands than mine.

"There is only a little water on the floor of the hospital huts, *mama*, and we have stacked cooking pots, one on top of the other, upside down, and have rested the sleeping mats on these supports."

What would the women use to cook with? Few families had more than one or two pots. Then I realized that there was no place for most of the people to lie down, no place where a woman could light a fire. "Where are the villagers now, Aganza?" I asked.

"The men are gathered about the hospital huts and are making a big palaver. Those who have hunted far away on higher land are speaking of places where a village might be located. The women sit behind the men of the council, but now and then one of them hurries off to her hut to search for what she might have overlooked and which she should take with her to the new home. They will not leave until light comes, for the spirits of evil love the darkness and man is most helpless when he cannot see where to place his feet."

The hours until dawn were a nightmare. The muscles in my leg were beginning to draw, and I knew that if we did not set the bone immediately, removed from skilled medical help as we were, I should be a cripple for life. We called in Job and Jackie and Achmed, and somehow we pulled and pushed the two edges of bone back together. Then Aganza placed and bound the splints, while inwardly I bemoaned the lack of anything with which to make a cast. I looked across the room at the row of Dr. Mary's medical books. What help were they in a real emergency? Then I fairly whooped with the joy of my sudden inspiration.

We too must leave N'zem, and there wasn't the faintest possibility that we could take the books with us. After all, there wasn't one that was irreplaceable—or as valuable to me as a sound, straight leg.

"But how will we grind up the paper?" I wailed, when I had told Aganza my plan.

"In the same way women grind corn when they make *ksava,* maize beer," she answered. "Chew it up."

We made a ridiculous picture—three grown men and two women, tearing page after page out of medical journals, chewing the pieces industriously, and spitting the gooey paste into a cooking pot. My jaws ached long before we had enough, and the false dawn had faded into the true morning before Aganza stirred salt and mealie flour into our sodden paper. But I had a cast for my leg, though I may as well say right now that something was wrong with our recipe for papier-mâché. It never really dried properly. It molded too, and within a few days it stank to high heaven, but it hardened. And the bones knit and my leg healed as it should. All that is left now of that experience is the heart-warming memories of the devotion of true friends, a slight ridge just above the ankle, and a tendency to rheumatism in wet weather.

Long before we had finished with my leg, a deputation of elders came to my hut. I knew before they spoke that they had decided upon a new village site. My first concern was the patients in the hospital. With the exception of two, all of them could rise to their feet and walk. Very well, they would walk, with an arm across the shoulder of a brother or friend; they would stop to rest frequently; and they would lie down as soon as camp was struck for the night.

"For the other two, and for you, *mama,* we will lift your beds upon the shoulders of four men and you will not need to put your feet to the ground."

This was a complication that I had not thought of. I had become as big a burden to my people as any patient in my hospital. I couldn't walk! Or could I? I called for a pencil, turned to a flyleaf in one of the remaining medical books, and rapidly sketched a crutch.

"Can someone make me two of these?" I asked the headman. "If so, then I can walk. They should be as long as from the pit of my arm to the sole of my foot."

While I waited, I talked with Aganza, Jackie, Job, and Achmed. I knew what I must do, and I thought I knew what they should do, but I wanted their free consent. I had it. The village had elected to move westward toward a small ridge of rolling hills ending in a well-wooded plateau where there was game and rich earth for gardens. I would only be a burden to them while they built their houses and cleared the land for planting. I would have to go on crutches to Tani, two hundred and more miles of jungle in a nearly opposite direction. I was frightened, but when these people, who had lost infinitely more than I, uttered no words of complaint, how could I whine? The last thing they did for me was to fan heat from glowing embers across the heads of their big drums until the membranes were dry enough to produce their normal rich tone and pitch. Then they sent word to Tani that I was injured and had started back to the Central Mission.

I watched my N'zemi file out of their village and off into the unknown. They carried with them as much as any group of black folk on trek, but it was so pitifully little: the men had their weapons and perhaps a little bundle of feast-day ornaments; the women carried their hoes, their chickens in wicker cages piled on top of the cooking pots on their heads, and the few surviving older babies on their backs. I promised that when my leg was well, and after I had visited my brothers and sisters far over the big, big waters, I would come back to them, but that promise was maudlin emotion born of the moment. I knew that my work from then on would not be in Dr. Mary's footsteps, that my path stretched beyond the one where pioneer feet had already trod. I watched and waved until the last straggler had disappeared among the big trees. Then the five of us—Achmed would not let me count Mata Kwan because that toddler was as yet but a bud, a mere fraction of a man—turned our faces southeastward.

We carried very little more than the N'zemi—food, my big rifle and shotgun, a blanket apiece, and a couple of cooking pots. Hospital supplies, instruments, drugs, records, personal items—all had to be abandoned. I picked up the little hinged frame holding my father's and mother's pictures and was on the point of tucking it into my bosom when I looked up at Aganza.

The pile on her head seemed mountainous: two blankets, one cooking pot, a measure of mealie flour, a stalk of plantains, a meager roll of garments for Mata Kwan, and the child himself slung over her hip in a fold of cowhide. I laid the pictures down and picked up a little tin first-aid kit instead.

I took a half dozen steps on my crutches, and then, when I slung my good leg forward, my foot struck a patch of mud as slick as grease. I sat down flat on my rump—at the same time clutching my right knee so that my broken leg was lifted off the ground. I felt like weeping, but there was nothing to do but get up and struggle on. I can't describe the horror of that first half hour. Normal crutch walking was an impossibility in the flood slime underfoot. I could only shuffle forward a few inches at a time and still I slipped and slid until every muscle in my body was strained and my arms felt as though the crutch heads were tearing them out of their sockets.

Finally I had to admit that two hundred miles of this was beyond my strength. I stopped and panted, waiting for breath with which to tell the others that they must go on without me. They wouldn't want to, but I must make them. We were still within sight of N'zem. I could get back there somehow and wait for whatever fate God might send. I looked back at my hut and saw—I rubbed my eyes with my knuckles and looked again—no, I wasn't dreaming! A string of the little men, Pygmies, a whole baker's dozen of them, trotted into view. I stretched out my hand and pointed silently.

"*Halaa! Muungu wa tesi,*" I heard Jackie murmur behind me. "God has sent them."

Aganza was more practical. "They heard the drums, *mama,* and they have come to help you."

CHAPTER
16

THE Pygmies reached us in a matter of minutes, jabbering
away, although not a one of us could understand them.
Two of them put their shoulders together, while a third wound
a green vine loosely about their two necks, making a rude sort
of saddle. But when they knelt, motioning for me to sit down,
I hesitated. I am not a particularly big woman, but they were
so tiny that I didn't see how they could get up again if I once
crushed them with my weight. Jackie solved the problem by
lifting me up as though I were a child and settling me firmly
where the Pygmies wanted me. A third stepped in front of
my two "pack mules" and lifted my legs across his shoulders,
straddling his neck. A fourth pressed his open palms against the
small of my back and with scarcely a grunt we splashed off,
south by southeast.

We made good time. My carriers changed about every ten
minutes, and before night fell, we were out of flood territory
and it was possible to make a comparatively dry camp. None
of the Pygmies seemed more tired than my own people. We
shared our food with them, and they ate voraciously, their
stomachs visibly swelling before they stopped. It made me
wonder if we should have enough food to last to Tani.

And how long would it take us to reach Tani? I had no way

of estimating our speed or the distance we traveled each day, and I knew better than to ask my companions. To the ordinary African villager distance is either "a big walk," or "a little walk," and both measurements are comparative, according to whether the speaker wishes to please the one spoken to or not. I have known "a big walk" to be completed in five minutes, and "a little walk" to stretch out into a week's trek.

Hour by hour I scanned the forest through which we passed, but when wild animals flee, they do not stop on the rim of danger, and for the first three days I saw nothing except two monkeys swinging along through the treetops. My people wanted me to shoot, and the Pygmies pointed excited preemptory fingers at the pair. I had never killed a monkey, but I would have tried for one now had they not been too far away for me to do more than scare or wound them superficially.

The morning of the fourth day we flushed a few guinea fowl, some of which did not fly until we almost stepped on them. It was a small flock, as guinea fowl go in West Africa, perhaps no more than a thousand. Jackie, who always trod at the heels of the Pygmy supporting my back, handed me my shotgun, and I fired into the mass of fluttering birds. I forgot that my Pygmies had probably never heard a gun discharged before. At its roar the men at my feet and back and those unencumbered simply melted into the jungle about us while I teetered precariously on the yoked shoulders of my frantic bearers. Undoubtedly I should have taken a pretty bad tumble had Jackie not wrapped one great prehensile arm about the two men and the other about me and held us in a viselike grip until the struggling ceased. Then, gently, he lifted me down and set me on the root of a tree.

By that time Achmed and Job, scurrying about like two terriers, had retrieved twenty-six birds. We built a fire right there, skinned and drew the fowl, spitted and roasted them. Long before the meat had started to brown, our Pygmies were back, sniffing like puppies. Many of the birds were eaten half-raw. I hadn't thought of myself as being really hungry, but I devoured a whole one, and little Mata Kwan did almost as well.

That afternoon I got more guineas—not shooting from the Pygmies' shoulders, however. And the next morning there were lesser bustards and spur-winged geese. There is no better recipe for contentment on trek than meat in the tummy. The Pygmies began to chant and to toss me up and down a little bit—perhaps just for the deviltry of it. Jackie began to sing the old hymn "Shall We Gather at the River," which I thought hardly appropriate, but he carried through, all six stanzas of it triumphantly. The cocky Achmed, not to be outdone, began a ribald chantey which he must have learned from some mining fugitive from a British battleship. Its sentiments were so frank that, alone as I was with sixteen men and one woman, none of whom—not even Achmed himself—could have completely understood its bald insinuations, I was numb with embarrassment. Fortunately he knew only one stanza, and when he attempted repeating that, I started the group telling stories. This, I felt, would save us from Achmed's songs, since most African folk tales take days, or even weeks, in the telling.

Many times as I rode along I wondered just what I should give the Pygmies in payment for my rescue. Salt, of course, would have been the ideal gift—but I had none. In fact, leaving N'zem under the circumstances we did, I had nothing. Then I noticed that their eyes gleamed whenever my gun ejected an empty shell, but these, by unwritten law of the jungle, belonged to Jackie, my gunbearer. Normally he traded them off to his companions and to the folk in the villages we visited, thereby augmenting the salary I paid him. He would sell them back to me as readily as to anyone else, I knew, but, while he was a good and faithful servant, he also drove a stiff bargain. I approached him on the matter one day—foolishly,

I suppose, telling him why I wanted the cartridges. He nodded understandingly and named a price slightly in excess of what I paid for new shells.

I told him so. He was surprised, but answered with perfect logic: "You could give them new shells, *mama;* those do not belong to me. But you will not do that because they might kill themselves with the new shells. And when you fire the shells, the empty cartridges become mine. Still—" and he came down to the exact price of new shells.

"Certainly not!" I answered. "I'll give the Pygmies something else."

"What, *mama?*"

"I don't know," I replied. "I haven't put my mind to it yet. Don't forget, you fellow, that the blanket you sleep under belongs to me, and I might give that to the leader."

My bluster didn't fool him for a second. Again unwritten law secured him his blanket as certainly as if he had laid cash in my hand when I passed it out to him.

When we reached Tani, a blanket for each one of the Pygmies, I promised myself. Tobacco too, if Dr. Early had left any behind. And what else? Salt! Lots of salt. After all, it was my life these little men had saved. I looked up into Jackie's curious eyes. He had been reading my mind, I suppose. Anyhow, he smiled, with all the assurance of a merchant who loves to haggle and who knows that when the bargain is concluded, he will come out at the long end.

But Jackie's confidence was misplaced, and I might have spared myself worry, for I never paid the Pygmies in any slightest measure for their great service to me. They left suddenly on the ninth day, without warning or leave-taking of any kind. They simply stopped, all thirteen of them, as though by signal, and muttered to each other so low in their throats that the words sounded like stomach rumblings. Then, gently and calmly, but without any waste motion, they deposited me, flat on the ground. My two pack animals unyoked themselves and, before our astonished eyes, melted into the jungle like shadows, without rustling a leaf or stirring a twig underfoot. It was Achmed, more Occidentalized than his companions, who broke the silence.

"Perhaps—they will come back?" I sensed fear in his voice, and turned quickly to the others.

"No." "No." The words were the merest shadows of sound, but they were emphatic.

I felt childish sitting there on the ground. "Well, help me up, somebody, and give me crutches," I commanded. "If we've got to make the rest of the way alone, let's get started."

Jackie put his hands under my arms and hoisted me to my feet as easily as though I were Mata Kwan. Achmed handed me my crutches. But Job was sniffing the air like a hunting dog. Any other time I would have laughed at him. Now I stood tense and silent like the others, waiting for him to identify whatever it was that teased his sensitive flaring nostrils. Suddenly all uncertainty vanished and his broad face split into a toothy grin.

"I smell a white man," he announced simply. He continued to grin like a minstrel caricature, and the relief shared by everyone was as tangible as the crutches under my shoulders. A minute later we heard men talking, and then Dr. Charles came into view with a string of porters. I had forgotten the message my N'zemi sent to Tani via the big drums. Nor had I thought of it at the time, but Dr. Charles—or someone from the Central Station—would have trekked clear to N'zem after me had that been necessary.

We camped where we were for that night and Dr. Charles examined my leg thoroughly. The injury had caused me no more discomfort than I had a right to expect, nevertheless, being both patient and nurse in this case, I watched him carefully. When he looked up, he started to nod his satisfaction, but checked himself quickly. Turning his head to one side and pinching his nostrils between thumb and forefinger in an exaggerated gesture, he tried to assume a dictatorial air while watching me out of the corners of his eyes.

"Nurse Ellen," he began in severe tones, "positively the rottenest cast I've ever examined."

For a moment I was bewildered, for my cast, which now actually was sprouting a coat of moss, had become so much a part of me that I had forgotten its rank character. We were both on the point of laughing when, with a single movement, Aganza stood between Dr. Charles and me.

"*Bwana*, my *mama* has done the best she can, and she has done well."

The words were simple, and the woman's tone was even soft and gentle, but there was something about it that cut through one's ears as easily as an iron hoe, fresh from the blacksmith, cuts through weeds in a garden.

Dr. Charles actually took a step backward, but I could only stare at Aganza. She spoke in Hausa, but she had understood our English. I had taught her to read English, but I had never spoken it to her.

"What— Who—is—this?" Dr. Charles was groping for words.

"Her name is Aganza. Mother Aganza, we all call her. She is my—slave. I bought her for a bit of salt and calico and two empty tomato cans. She is the best helper a missionary ever had and she is a wonderful nurse. Not the kind you're used to, you understand, but still she is wonderful with children and old folks and those really sick."

His eyes flashed interest and he looked her up and down like a white trader evaluating a tusk of ivory. "H'm," he breathed finally, and then pointed at Mata Kwan. "Her child?"

Aganza's body tensed.

"She gave him life," I answered. "Yes, he belongs to her. Completely!"

Aganza turned and looked at me, all primitive savagery gone now.

"H'm." It was Dr. Charles again.

Aganza took a step backward and laid a hand on my shoulder. I was conscious of a warm, comforting peace. She and I together could face the world.

"We can use her at Tani," Dr. Charles stated in that impartial tone doctors cultivate for use in tense moments.

His words were addressed to me, but his eyes still swept Aganza's gaunt frame. From crown to toe, and every muscle in between, her body bespoke health and strength. The ghost of a smile and the barest suggestion of a nod spoke more emphatically of his approval of what he saw in her than a garrulous discourse would have.

I breathed a huge sigh of relief, and Aganza again patted my shoulder. All three of us turned back to my leg.

"Do you want a new cast?" Dr. Charles asked. "I brought plaster of Paris for just that purpose."

"What do you advise, doctor?" I answered in my best professional manner.

"I'd say let it alone—if you can stand the smell," he replied. "It takes time for a bone to knit, as you know, and there is always danger of additional injury when cracking off a cast."

"I'm used to the smell," I answered. "And maybe the others won't mind me too much if I keep sufficiently distant. Besides it may dry out at Tani."

"Maybe," Dr. Charles agreed, and I thought I read approval of my decision in his eyes.

A week later we reached the Tani. The bulk of the floodwater had long since washed down to sea, but the river was still red from upcountry silt and the current was a gigantic millrace. Dugouts were waiting for us. We carried these two miles upstream, and then aimed as though to cut straight across. Five minutes later we landed about a quarter of a mile below the Tani dock.

No missionary ever fully realizes how much she has missed

the companionship of people of similar background until she returns to them from a long period of lonely service.

"It's heaven, isn't it?" I said to Aganza one day when she was helping me in the bathhouse.

I don't remember that she replied. She had learned long since to let patients talk their hearts out if the fountain of words bubbled up within them.

"I wish I could do something about this cast," I went on idly. "I feel as though I ought to stick my leg out the window when I eat."

An hour later Aganza came to me with some strips of bark in her hand.

"Do you like the smell of this, *mama?*" she asked, holding the fragments under my nose.

"Yes," I answered sniffing. "It's sort of like spice. Spice is something we put in food to make it taste different, and better."

"We put this in food too, *mama*. In my youth, when warriors ate the men they killed in battle, sometimes they emptied the stomach and filled the hole with corn and shreds of this bark, which comes from the roots of the *llmimi* vine, then they roasted the men above a fire. And they say the meat was very good—and the corn too."

"Did you ever eat man's meat, Aganza?" I asked idly.

"Oh, no, *mama*. Women never ate man's meat. And only the men who were too lazy to fight ever ate woman's meat."

"What are these strips for? Are we to have a special roast?"

"They are to bind over your cast, *mama;* they will take the bad smell away."

She was right. When next I hobbled into the hospital, Dr. Charles looked up inquiringly. "What happened to you? It seems to me that your personality is not quite so—uh—aggressive today."

"Oh, just a little native medicine," I answered airily. "Wait until you've been here long enough to really know Africa, and then—"

He cut me short. "How would you like to help my head nurse today?"

I looked at Madame Doctor inquiringly, but to my surprise, she shook her head "No." Dr. Charles pointed across the room to where Aganza was dressing an ulcer.

"My wife is going to have a baby one of these days, as you may have guessed," Dr. Charles went on. "That'll take her out of the hospital for some months. You're on your way to the States on furlough, but you can't take Aganza with you. The woman might as well earn her board and keep."

His light manner didn't fool me. "You feel the same about her as I do? That she is wonderful?"

"She has a good mind, and imagination plus balance. And she seems thoroughly trustworthy." It was a sober attempt at honest estimate.

"Thank you," I said, as though it had been I he was evaluating.

"With her help, I believe I could train an efficient staff of native workers that would multiply our outreach tenfold," he added.

I had never thought of Aganza as a teacher. It opened up endless possibilities. The rest of that day, as she and I worked together, I found myself staring at her as though I had never really seen her before. Nor had Dr. Charles spoken idly. As the days went by, his wife spent fewer and fewer hours in the hospital and Aganza took over like an old hand.

"Good heavens, do you know what I found her doing when I came back from lunch?" Dr. Charles said to me one day. He pointed to a huge volume on the table at his elbow. "Reading that—my old textbook on obstetrics."

"Well, can you think of anything the ordinary African village needs more than a good midwife?" I asked.

"But reading!" he went on. "Reading a technical treatise.

203

And in English! I thought at first she was just looking at the pictures, but there weren't any pictures on that page. I questioned her on the text, and her replies were intelligent!"

"Of course!"

We stared at each other for a moment, and then I said something that had been on my mind for some days: "Dr. Charles, when your baby comes, I'll assist you, of course, but Aganza would be an awfully good person to have there too."

He turned the idea over in his mind. "Yes!" he murmured. "Yes!" And we both understood the volumes of satisfaction so tersely expressed.

Thereafter she assisted him with all deliveries, and apparently he looked upon every expectant mother who came to him as a classroom demonstration for her benefit.

I thought I had come to know Aganza so well that nothing she said or did could surprise me, but I was mistaken. One day Dr. Charles raised his head from his microscope to remark: "I've suspected for some time that I was going to be the father of twins. Now I'm sure."

"Wonderful!" I exclaimed. "Mission twins! Could anything be nicer? You know all of us— Oh, oh!"

"What do you mean by 'Oh, oh!' " he demanded.

"It's all right, here at Tani," I answered slowly, "but I was thinking of Aganza. How will she react to twins?"

"What's she got to do with my twins?"

"You've worked pretty hard, haven't you? Haven't got out and traveled much, if any? That's a mistake for any missionary—"

He tapped the base of the microscope with an impatient forefinger. "Get back to the twins."

"Well, it's just that native peoples react differently to twins. In some villages a multiple birth is looked upon as a divine blessing, we'd say—as expression of the good will of the jungle spirits. In other villages, sometimes only a few miles distant, it's

204

proof of infidelity. I knew a woman who gave birth to twins and was beaten to death by *kiboko*.

"Every man in the village gave her at least one blow—to show how he felt about adultery. The babies were thrown into a huge jar, and every woman in the village dropped a stone in on top of them—proof of her attitude toward an erring sister."

Dr. Charles whistled softly. Then, "Let's find out right away how she feels about it."

His bellow could have been heard clear across the Tani, and it brought the woman on flying feet.

"Aganza, I'm going to be the father of twins," Dr. Charles announced aggressively before she was inside the door.

She stood there a moment panting, and then asked simply, "Is that why you shouted, *bwana?*"

We looked at each other foolishly. "Aganza, we didn't know how you personally would feel about twins?" I half questioned, half explained.

"They are not my twins, but the doctor *bwana's.*"

"All children that are born belong to every woman in the world, and every woman has a responsibility for them."

I looked at Dr. Charles quickly. Was fatherhood making a sentimentalist of him? Or did he really believe that?

Aganza's face was a conflict of emotions. "Am I a good enough nurse to help the little white sister?"

Dr. Charles drew a deep breath of relief. "You are to take Sister Ellen's place here in the hospital with me while she is gone," he said. "Would I ask that of you if I didn't think you were able to do her work?"

"Her work, yes, *bwana,* I will try. But no woman, however hard she may try, treads the path *Muungu* has laid out for another."

"But about my wife, Aganza. You haven't told us how you feel about twins. Are they a blessing? Or—do you feel my wife has been unfaithful?"

Aganza almost laughed. "*Bwana,* every woman looks at her

205

own child and is sure it is a blessing. Every other woman looks at it and knows that only the years will disclose whether the spirit of good or the spirit of evil has taken possession of the body. As for adultery—*bwana,* the black man says of his wife that she is merely a pair of hands and stupid as a hen. The white man walks beside his wife on the path, and he talks to her as though to a companion hunter. Hunters must depend upon each other, for their lives sometimes depend upon each other's skill and courage and honesty. Surely, *bwana,* if you treat your wife like a companion hunter, you must know whether or not she can be depended upon?" Aganza spoke slowly as though she were putting unfamiliar precepts into words for the first time, and her last phrases were half inquiries, half rebuke.

Dr. Charles fiddled with his pencil for a moment, and when he looked up, asked me, "Have you ever heard a preacher put it better?"

I hadn't.

I did not bring up the matter of twins again until after the children were born. The little boy came first—which was as it should be, Aganza told us. The elephant is the greatest of all beasts, and the hippopotamus the second greatest. The first-born of twins must be called *Tembo,* the Elephant, and the second, *Ngana,* the Hippopotamus. It is an embarrassment to a family to call a daughter by a greater name than her brother of the same age.

"Even in a family blessed by the spirits, Aganza?" I teased.

She glanced up quickly from the child she was rubbing with oil. If she was troubled, she overcame it immediately, for she chuckled and murmured: "Black or white, twins or lonely, they all look like fowls ready for the spit when they come fresh from their mother's bowels. Do you not think so, *mama?*"

"Well, I certainly think twins are a blessing," I remarked, as I laid a beautiful little girl beside her brother. "Don't you agree with me, Aganza?"

The old woman wrapped a towel about the boy, moistened a

206

dab of cotton with oil, and turned to the little girl before she answered. *"Mama,* I have lived with many different men in many different villages. Each man believed something a little different about the spirits. Some of them had to be mistaken, but who can say which ones? And why should a woman be beaten to death and her babies crushed in one village, when, if she had been sold into the village just across the river she would have been made much of? And all for exactly the same reason!"

CHAPTER
17

I spent fourteen months in the United States—hectic, frantic months—rushing from engagement to engagement;
crossing the continent four times; doing secretarial, deputation,
and ministerial work—and heaven only knows what else. I had
fragments of time with members of my family and a few
friends, who exhibited me to other friends and relatives at
luncheons, teas, and dinners as though I were a prize heifer at a
county fair. And I tried to study. Long before my year of rest
was up, I was exhausted, and I began to long desperately for
the peace and quiet of my primitive jungle, my hundreds of
patients, my simple schedule of ten to fourteen hours a day
seven days a week. I wanted to go home.

"Ellen, I believe you're positively glad to leave us!" Sister
Alice whined when I kissed her good-by at the train. I looked
over her head at brother John. He nodded his understanding as
my father would have done. As the whistle blew and I mounted
the steps, my face turned toward Africa, my heart was
singing.

This time no one from the mission met me in Léopoldville. I
was an old hand now, and supposedly able to take care of myself. A runner from one of the hotels was a *boy* who had left
Tani only a year or two before. He was as good as a nursemaid

until our side-wheeler chugged away from the dock four days later, and we headed up the Congo.

At my bank, I picked up messages from Tani and two or three neighboring mission stations. All missives welcomed me home and then went on: "Will you please—" The errands were legion, mostly shopping—from diapers to perfume. Naturally, I called on Achmed, or rather on the family with whom I had left him as houseboy a year before. They were delighted with him as a servant, except, as his mistress put it, "He suggests to me, at least once a week, that since he is now of an age when a woman would be a great comfort to him, I buy him a wife."

"I suppose he's still always broke? Knucklebones?" I asked.

"Oh, no. Dice! He doesn't play knucklebones at all now. He can lose faster at dice."

It was pleasant to talk with Achmed himself. And as a servant, he was a refreshing sight. Clad as always in a spotless *kanzu,* he had perched the scantiest of red tarbooshes over one ear, and pinned to each side were two immense orchids.

"It is the very latest style, *mama,*" he assured me. And by way of proof, he pulled out of his pocket the picture of a bullfighter's cap.

I didn't ask him to return to the bush with me, for he was well satisfied to live in Léopoldville. He had a request to make of me, however.

"As a *presenti, mama,*" he urged. "We meet, and we say good-by. It is so brief; but with a woman always to remind me of your goodness—"

"Absolutely not!"

"I know a man here who is in debt, and he is willing to sell one of his wives for ever so little." Achmed measured the infinitesimal price between thumb and forefinger while watching me narrowly for any signs of weakening.

I pushed my lower lip halfway up to my nose and swung my head slowly from side to side in exaggerated refusal. He shrugged his shoulders ruefully, and we parted good friends.

The mission *shimbeck* and Dr. Early met me at the confluence of the Tani and the Congo. Again he complained of my luggage.

"You would think that after Mother and I brought back mountains of bundles for everyone last year, nobody would have any further wants," he grumbled. "But look at this!"

I looked and let it go at that, while my boss and his *boys* loaded and reloaded the *shimbeck*. Seven short years earlier, I would never have believed the unwieldy looking craft could have survived the turbulent water of the lower Tani. Now I knew that we would creep along, often so close to the bank that I could pick flowers from overhanging branches, and that in due time, singing an appropriate chantey, we would nose in to the bank above the dock at Tani and let the current anchor us broadside against the piling.

Among other things the chantey this time called me their "goat-faced *mama*." This was not derisive by any means, but a lament that America had bleached the sun out of my skin and that I had returned as frail and delicate-looking as the little goat of the heavens, that is, the moon.

Everyone met me at the dock, and we laughed and chattered like monkeys in a treetop—and now and then I had to sniff hard to keep back the tears of happiness. With the exception of Mata Kwan and the twins, everyone looked exactly as when I left: Dr. and Mrs. Early perhaps a bit rounder, plumper; Sister Susanne a bit thinner, Dr. Charles broad and handsome as a professional cover boy; and Madame Doctor as stiffly starched in a house dress as she had looked in a nurse's uniform. The twins were almost as broad as they were tall. I was assured they could talk, but for the time being all they would do was nod and blink and waddle about like automatic dolls.

Aganza was wrapped in a single length of white *merikani*, her version of a suitable African nurse's uniform. I would not have recognized Mata Kwan had he not attached himself to

Aganza as tightly as the twins were anchored to Madame Doctor. I picked him up in my arms, but after five seconds of wondering acquiescence, he came alive and I might as well have tried to hold a forty-pound eel.

Job seemed a little different too, a mite straighter of body—or perhaps I should say, a mite less crooked. I looked at Dr. Charles questioningly.

"Just removed some scar tissue and grafted on skin. It permits freer movement," he murmured casually.

It is remarkable how quickly a missionary slips back into the life of a station. Before I had unpacked my traveling bag, I was helping in the outpatient clinic. The entire staff had dinner together that night in the Earlys' dining *dukas,* but after a little gossip and a few records on the phonograph, we settled down to planning for the new station I was to establish at N'Titierte, or "Big Bush," as it became known.

"What have you taught Aganza?" I asked Dr. Charles.

He looked baffled for a moment. "Well, nothing really that I can take credit for," he answered. "But she's learned a lot. She doesn't need teaching, that woman. She just seems to absorb knowledge without effort."

A few minutes later Dr. Charles spoke up, "I suppose you will want—you're planning of course—to take Aganza with you?"

I looked at him in amazement.

"Hang it all," he burst out, "the woman's the best assistant I ever had."

Without thinking I turned to Madame Doctor. She smiled and nodded. "I'm not jealous," she explained. "I learned to do what I'm told and when I'm told. Aganza's different. She really *assists.*"

He never really asked me to turn Aganza over to him as a worker, and I joked somewhat about wanting to get full value out of the empty tomato cans I had paid for her, but I felt that the decision did not properly lie with either Dr. Charles or me.

Aganza's reply was gratifying when I asked her if she would prefer to stay at Tani or come to Big Bush with me.

"We are old women, *mama,* you and I, old and worn out and soon we must turn our faces to the wall so as not to be a burden to those who are young and strong and vigorous," she began.

This was a new thought to me, and when I dwelt upon it, a distinctly irritating one. True, I had twinges of rheumatism in my leg where it had been broken, and gray streaks in my hair, and during my year in America I had acquired an upper plate, but I didn't feel old. On the contrary, I felt vigorous.

"How many years are left to us, only *Muungu* knows," Aganza was murmuring. "And we must prepare Mata Kwan."

"Prepare—Mata Kwan?" The grave emphasis surprised me. I sometimes forgot about the child for days at a time, but always he lay uppermost in Aganza's mind.

"There are so many things I would do if I were young once again and not compelled to hoe in a garden from dawn to dusk. Mata Kwan must be taught to do them. Already he can read, *mama.*"

I blinked. Mata Kwan was not yet five years old.

Aganza was a curious woman. I'm not sure she even understood the word "immortality" as we use it. Perhaps not, for more than once I heard her indicate that this little Son-of-a-Goat was to carry on for her. Was his life to be her immortality? I thought of the many American mothers, and fathers too who had tried to force their children's lives into the molds that had shaped their own personalities, and I protested.

"When Mata Kwan is old enough to judge, he will want some voice in choosing his work," I murmured.

"It is too late for a hunter to learn the use of a spear when a beast is charging," Aganza remarked simply. "We will build a station at Big Bush, *mama,* you and I, a station that will be like Tani. And we will train many young men and perhaps some young women to heal and to teach. And Mata Kwan—" her eyes glowed when she spoke of the child—"Mata Kwan, you will teach him everything there is for a man to know. And then, Big Bush will be—heaven too."

It took us some weeks to prepare for the move to Big Bush. There was no need to go back to N'zem and try to rescue anything abandoned there. By now, mold, white ants, and rust would have destroyed all of it. I had brought back from the United States what I could, and, as I had shared with Dr. Charles on his arrival, he now divided equipment with me.

It was evident that Dr. Early too expected the station at Big Bush "to amount to something." He chose with great care the *boys* who were to serve as my porters on the trip in. They were all mission *boys* skilled in some form of handicraft and construction, and each was to stay with me two seasons if I wanted him that long.

"It won't be clear sailing for you at Big Bush," he warned me. "I made a trip up there for general observation. I've talked with several traders too, and Monsieur l'Administrateur, of course. There are three witch doctors there: one good, one bad, and one indifferent. The chief, old Z'Nbolo, is a mean one, and watch out for the witch doctor N'Devli. Monsieur l'Administrateur tells me he visits that village at least twice a year and never sees a thing out of the way—in fact, he never sees Z'Nbolo, who has always just left on a hunting trip or has some other convenient excuse. And Monsieur has never been able to get a census of that village that is in proportion to the number of huts. The kola nuts with which they pay their hut tax are always of inferior grade. And there is an awful lot of tattooing of tribal marks and all that sort of thing—devil bush, long-drawn-out initiation rites, and vague tales of palm-wine orgies that have lasted weeks.

"Really want to go up there, Ellen? Or—stay here while I scout around for another likely place?"

I had been listening with that unheeding sort of attention one pays to the familiar. Was there a village in Africa that did not try to evade some portion of its taxes? or did not love the combination of religious rite and social orgy evolved throughout the ages? These were everyday facts in the life of a missionary, and I was surprised at Dr. Early's questions.

"Monsieur l'Administrateur says what he likes least about the village of N'Titierte is that he has sometimes walked there without a man, woman, or child seemingly being aware of his existence. It isn't that they stop talking when he's around or drop their eyes or look away. They just keep right on talking, arguing, and looking right through him as though he were thin air. And he says it is a village of no laughter . . . Still want to go?"

"Of course I'm going."

It was a beautiful morning when we started out, Aganza, Mata Kwan, Job, Jackie, myself, and some sixty-odd porters. We carried food for a month, some barter goods—salt, of course, *merikani,* safety pins, and such—a tent, and what medical equipment we could manage. Two *shimbecks* took us downstream to the confluence of the Tani and Congo, and then about a hundred miles west on the Great River, where we landed and struck cross-country almost due north.

There was a new *tipoye* for me, but it was mostly Mata Kwan who occupied it. I enjoyed walking, for the going was not too difficult. In the wooded sections we followed game trails which were sometimes as smooth and pleasant as the bridle paths through a city park. It was about a month after the rainy season had stopped and the open spaces were spread with a bright new coverlet of flowers. We tramped one whole day over a plain where every footstep fell on a cushion of blossoms and that night each of us slept on a mattress of flowers.

We had to cross a river twice. I thought at first it was the Congo again, but Job told me that this was the Oogau, the river that our new home overlooked. At the last crossing, we found a young man with a dugout, a Government ferryman.

He took us across, a few at a time, finishing after darkness had fallen, and we camped almost on the landing. I had bathed, eaten my supper, and was ready for bed when there was a gentle cough outside my tent. I went outside and there stood the ferryman.

"My wife, *mama*," he began without preliminaries. "She is a cripple. That is the only reason why I could buy her. But she is young, *mama*, and should be strong. However, instead of planting a garden and gathering greens for her cooking pot, she lies on her side on her sleeping mat and moans that she is beset by devils. I have traveled much, *mama*. I have worked in the mines at Katanga, and on the Government roads, and once I went down the Great River to a white man's village. It was an immense village, with huts as thick and huge as trees in a jungle, and there were other marvelous things, *mama*. There were huts upon huts, and when it rained, one walked between the huts and did not get one's feet muddy. Have you ever seen such a village, *mama*?"

I nodded, although I wondered what town he meant. Léopoldville? Stanleyville? or maybe just a more or less permanent construction base?

"But the most marvelous thing I saw, *mama*, was men who were not afraid of devils. They fought with them and conquered devils. I have tried to fight devils too, and my village has driven me out. They sold me a woman, a cripple, but the witch doctor has put a curse on her."

I was curious, but tired, so I merely picked up my emergency bag, and followed him, murmuring as I did so, "Who would hire a witch doctor to put a curse on a cripple?"

"There is one, N'gana," he answered, and that was as much of his story as I got from him that night.

The ferryman held back the cowhide door of his hut and I entered. Aganza slipped in behind me, and together we examined the wife, a child not more than thirteen or fourteen years old. It was apparent at the first glance what had crippled her.

215

As a small child she had crept or tumbled into the fire, or—as is so pitifully often the case with African children—she had suffered an epileptic seizure and had fallen on a firebrand. Her left leg had been terribly burned. I couldn't find another thing wrong with her, however, and I told her husband so.

"She'll have to move slowly. She can't do as much as the ordinary woman because she has to struggle against those scar tissues," I explained. And I urged the girl to stand up and let me see how straight she could get herself and how much she could move about, but she only rolled her eyes at me and moaned, "I am to die."

For the first and only time in my life I heard an African husband plead with his wife where the normal procedure would have been blows. As I watched the girl on the floor, I wondered just how large a part what we call neuroses play in witchcraft. I was reminded of the old legend of the fearsome spirit who is the tribal bogeyman of refractory wives:

" 'What shall I do with my female *cattle* to teach them obedience?' moaned the wretched husband.

" 'Let Mumbo Jumbo beat some sense into their stupid heads,' advised the old men resting in the shade of the palaver hut."

Perhaps Aganza was thinking of this legend too, or possibly this elemental marital precept merely coursed through her veins. In any case, the child wife on the floor heaved an immense sigh and rolled over and, as she came to rest, Aganza implanted a powerful kick in the exact middle of her buttocks. Even witchcraft is not powerful enough to overcome surprise, and the girl was on her feet instantly. On one foot, I should say; the other she held a good twelve or fifteen inches off the floor to ease the strain of the scar-puckered skin.

"Cook your husband's supper," Aganza ordered. "What kind of old women are there in your village? Did they think they were preparing you for marriage without teaching you obedience? When night falls, a man's belly clamors for food,

216

and it is your duty to fill it, no matter if you are tired or in pain."

The girl touched the floor with the toes of her injured leg and, only slightly bent, scurried past Aganza, gathering up her cooking pot as she slipped out the door. Back in the United States, I thought pityingly, a few simple operations and the child would be as straight as any other woman. I turned to Aganza for the bolstering advice I knew she would give, and caught a glimpse of the openmouthed ferryman.

"She is too little to kick, too little and delicate," he was babbling.

"Fool!" Aganza snorted. "All women are little when they are young, but it is then, when they are 'little and delicate'—" the scorn with which she mimicked his words was superb— "that they form the habits nothing but death can break."

As we went back to our tent, a cooking fire was already twinkling in front of the ferryman's hut and his wife, watching us out of the corner of one eye, bent over it. I explained to Aganza about removal of scar tissue and skin-grafting.

"Very well then, *mama,* we will straighten the little slut out," was her only reply.

"We would have to take the girl along with us to Big Bush, because the operations would take time, and I would have to watch her while they were healing," I explained.

"Then we will take her," Aganza answered. "The man needs a wife who can work."

"But I doubt if she will want to come with us," I half suggested, half asked. "If she whines to her husband, he won't send her."

Aganza's reply, whatever it was, sounded very much like a contemptuous snort. And when we started off down the trail the next morning, the ferryman watched us out of sight, for sharing my *tipoye* with Mata Kwan, and keenly cautious of Aganza, was his "too little and delicate" wife.

217

CHAPTER
18

Our entrance into N'Titierte caused very little stir. The village knew who I was and why I was there; Dr. Early and Monsieur l'Administrateur had taken care of that. There was no particular welcome, and, despite Dr. Early's warnings, no more animosity from the villagers than a primitive people naturally show the stranger who may be either friend or foe.

Concerning me, however, there was a great deal of curiosity. What seemed to be the entire female population of N'Titierte followed us out to the spur of land overlooking the Oogau River, where the mission station was to be built. My *boys* pitched the tent that Aganza, Mata Kwan, Laii—the ferryman's wife—and I would occupy until permanent buildings were constructed, and then threw up bamboo and palm-leaf shelters for a kitchen and a dining room. Lastly, because I insisted—otherwise they would have slept in the open around a fire, scorching the soles of their feet and their blankets with equal unconcern—they built tiny palm-leaf lean-tos for themselves.

I missed Achmed during this settling-in process. Job took his place with good spirit, but he was definitely not cut out to be a head houseboy. Jackie made a wonderful headman, and Yedou the cook, lent to me from Tani, constructed a sunken fireplace and had water for tea and baths bubbling in less than an hour's time after our arrival.

Established, clean and comfortable, I sent Jackie with a half dozen *boys,* each bearing something by way of *presenti,* to the chief. I had spent much thought on the choice and amount of these gifts. If I were too generous in the beginning, the precedent might be a burden in the years to follow. On the other hand, my gifts must not appear stingy to the man who was in so many ways my host and who could help or hinder my work immeasurably on a mere personal whim. I had heard of villages whose children were fat and lively, and whose shambas were lush, which nevertheless suffered from acute and sudden famine whenever traders or white hunters who had offended appeared on the scene. Finally I halved what I had originally laid out and supplemented the smaller amount with diplomacy. I instructed Jackie to ask for the services of half a dozen bearers for the rest of the afternoon, because my own bearers needed meat, which I would shoot for them, but that they were tired. Bearers on a hunt always receive a liberal share of the meat, and the inference was that, luck being with me, the whole village would feast that evening.

Jackie was back in a few minutes, minus my gifts but with the information that His Royal Highness was resting. There was no invitation for me to visit him, or intimation that, once refreshed, he would visit me. This could mean only that either I was unwelcome or the chief was sick. The man who had received the *presenti,* had done so at the door of the chief's kraal and Jackie had not been invited to enter. Neither of us knew what to make of it.

But trailing behind my gunbearer were at least two dozen men, proof that the possibility of meat was highly pleasing in some quarters. In less than an hour and no more than half a mile from the village, I shot four zebras, a reedbuck, and two tommies—as the tiny Thompson's gazelle is known all over

Africa. I kept the reedbuck for my *boys* and the tommies for us women, and gave the zebras to the N'Titierteans.

When the cook cut up the tommies, I had him wrap one of the livers in the leaf lard stripped from the inner surface of the ribs, and take it to the chief. I knew the old man, if well, would eat the whole gift raw, both fat and organ. Or, however ill, if any semblance of appetite remained to him, the delicacy would set his mouth to watering. The cook brought back thanks, and a dozen eggs, so I knew that the thanks were sincere. Other, similar gifts would be appreciated—but the cook, like Jackie, had not caught even a glimpse of the chief.

Two of the eggs were fresh, a good percentage for an African village. We fed them to Mata Kwan. The other liver and leaf lard we gave to Laii, in order to build her up for what was ahead of her. She seemed afraid to take the meat. In her bewildered eyes one could read the question: Why should anyone give me, a female, these choice bits? She didn't touch them until Aganza arose, as much command in her manner as in her voice, and then the child bolted both fat and liver almost whole. Little Laii would not forget in a hurry that the old woman's stubby, chigger-scarred toes could inflict very real punishment.

Before supper Aganza and I walked over the knoll which was to be our future home. Lengthwise and crosswise, we covered every foot of the ground, and I made a map as we went, marking in the contour as best I could, locating every clump of trees. In Africa, as elsewhere, it takes God and sometimes a hundred years to make a forest giant, and I had no intention of denuding my knoll so that the plans for future buildings might look neat on paper. At present all we needed was a *dukas* for me, one for Aganza and Mata Kwan, and a third which would be dispensary and incipient hospital. They would be of wattle and clay with thatched roofs.

As for the *boys*, the temporary shelters answered their own ideas of comfort. When the wind and rain tore holes in their roofs, a forest full of green shingles was at their back door, free for the gathering.

With many hands helping, our three *dukases* were completed in a day; then, with a slow fire burning in the center of each to help dry out our plaster, they were ready for occupancy in a week.

The evening of the day we moved into our new homes, Aganza came to me and asked for Christian baptism. I had almost forgotten that she was not a Christian. Surely she had been one in the truest sense of the word for several years now. There was no need for me to catechize her; she understood as well as I what she was doing; she understood better than many who have grown up in so-called Christian communities.

I recalled the evening when I had asked her if she did not want "to become a Christian," and she had answered that she could not believe in heaven until she had seen it. I suppose that in those early years I had made heaven seem an integral part of Christianity; inexperience is apt to lay stress on nebulous detail. Now I merely asked Aganza if she was very sure, no doubts at all.

"I have seen your heaven, *mama*. I have lived in it for more than four seasons," the old woman answered.

She went on to talk about the Tani Station, the love and gentle care of every inhabitant there for every other person. Tani, heaven? The place where I myself had lived in such vexed bewilderment, critical of the work and even the personalities of others about me?

"And *mama,* will you baptize Mata Kwan at the same time?"

"But Mata Kwan is little more than a baby," I answered. "He must reach the age of accountability and make that decision for himself."

The old woman was silent for a moment. Then she asked: "Did you make that decision for yourself, *mama?* I thought everyone in your home village was born Christian."

It was my turn for silent thought. Technically, I had made that decision. I had made formal confession of faith at the age of thirteen, along with a dozen or so other little girls for whom the whole affair had been something of a long-drawn-out party with its solemn—or at least quieter—moments. Actually, no decision had really been made. Confirmation was something nice little girls of good family prepared for and went through— just like graduation from grade school.

The next day I baptized the two of them and received them into the membership of the newly founded, and as yet homeless, little church of Big Bush Station. I suppose the parish of Big Bush was born automatically at that moment. No one to my knowledge has challenged it since.

My own people were present, of course, as well as the porters from Tani. Back of them, in shifting, goggle-eyed groups, was the entire village of N'Titierte, with the exception of its chief. Two men of striking appearance were in the forefront of the N'Titierteans, and I could not help wondering about them. Our simple ceremony over, one of these men turned and stalked off, and the villagers made way for him. As I watched the arrogant swing of the man's shoulders, I knew that he was a witch doctor. Even a village chief, no matter how rich or powerful, never equals that air of insolence. And he was an unfriendly witch doctor; nothing could have been more evident.

"N'Devli!" I exclaimed in a whisper.

I turned quickly to Aganza, but if my newly baptized convert had any premonition of evil, it did not show in the angular lines of her calm face.

The second man stayed to talk with me. I have called him N'Derfi (friend) and he has been just that throughout the years. He remained behind to offer advice as from one practicing craftsman to another. It was a neat little lecture on the value of mob psychology that would have done credit to the most accomplished propagandist. People like a show, he told me, and if it is good enough, there can be complete identifica-

222

tion of self with the performer, he averred in essence. It must be of the familiar, yet at the same time stimulate each mind into assurance of uniquely personal exploration of the unknown beyond one's fellows. I listened fascinated while he advised change of costume to inculcate physical or mental fright. And had I no spirits imprisoned among my belongings? Spirits that spoke to me alone, using me as a channel for voicing their desires and wisdom?

I tried to explain to N'Derfi that I had no supernatural powers. He was an honest man who believed in his own magic, and my confession bewildered him. He advised me quite earnestly not to disclose my weaknesses to the general public. I told him that my work was to heal, and that I intended to remove some of the scars from Laii's leg that afternoon. I hoped, I went on, that eventually she could walk upright like other women and be able to be a good wife to her husband, the ferryman. Why did I not remove all the scars in one afternoon, the witch doctor asked? Was it because if the ferryman saw his wife just a little less crooked, he would pay more and more progressively as he saw her less and less crooked? When I told him I received no payment other than that joy which comes from relieving the pain and misery of others, his eyes narrowed in amazement and disbelief. I continued, however, to speak of shock, and the necessity for not stripping too large an area of skin off the girl's ribs in order to cover her legs.

"What will you do if N'gana objects to your straightening the woman?" N'Derfi asked.

"N'gana? The Hippopotamus? Who is he?" I countered.

"Tembo your ferryman's twin brother. N'gana was the second to tumble out between his mother's legs, and it was plain for everyone to see that even as a child he hated his brother because Tembo was first."

So this was one of the tribes that considered twins the greatest blessing that could happen to parents!

But N'Derfi was telling me, briefly, a tale common to many

223

families, regardless of time, race, and geography. It was of two brothers, one good, kind, well-liked, and not too bright—misfortune's stepchild. "As for N'gana, one passes him quickly on the path, *mama*. Few sit beside him in the palaver house, but everyone likes to hunt with him for truly he is beloved of the spirits. There is always game for his spear and his flying weapons are as unerring as a diving hawk. He is only a young man, but, *mama*, he already has many wives. More wives than some of the old men upon whose wisdom the chief has leaned for many years. But Tembo is the elder; that is one thing N'gana cannot take away from him, and he hates him because of it."

I waited for more, but N'Derfi did not go on. Then my mind veered to something which at the time I thought more important.

"When will I see the chief, N'Derfi?" I asked.

The witch doctor shifted from one foot to the other and back again. He touched the ribbon marker hanging from my prayer book with a tentative finger and seemed to study the bit of satin with absorption. I waited until he raised his head.

"May I see you cut away these crippling scars and replace them with new skin, *mama?*" he asked.

I considered a short while. "If you will wash yourself well all over, scouring every part of your body with wood ashes, and if you will stand back against the side of the hut and neither move nor speak until I am finished, you may watch."

"I will do all these things, *mama,*" he answered.

"And—" I hesitated again. "If we, you and I, do not speak of what I intend to do to Laii, N'gana need not know anything about it. Then, no matter how spiteful he is toward his brother, he can't do anything to hinder us."

"N'gana will know," N'Derfi answered calmly.

"How can he know if neither of us tells him?" I demanded.

"N'gana will know," the witch doctor reiterated. Then he leaned forward and spoke in a very low voice. "One never knows what spirits may be listening and take offense at man's least words. N'gana is beloved of the spirits. He will know what you intend to do."

I don't explain it that way. In fact, I can't explain it at all, but as Aganza and I began preparations for the operation—an amazingly clean N'Derfi pressed tightly against the side of the hut—a messenger came from N'gana demanding that I turn Laii over to the ferryman's brother "for safekeeping and return to her husband." I shooed the messenger away with scant ceremony and called for Job to bring us more water. During the operation we would sweat like horses in the still air of the hut, and drink like horses following it.

Finally everything was ready. Aganza had given Laii a local anesthetic—Dr. Charles had made a beautiful anesthetist of her—and I was washing my hands when a drum began thumping right outside my door. I straightened up in annoyance. Then I caught sight of Laii, reared upright on her elbows, stark terror in her face. I walked to the door and pushed back the curtain. There, not ten feet away, was N'Devli in an outlandish getup of claws, feathers, and fur. Behind him squatted a naked child, busily thumping on a small drum. N'gana leaned against the trunk of a coral tree and grinned at me. He had paid for the performance, and he intended to miss none of it. As I looked, N'Devli raised a hand toward me and shook a rattle, then he advanced with a little stamp of one heel. The other hand raised, its rattle clattered, and the second heel stamped, and N'Devli howled.

"Boo!" I said suddenly.

N'Devli stopped and looked at me in some surprise. The drummer boy faltered in his rhythm, but N'gana screamed at both of them. Then N'Devli bent nearly double and, shaking both rattles, leaped a good three feet straight up into the air. He leaped again and came down with a tremendous howl. Behind me I heard a whimper, and I turned to see Laii, normally the hue of a ripe eggplant, now the color of dirty ashes. Aganza's eyes were wide and staring, but I couldn't tell whether it was from anger or fright.

By chance my eyes fell on the pot of water that had been heated for us to wash up with following the operation. It was not boiling, of course, but it was hot and a faint vapor hung above it. Without hesitation I picked up the pot and pushed through the doorway, straight up to the howling N'Devli. He stopped his gyrating and pranced in front of me like a skittish colt on a cold morning.

"There is medicine in this pot stronger than any of your spirits," I told him, and with a long swinging motion I dashed the water full in his face.

The deep-throated howl he had begun ended in a tapering squeak. As I drew the pot back in order to empty the remainder upon him, N'Devli shrieked once more, and leaped whirling in the air. When his feet struck the earth, he was already running, and seconds later he had disappeared in a cloud of steam. The tiny drummer scrambled to his feet and made off in another direction. I turned toward N'gana, who was staring at me openmouthed, and swished the water in the pot meaningfully. He too fled. The rout of the devils was complete.

Back in the hut, not a person had moved, even to the shade of expression. I walked over to Laii and tried to conquer the tremor in my voice as I told her: "There were three devils outside the hut that hate me—me, not you. But I am not afraid of devils, child, because I have medicine that is stronger than any of their magic. You heard one of them screaming in fright, and all of them have run away. Lie down now, and we will go about straightening your leg."

For a moment she did not move, but it seemed to me that I could see the tension easing in her face. Then Aganza laid a hand on her shoulder, and Laii looked up into the old woman's face.

"What the white *mama* says is true, little woman. Lie down now," with a gentle shove. "*Mama* cannot be bothered with talking to you while she is taking the bad things out of your leg."

Three weeks later when Laii was on her feet again, inches taller, I learned a curious thing about witch doctors through N'Derfi. No full-fledged, practicing witch doctor, in our part of the Congo Territory at least, ever has his kraal in his village. In Africa, as elsewhere, familiarity breeds contempt, and a witch doctor secludes himself somewhere in bush or jungle so that the imagination of his clientele can work in his favor. N'Derfi had four wives, and accordingly he had four homes, located in four different directions from Big Bush.

"The plants I need for my medicines do not all grow in one spot," he told me once. "This way, no matter what the direction I must travel, there is always the comfort of a wife nearby. And," he smiled slyly, "there is also absolute peace among my *cattle*."

Now, after Laii's operation, N'Derfi brought a wife and settled down in the village, so that he could watch the effects of my white magic on Laii. When he saw the ferryman's wife walking again, straighter and obviously with greater ease than before, he asked, "Can you straighten all crooked people, white woman?"

"Not all crooked people," I answered. "I would have to see each one and find out what made him crooked."

He pointed at Job. "Can you straighten his legs?" he asked.

"No. It is the bones underneath the skin that have been injured, but there are other white medicine men, ever so much more skilled than I, who could straighten him."

Many times after that I saw N'Derfi watching Job speculatively, and I would have given a good deal to know what thoughts were taking shape between those two black ears of his.

In six months, Laii was ready to go back to her husband, tall, straight, a really comely young woman, whose only blemishes were a few hairline scars on her thighs and ribs where skin for grafting on her legs had been taken. There were heavier scars on her leg—I was a surgeon by necessity and with no particular training, you must remember, but there was buoyancy in her step and the joy of living in her face. I was proud of her, and my success added infinitely to the prestige a white person must always build for himself in a native village if his work is to have any lasting effect.

I sent her back to her husband with the Tani porters, who had stayed with me long enough to mold and burn brick for the foundation and lower walls of a hospital that could be kept clean of vermin. They also dug me a latrine and, using bamboo joints, piped spring water down from a nearby hill. Since we had no spigots, the water ran continuously, and, except for the time a herd of playful elephants destroyed about an eighth of a mile of this primitive pipe line, the water was a very real comfort. I shared it with the village of N'Titierte, and·earned the gratitude of both men and women. The women, who had carried their water from the river before, were saved hours of backbreaking uphill toil. The men were pleased because no crocodile ever seized one of their *cattle* while drawing water from my "infant river," as they called it. I pointed out that there was no sand or fish or other little wriggly things in my water, but that was shrugged off as not being really important.

We started a school too, with Aganza as teacher. At first only two of N'Derfi's sons attended. Aganza taught them to read while a raft of village tots stood about in a close-packed circle, wriggling, giggling, staring, and pointing. Aganza was an excellent teacher. We printed books in Hausa by hand, she and I together, during the evenings, but we were seldom more than one page ahead of our pupils at any time. I supplied the textual material at first and, being a soul without much imagination, it was the fatuous:

"The cat ran up the tree.

"The dog ran after the cat.

"The cat looked at the dog.

"The dog looked at the cat.

"The cat miaowed at the dog.

"The dog barked at the cat."

228

I ran through the exceedingly brief gamut of domestic animals and common birds—at least, I did have the sense to stick to those known to Africa—and then Aganza took over. Her first product was the fairy tale that explains why the huge elephant is afraid of the mouse. It is a tale of brute strength outwitted by cunning.

Every child in the village knew the story by heart. The day Aganza showed this copybook to her two pupils, the circle of curious young onlookers tightened, pressed forward, sank down onto their haunches—and thus informally enrolled themselves in the first mission school in Big Bush.

Other fairy tales followed in quick succession: "The Crocodile-headed Boy," "The Sloogeh Dog and the Rich Man," and many items of folk history. I have since heard a great deal about progressive education, but I don't believe any group of children learned with greater ease or pleasure than our young N'Titierteans. Nor was school a matter of "Do as you please, dear little one." The pupils did as Aganza pleased, and on more than one occasion I have seen her pick up a youngster who was experimenting with insolence as a normal phase of his growing-up process, and warm his buttocks with the palm of her hand until they glowed a brilliant rich purple—red being an impossible color for them under any circumstance.

And it was with the young men from among these pupils whom Mother Aganza loved and paddled into some state of formal knowledge that my superiors on the African staff sowed literacy throughout the country to the north and west of Big Bush not so very many years later.

It was Aganza too who worked out a system of securing nurses for my growing hospital. We received many gifts for our medical services: "For her who bore you, *mama,*" is the way in which they were usually offered, since, according to some African minds, all of good or evil a woman accomplishes in this life stems from one's mother and her conduct before one's birth. Therefore, it is to one's mother that a gift is tendered, whether or not the mother is living or dead. We charged no fee, however, until Mother Aganza began looking over all the adolescent boys with a speculative eye. If the young male patient were strong and healthy and his illness or wound superficial and not incapacitating, Mother Aganza demanded personal service in return for medical attention. Some of the boys were inept or unwilling; some few liked the work we set them at so much that when we offered them a few *sous* by way of salary, they stayed on and eventually studied medicine, after a fashion —under Mother Aganza's direction, of course.

I remember the first time I ever saw one of those boys. He had come to me with a superficial wound which laid back the skin over the big muscle on his left arm. All I needed to do was cleanse the wound and sew it up, but when I brought out my needle, the boy took one look at it and drew back.

"Afraid?" I taunted. "A great big boy like you who will surely take part in the next lion hunt? What will you do when *simba* charges? Crawl under your shield and curl up like a chinch bug with the haft of your spear frozen to the palm of your hand?"

The urchin grinned impishly and waved a supercilious hand at a companion. The latter dashed away. I took a step forward with my needle, but Aganza touched me on the shoulder and whispered in my ear.

"Wait, *mama*. I think he wants to show you something."

He did. The whole thing was prearranged—possibly even to the wound.

In a few seconds the companion dashed back with a calabash dipper covered by a leaf. Nonchalantly my erstwhile patient thrust his right hand into the gourd and picked up a vicious black driver ant. Calmly he ripped off one of the insect's pincers, and then held the other at the exact point where the tear in his skin ended. With almost lightning speed the pincers clamped shut through the skin, drawing it together in as neat a stitch as I have ever seen, a stitch which I knew

230

would never loosen its hold until pried out later. A fingernail severed the body of the ant from the pincer and tossed it away. The boy grinned at me again. A second ant, a second stitch, and another grin.

When he had finished, I examined the primitive "seam" carefully and then said with perfect honesty, "I couldn't have done a better job myself."

His reply was as surprising as his conduct had been, "Now, *mama,* what must I do in order to pay you?"

"Why, you don't owe me anything!" I exclaimed.

For a moment I thought he was going to cry. Again Aganza touched my shoulder, and when I looked at her she nodded briefly, peremptorily.

I turned back to the child. What would I give him to do? And then, as usual, "Mother Aganza will put you to work," I hedged weakly. I have no sweeter memory of all my African service than the happiness which flooded his face.

Eventually that boy went to the University of Chicago and worked on my brother's farm during the vacations. Today he is known and respected throughout Africa. And many a doctor whose skin was blanched by providence of God at birth reads his learned articles in medical journals, never dreaming that their author once sacrificed to tribal fetishes and still respects the rite for the place it holds in the evolution of mankind.

19

W HEN N'Derfi, the rain maker, as I prefer to call him—
because the popular connotation of "witch doctor" is
usually evil—asked me why I did not straighten out Job's
twisted limbs as I had Laii's, he planted a seed in my mind that
grew and vexed me almost daily. N'Derfi seemed satisfied with
the explanation I gave him at the moment, but many times I
noticed him watching my gnarled servant sidling along like a
monstrous land crab, and then looking at me with open question in his eyes. Just how great was my white magic? Just how
generous was I? I thought I read these questions on his face, in
spite of the fact that N'Derfi was a good and honest friend of
mine in deed as well as in word. It was he who secured an invitation from the Council of Old Men for me to assist in the
funeral obsequies of their chief. It was a signal honor and I
appreciated it as such. And, as I helped to coat the royal body
with clay and bind it in the funeral mats, I finally understood
why I had never been permitted to look upon him in life. The
man—everyone had called him old, but he was so mutilated by
disease I could never have guessed his age—was a leper.

Leprosy is one of the scourges of the tropical belt of the Dark
Continent, and the civil administration in our territory, in at-
tempting to deal with it, has established leper colonies at vari-

ous points. But the natives hate segregation and fear the camps, so that whenever a white man or woman or a black official visits a village, the lepers disappear as if by magic. The black man is voluble, not to say garrulous, but he can keep a secret, and no one, not even N'Derfi, not even Job or Aganza, if they had chanced upon the knowledge, had betrayed the villagers' prime secret.

Burial customs for important people differ from tribe to tribe and even from village to village in Africa. The N'Titierteans believe a dead ruler himself chooses the place of his simple interment, although the living must assist him. First, a funeral party of sixteen was chosen by the Old Men's Council. Then the clay-caked, mat-wrapped corpse was lashed to a pole and hoisted onto the shoulders of four of the honored group, two before and two behind. After that, the whole sixteen began circling the village, lengthening the radius of the circle by about ten feet at each revolution. The theory is that when the grave site chosen by the spirit of the dead chief is crossed, the corpse will indicate that fact by a struggle.

I was curious to see this "struggle," and since I could not refuse at least partial participation without giving offense, I started out with the other fifteen on the funereal merry-go-round. We trudged along for three days, camping at night wherever we happened to be when the sun set, with the villagers bringing us food and skins or blankets, and discussing volubly the stubborn immobility of His Royal Highness. I began to wonder what we would do when eventually we struck the riverbank. That question was partially answered on the third day when we cut across the edge of a small marsh created by a chain of springs. In we plunged, without deviation of so much as a foot from our direct line of march. The first round was muddy and unpleasant; the second, third, and fourth rounds progressively more so. Before we camped that night, the mud and slush were up to my knees and it took all my strength to pull my feet out of the mud and force them forward. It was hard to keep one's footing too and several times I sat down in the muck.

Long before we camped, I decided that I had paid our chief quite enough respect and that, regardless of the offense that might be taken, I was going home. But my curiosity was aroused again, just in the nick of time. That evening the villagers inquired most anxiously after the chief's behavior and informed his honor guard, somewhat plaintively, that the palm wine and banana beer with which his burial would be celebrated were perfect now, but on the point of spoiling. I stayed on into the fourth morning just to see how this pertinent announcement would affect the matter in hand, and sure enough, on only the second or third time around, right in the deepest part of the marsh, His Royal Highness must have had a postmortem epileptic seizure, for the movement was so violent that it apparently threw both of his forward carriers to the ground. Immediately all sixteen of us made a beeline for home by the shortest route possible; I to a hot bath and clean clothes, my companions-in-honor to a community binge of such proportions that they did not recover for a week. The corpse? Earth and water had taken it to themselves. Could living man provide a more sufficient grave?

As the village emerged from its stupor, three things happened almost simultaneously. First a ceremonial lion hunt was set up, and since I had been an honored member of the funeral cortege, my *boys* were invited to share in the hunt. All accepted with alacrity with the exception of Job, and his refusal was taken as indication of cowardice. Even I questioned him.

"I am not afraid, *mama,*" he assured me earnestly. "It is just that my people do not hunt lions. They are elephant hunters. Now if there is an elephant you wish me to destroy—"

The village, men, women, and children, howled with derisive laughter, but I believed Job. After all, he was a Batwa, a man from the deep rain forests where there are elephants aplenty but no lions.

He might, however, have spared himself much by simple acceptance to the lion hunt, for it was a "ceremonial" hunt: that is, a pantomimic dance. My N'Titierteans were famed all over West Africa as lion hunters, but for some strange reason there had been no real lion hunt from this village in a generation. Again, I asked Job why, under the circumstances, he had not joined in the "hunt."

"I do not hunt lions, *mama*. Now elephants—" And that seemed to him all the explanation necessary.

The second event was Jackie's marriage to the granddaughter of the old chief. The wedding was a purely native affair, since Jackie had never become a Christian convert. He paid the equivalent of five goats for the girl—a good, round price— and the village feasted for a day at my expense.

As for the other happening—Monsieur l'Administrateur moved into N'Titierte with his entourage. Monsieur told me that theoretically the Old Men's Council chose a new chief, but that in the past each of the ambitious ones among the sons, brothers, and uncles of a dead ruler had used extremely strong and violently convincing methods to influence this decision in his favor. Three or four times within the history of the Belgian administration, N'Titierte had been plunged into civil war, among as many as a dozen factions. On those occasions, no man lifted the cowhide over his door without his spear in his hand, and few among them could name definitely the handful of neighbors on his particular side. The turmoil ended only when all but one of the male relatives of the dead ruler had joined him in the spirit lanes under the big trees. Monsieur was present now to make certain that the choice of a new chief rested solely with the Council of Old Men, and to threaten truly frightening punishments if that choice were not respected by all and sundry.

"But what is this I hear about your scalding old N'Devli into tractability?" Monsieur demanded.

I was astonished and embarrassed, and it made me a little incoherent.

"N'Devli has never been—tractable," I burst out. "If ever a thorn in missionary flesh existed, it's that blackhearted old scoundrel. He can think of the meanest things to do! Nothing much you can put your finger on, but irritating to the point of madness."

Monsieur laughed heartily. "I'd have given a year's salary to see the old devil scampering off into the brush steaming like a geyser."

"The water wasn't really boiling," I defended myself, although his laughter had assured me that no excuse was necessary. Still it all sounded so childish now, that I kept on making words. "I had washed my hands in it, or was just going to, and it wasn't really so hot."

Monsieur laid a hand on my knee. "Never mind, *mama,*" he began, giving me a quizzical sidewise glance as he used the natives' name for me. "Officially I haven't heard a word about the affair. Strictly gossip!"

Monsieur came to N'Titierte without his many-petticoated Madame. I missed her, for this plump little robin of a woman was an event in any missionary's life.

The Old Men of the Council took almost six weeks to reach a decision, and Monsieur sat with them every hour of every day of every week. Finally he could wait no longer; a messenger had arrived with a letter for him in the cleft of a stick. He gave the Council twenty-four more hours in which to make up its collective mind and suggested that Kdogoluc, one of the dead chief's older sons, was a wise, strong, and temperate man. The next morning Kdogoluc was informed that henceforth the men of N'Titierte, including the graybeards of the Council, would defer to his judgment in all matters of village government. Monsieur had a long talk with Kdogoluc in the privacy of his tent, bade me a hurried good-by, and left.

I was oblivious to my good fortune in the choice until Jackie presented himself to me swaggering with importance. Kdogoluc was his father-in-law. I am quite sure Monsieur would never have nominated Kdogoluc had he not thought him competent. Still, the old chief had had many sons, and there might have been others among them as well fitted for the position. I couldn't help believing that the choice was simply one more instance of a very fine gentleman's kindness. The Big Bush Outstation now truly had a friend at court.

It was during this period that I became much better acquainted with N'Derfi and one of his families: a wife and two little daughters. They were charming elfin creatures, whom I saw playing about his hut, and it was obvious that he loved them as dearly as any white man loves his children. I didn't know of the existence of a third daughter by this wife until one day he asked me if my magic were great enough to cure a girl who was not yet old enough to have lain with a man and yet suffered an enormous swelling in her stomach. I went with him to his hut and found the tiny creature, probably nine or ten years old, seated on a low stool and nursing a huge belly on her thin little knees. Her face was drawn and lined, and there was nothing of merriment or roguery in it. In the background her mother hovered within easy hearing, but beyond reach, like a tabby cat when visitors cluster around her litter of kittens.

I examined the child and, as nearly as I could guess, it was a freak tumor. Whether or not I could have operated, I don't know; but I was afraid to try it, and again I spoke to N'Derfi of Dr. Charles.

"Is this witch man, Dr. Charles, like you, *mama?*" N'Derfi asked anxiously.

"What do you mean?"

"Will he drive the devils out of my daughter's body? Or is he like N'Devli? Will he demand many chickens and goats, and then find that the devils are very stubborn and that he must have more chickens and goats? And always more and more chickens and goats until I must sell my wives and other daughters in order to pay him! And then, when everything is gone, will he tell me that it is the spirit of a crocodile that has taken up its abode in my daughter and that it is *Muungu's* will that she go on all fours and drag her belly on the ground like the crocodile?"

I could only wonder what bitter experience was back of the man's word, and I hastily promised him everything he wished through Dr. Charles's magic.

"God help us!" I whispered under my breath as I turned to leave.

Just outside the door, Job was waiting for me, and nearby two urchins were playing a game that had become fairly popular since the ceremonial lion hunt dance: "Job and the lion"!

"Grr!" went one urchin with a tremendous gust of breath, arms extended and fingers curved rigidly into claws.

"Wah-ah-ah-ah!" whimpered the other like an old nanny goat staked out for leopard bait. Then he took a few faltering steps, fell to the ground, rolled over and curled up, shaking as hard as he could. When they saw me, they turned and scampered away.

Job's face was gray and his eyes were sick-looking. I would have put my hand on his shoulder, but he stepped from under the gesture.

"Don't, *mama*." The words were a plea that he be allowed to preserve his manhood, but there was heartbreak in them. If I had had any doubts before, I knew from that moment on that Job was a brave man.

Back in my hut, I told Job about N'Derfi's daughter, and that her father and I were going to take her to Dr. Charles.

"I want you to come along with us, Job," I told him, "and let Dr. Charles look at your legs and back again. If there is anything he can do for you, you will let him—for my sake! Won't you?"

The man looked me straight in the face and answered, with far more calm than I possessed at the moment, "It is not my back or legs that made me an elephant hunter and not a lion hunter, *mama*."

238

"But you would like to have your legs straight again, wouldn't you?"

The moment I uttered those fatuous words I could have bitten my tongue out. But Job only looked at me with the ageless patience of the cripple.

N'Derfi was ready to leave immediately; for his sake I hurried preparations, and we set out for Tani less than a week later. When I told Job I wanted him to go along, it was hard to look into the man's eyes.

"It's no use, *mama*," he chided gently. This time I had not mentioned Dr. Charles but he knew what was in my mind. "It is the will of *Muungu* that I walk like a crab and not like a man."

But he trotted along with the other porters, his cooking pot and tin oven balanced lightly on his woolly head. N'Derfi's daughter rode in my *tipoye*. I fastened a band of cloth from arm to arm of the swinging chair, a band that supported the monstrous stomach so that the child's thin arms and swayed back might have a little rest.

That first night we camped near the hut of Tembo the ferryman, and I was glad to see his wife again. Three seasons back I had delivered Laii of her first baby. It had been a beautiful child, and I was as happy as the parents. I was just as sad too when I heard, a few weeks later, that the little one had coughed and coughed until the weak spirit fled from a body so racked by convulsions. Now Laii was great with child again—did I think the spirits would let her keep this one? How could I say, when infant mortality is so appalling in the Congo Territory that no native woman expects to rear more than a fourth or a fifth of the children she bears? With the good will of the spirits, that is!

In the hut I noticed that all the bed skins were in one heap, which meant that only one person slept warm at night. Knowing Africa, I took it for granted that it was the husband, but when Laii sat down on the heap as we talked, I knew I was wrong. No African wife would so defile her husband's bed as to use it for a seat. I was touched that Tembo should sacrifice his own comfort to hers, and on the spur of the moment I made him the gift of a blanket.

"It is softer and warmer than many skins," I told him. Tembo was not a rich man, and his eyes shone at the magnificence of the gift. I knew it pleased him exceedingly—and that Laii would lie wrapped in it that night. But at least Tembo would have his skins back again.

When we reached Tani, Dr. Charles removed N'Derfi's daughter's tumor easily, but he shook his head when I argued the case of Job.

"But it can be done, can't it?" I pleaded.

"Yes." But there was something of denial in his affirmative. "Yes, it can be done, and if Job were a rich man back home—really rich, I mean—I know just the surgeon to whom I'd send him. But even there it would take a long time, much patience, and a lot of pain. Each leg would have to be broken in a couple of places, then traction splints and months in bed and on crutches. Then more breaks, more weeks in bed and on crutches. All in all, it would take at least a year, maybe longer, before we were finished. It wouldn't be fair, Ellen, to give that much time, and tie up so much of our meager equipment for just one man when we have hundreds needing our attention, often people whose lives can be saved by ten or fifteen minutes' work, and two or three weeks' care. After all, Job can get around quite well as he is."

I didn't give up then, but I had to in the end. If I had aroused false hopes in Job's mind, he hid them from me completely. Perhaps his terrible calm was merely born of the fatalism of the cripple.

Our stay in Tani was brief, and without notable incident. On the trip back to Big Bush, we camped again, on the last night, near the hut of the ferryman, but not at our preferred site. That we found already occupied by N'gana and four of his wives. Since our movements were known, via the drums, by everyone in Big Bush, there can be no doubt that the second twin had timed his arrival to coincide with ours. He had never forgiven me for routing his hired witch doctor, and he lost no opportunity to inflict petty irritations. Now I think he simply meant that I should see him lord his wealth over his poorer brother.

"I could have gotten along with only one wife, I suppose," I heard him say in a disparaging tone to Tembo, the single-wived man. "But I like comfort. And of course there are *cattle* back in N'Titierte to care for my gardens and goats."

The ferryman nodded. He had lived so long with poverty that I doubt if he actually grasped the insult of the words. Instead, his eyes glowed with interest in his brother's good fortune. Or perhaps he was dreaming dreams: How wonderful it would be to settle down in his dugout with Laii and a fat *pickinin* behind him, and let the current carry him down to the Great River and out into the wide world where people were strange and different and did unusual things!

Then I came to with a rude jerk. "Perhaps I shall buy me one of these white-skinned women for a wife," N'gana was saying, with a leer and a sidewise glance at me. "They are no good, of course, barren and lazy, but N'Baganza had one, and my wealth is as great as his was."

I knew of M'Baganza. He was a chief who had been deposed by the white civil administrator for his excesses and rumored orgies. It was said that he owned somewhere between three and six hundred wives and female slaves, including, for the sake of variety, representatives from every tribe of which he had ever heard. After he was deposed, he suddenly decided that he wanted a white woman, thinking, perhaps, that such a wife would restore his prestige. In any case, he approached white trader after white trader until he found one, a Portuguese quadroon, who sold the old man his own half-caste daughter for a fabulous price. It is said that Madame, as she insisted upon being called, made his declining years wretched, and that he was afraid to turn her over to Mumbo Jumbo for fear of reprisals from her relatives.

I'm afraid I sneered contemptuously at N'gana's boast, and arose to go to my tent for the night. But at the moment, Laii, being all woman, and perhaps feeling the shame of having no sister wives to show her in-laws, came out of her hut with the only thing she possessed that they might envy—she was wrapped from shoulder to ankle in the red blanket I had given her husband. She drew the blanket closer about her and squatted down, not too near to her relatives, but not so far away that they would fail to see that she was more comfortably clothed than they had ever been in their lives. They fairly drooled with envy, and N'gana's eyes almost popped out of his head. Simply, as though he were in the habit of receiving such magnificent gifts every day of his life, the ferryman explained the acquisition of the red blanket.

N'gana turned amazed eyes on me. "But, *mama,* you and I have been friends—"

"Friends! You and I?" I snapped angrily.

But N'gana had flung up both hands, fingers rigidly extended and was staring at them helplessly. How could he number the seasons we had known each other? He gave up with a great shrug of his heavy shoulders.

"—for ever so long, *mama,* and you have never given me a blanket."

"Why should one so insignificant as I offer *presenti* to a man as rich as you?" I snorted contemptuously, and turned on my heel. But I did not feel triumphant; N'gana was cunning and cruel and unscrupulous. Should I warn him of my anger if he tried to take the blanket away from his brother? I faltered a step, then caught myself and went on. Heaven forbid that I should put anything in that evil mind the devil had not already put there.

The next morning I made arrangements to be sent for when

the time came for Laii's confinement. N'gana stood within hearing all the time—perhaps he was waiting for the presentation of other gifts in which he might share. As his brother and I laid plans, the sneer on the face of the Hippopotamus deepened, and he could not forbear telling us that his *cattle* scarcely laid aside their hoes when the time came for them to drop their human calves. I was more than glad to turn my face toward Big Bush.

Laii's second baby also died. The birth was a normal one and the infant was a beautiful child, perfectly formed and, if his squalling were any measure of his health, vigorous. I suppose that after I left her, in spite of my instructions, Laii forced too much half-cooked, coarse corn meal mush down the child's throat with her forefinger, or perhaps she gorged it, using the same method, on caterpillar paste, or drenched its insides with banana beer. She and Tembo would have said that the jungle spirits were jealous of them and had taken the beautiful child away from them out of ghostly malice. It was too bad, but that was what happened to most of the children born to any woman, and Laii could normally be expected to conceive again almost immediately.

After the night we met at the ferry, the Hippopotamus and his four wives were gone from their village a year. When N'gana returned, he traveled with six wives, three new ones and three of the old ones. The fourth "old one" had sassed him once too often, and he had sold her to a soldier. Perhaps her price had been the soldier's red blanket. At any rate, the Hippopotamus had a fine, soft, practically new, red blanket of his own.

By then, Laii, the Elephant's only wife, was pregnant again. And this time, the insatiable, unseen evil ones did not wait until birth, but entered the woman's belly and gnawed and tore at the baby while it still grew there—or that is the way my neighbors in N'Titierte described Laii's illness. I had planned to be with her when the baby came, of course, but the birth was premature and I was away on itinerary in The Hungry Country. I did not get back from that trip until it was all over with Laii—and Tembo.

Perhaps it was fate that she died the night N'gana and his six *cattle* camped near the Elephant's kraal on their way home again. She died, and the Elephant did not slide her into the river, where the crocodiles would have made short work of her body. Nor did he drag her to the nearest sunny glade, where the kites and jackals would have disposed of her with equal speed. Tembo, ever the fool, interred her as though she had been a chief or a great and brave man. Such behavior could not fail to offend the spirits, and N'gana had had no part in it, nor would he permit his wives to assist, not even to the extent of tossing one stone upon the cairn that would prevent the jackals from digging up Laii's beloved body.

But undoubtedly he saw, as his wives must have seen, that the ferryman's wife went to her long sleep wrapped in a red blanket. If so, he said nothing about it, but when N'gana returned home, his own precious red blanket was found to be missing. Articles of value are never "lost" in an African village. They are always "stolen," and N'Devli was called in to "smell out the thief." Inevitably the ferryman was accused, and his wife was disinterred in unprecedented search of proof. But who, other than the jealous accuser, three of his *cattle,* and I myself, far away in the The Hungry Country, knew that I had given the ferryman such a blanket? Both hands of the proved thief were severed at the wrists and he was driven out into the jungle. The next morning they found, not far from my hospital compound, the little that the leopards, inevitably attracted by the smell of fresh blood, had left of the man.

I did not get the story of Tembo's trial, punishment, and death from the natives of Big Bush, for villagers do not like to discuss the practices of their witch doctors with white people. Aganza gave me the bare details, and as soon as I heard what she had to say, I sent for Monsieur l'Administrateur. He came to N'Titierte immediately to try N'Devli and N'gana for collusion and murder and our friend Kdogoluc, the chief, for misconduct of his office. In the long run, practically nothing could be proved against either of the first two men. N'gana had made a very understandable mistake; N'Devli had unearthed what he and everyone else in N'Titierte had taken as incontrovertible evidence.

Tembo had not thrown his dead wife to the crocodiles as any sane man would have done. Instead, he had buried her; and when the body was exhumed, by N'Devli's order, it was wrapped in a red blanket that fitted exactly N'gana and his wives' description of the one the Hippopotamus had lost. Urged on by his Council of Old Men, the chief had sentenced Tembo. Kdogoluc, really a fine, capable man, did not order Tembo's execution, although it amounted to the same thing. In the end, Kdogoluc was deposed by Monsieur and sentenced to a term of forced labor on the roads.

"It was one of the most unjust sentences I have ever had to pronounce," Monsieur l'Administrateur told me. "And, worst of all, I had to let the guilty ones go. N'Devli will be harder than ever for you to get along with now."

Monsieur knew men, black and white. His safari was not out of sound of the village before the guilty old devil was strutting before me a like a turkey gobbler in the spring. And I thought I could read in his eyes, "I got rid of Tembo in spite of you, and I shall plague you as long as the two of us live."

CHAPTER
20

AMONG the new workers our mission station acquired during my third term of service was the oldest Early boy, now grown a head taller than his father and also a Doctor of Divinity. The "doings" of the boss or any member of his family are always of interest and exaggerated importance to a staff, and a mission group is no different from any other. We all hung on young Dr. Early's lightest word. His father beamed, his mother loved us more than she had ever loved us before, and the young man accepted our affectionate attention—all of us old maids were like second mothers to him—and took our effusive behavior with a grain of salt. Everyone knew he would be appointed head of the denominational work in Africa when his father was retired. Of course there were many on the staff older than he, and as well prepared, but the mores of our denomination call for a minister in the chief executive's position. In this case, however, I don't believe there was any mistake in the choice.

For some reason, I was chosen to accompany young Dr. Early on his first extended itinerary covering all the outstations. It was almost like a vacation for me: trekking over new territory, visiting, and telling myself, with anything but humility, that none of these outposts could compare with Big

Bush. But then, I didn't find anyone to compare with Mother Aganza either on that entire trip.

I was gone from Big Bush about six months, and when I returned, Job was gone. I mourned his death, but I was proud of him, for Job had died a hero. I couldn't have wished more for the cripple than the place his dying won for him in the hearts of his neighbors.

The N'Titierteans had wrapped Job's corpse in primitive mats and slung it high in the air between two saplings. It was so preserved because Job was to have a hero's burial and the village had waited for me, his best friend, to share in the obsequies. As he was not a chief, his body had not been plastered with clay, and by the time I was back in Big Bush one could hardly get within a hundred yards of it unless there were a wind of gale proportions at one's back.

At this funeral I was only a spectator; I did not even have to furnish the meat for the inevitable feast. One morning eight goats were led into the little inclosure in front of my *dukas* and killed. First a long pole was laid in the crotches of two trees and eight jars were placed in a row beneath it. Then five men seized the first goat, one at each leg and another at its head. The fifth man pulled the beast's head back taut over the first jar, and, with a great sweeping stroke of his knife, N'Derfi almost severed its head. Not a drop of the blood was lost. When the animal ceased to struggle, its hind feet were tied to the pole overhead, and it continued to dribble until the wound was black and purple with clotted blood and clusters of flies.

Was the execution to my liking?

Someone prodded me in the back, and I answered: "Yes. Oh, yes."

The other seven animals were executed in the same way. "Why was the word 'executed' used?" I asked Aganza later.

"Because, *mama,* in the days of—well, not so very long ago —it was men, captives taken in battle, who furnished the blood for a red sunset."

So Job was to have a "red sunset"! His neighbors, men who regretted that they had not been his friends in his lifetime, were to bury him in what was to them symbolical of a blaze of glory. The earth below and above him were to be muddied with blood, as Mother Earth should be when she takes real fighting men to her bosom.

We buried Job deep, very deep, and heaped his grave with stones, so that the jackals, in spite of the reek of blood, could not dig him up. I stood beside his grave and prayed. I did not use the Hebrew name for God, nor the English name, but the one my N'Titierteans understood: *Muungu*. I called upon God in a loud voice too, for as my neighbors there knew, *Muungu* is often wearied and disgusted with the childishness and evil ways of men and goes far, far away in order to escape them. I shouted in the biggest voice I could summon, and then told my people that I knew *Muungu* had heard me and that Job was at peace in death as he had never been when alive.

Then the villagers presented me with the lone tusk of the elephant Job had killed, after which we ate the goats and all the bananas the elephant had left in the women's shambas, and I heard the true account of how my faithful old servitor had met his death.

Big Bush is called lion country, and in olden days the most prized ornament a young man could wear was a lion's-mane headdress won by his own spear, skill, and bravery. But now and then an elephant strays into our territory and then these men, whose courage before claw and fang is a byword all up and down the Congo and throughout The Hungry Country, spend hours in the palaver hut discussing the gargantuan beast and devising childishly cunning ways of enticing it to its destruction. The influx of elephants is small, and the number of those destroyed is even smaller.

Books have been written about the wonder of these great beasts, but there is still much for man to learn about them. The dull gray skin does not look like protective coloring, but

I have been told that one can pass within ten feet of an elephant in the jungle and never see the animal. On the other hand, when a herd of elephants is feeding peacefully, the rumbling of their stomachs can be heard for an unbelievable distance.

No one actually knows why these males leave the herd to lead a solitary existence, but the theory is that, from age or injury, they have become so irritable and cantankerous that the rest of the animals cannot live with them. I question this theory because no cow is ever driven out, no matter how old or sick or badly wounded, and I do not believe that in any species temper and irritability are solely male prerogatives.

The elephant that visited N'Titierte was one of these solitary males—"rogues," they are always called. He came in the night and announced his presence by very neatly and efficiently digging and devouring, root and vine, every yam in a half dozen gardens. Like a native woman hoeing, he had straddled the row as he dined; the great pockmarks his huge feet left in the soft earth detailed his activities in the garden as meticulously as a map. The next night he was back for more yams, and the next, and the next, until there was not a single sweet, mealy tuber left for the cooking pots of N'Titierte.

The beans and groundnuts followed in rapid succession, and a start had been made on the manioc, when he discovered the banana plantations. Apparently bananas are to the African elephant what banana splits were to my high-school generation. In any case the rogue did not disappear with the coming of the false dawn, which is the earliest hour any African however brave will venture away from campfire or kraal. The glutton stayed all that day in the banana groves, trampling down the succulent plants and small fruit and devouring stalk after stalk of the ripening clusters.

Pandemonium reigned in the palaver hut, for everyone saw the vandal and knew without question that it was no mere hungry beast with which they had to deal. Sportsmen's tales can be trusted as little in Africa as elsewhere, otherwise I would have to report an elephant at least fifty feet high and probably weighing as many tons. The tusk of ivory given me was a huge one and the animal must have been big to carry it, but, big or small, any elephant is formidable where mere puny man is concerned.

The elephant had broken off its left tusk up close to its head, and inevitably, as with any uncared-for, broken tooth, ulceration had taken place.

Jackie, who was no fool and certainly no coward by any man's standards, told me: "When the great beast turned its head, *mama,* I knew it was a rogue. There was a sore where its tusk should have come out, a sore as big as one of your plates. The side of its trunk was shiny with pus, and the foul stuff was caked along its left leg, right down to its toes."

Anatomically, the tusk of an elephant is nothing but a monstrous eyetooth, and like any tooth it has a nerve. But what a nerve! From three to eight inches across at the top and anywhere from two to five feet long depending on the size of the tusk.

Jackie told me, with the simplicity of a man who has nothing to fear so far as his own reputation is concerned: "When I saw that sore, *mama,* I was afraid. And so was everyone else—everyone but Job; and if he was afraid, he didn't show it."

The folk at Big Bush said Job took charge. He ordered the women and children back—not into their huts, for those flimsy structures do not even slacken the stride of a rampaging elephant—but far into the forest. The men climbed trees, they told me without the least bit of shame. And why should they be ashamed? After all, "We are lion hunters, not elephant men, *mama,*" they said.

Job took his spear, that curious weapon with a forged iron head shaped like a new moon and with a short handle of tough thorn wood thick as a man's wrist. His elephant spear, he had always called it. The children of N'Titierte had laughed at it, and I had wondered how such a peculiar thing could more than tickle any animal.

Next he tested the wind with extreme care, dropping many pinches of ashes to determine the direction, steadiness, and velocity of any currents. Then he placed himself so that not even a vagrant, swirling breeze could betray his presence to the sensitive nostrils of his prey. Finally he disappeared into the herbage.

"Whether he walked or crawled, who can say?" more than one person remarked at different times. "But we who saw him disappear into the grass could not mark his progress by so much as one quivering blade."

"It took a long time, *mama*. A long, long time for him to reach the elephant," one of the many who helped tell the tale went on.

"I was tired out with waiting and ready to come down out of my tree. Besides, I was hungry and my stomach was growling in protest."

"To be honest, *mama,* we still thought he was a coward, and that he had run away into the forest to hide his shame."

Then they saw Job crouching under the beast, between the four legs, and they understood why the handle of his spear was so short.

"He was very fast, *mama*—very, very fast—and extremely skillful for a man who walked like a crab."

"He had to be swift, for the elephant would smell him in an instant. Then everything would be too late."

"He bent double—even more double than *Muungu* had made him—grasping the shaft of his spear; then he straightened up—"

"—as well as he could straighten up!"

"And the spear, *mama,* the spear buried itself in the soft belly of *tembo* up to the man's hands."

Thus, in this fragmentary fashion, from many people, I learned Job's story. The deathblow delivered, he did not seek protection as the lion hunters would have done. But then, there was no companion hunter with poised spear for him to step behind. No rhino-hide shield to fall under. And what protection would such a shield have been had several tons of flesh fallen or knelt upon it?

The great beast quivered like the top of a forest tree just before it falls, and then the rogue began a blind, insane running, here, there, anywhere, almost bouncing off the trunks of the big trees, crushing the small ones like dried leaves, and all the while dragging with it a helpless Job, who never relaxed his hold on his spear for an instant. Then a loop of intestine slipped out, hooked over a horn of the strange, crescent-headed spear. Then another and another until presently Job lay still and the monster's belly was empty.

"*Tembo* fell. No man or animal, however huge or strong, lives without guts," someone remarked succinctly.

"We ate him. We could not keep the flesh until you returned, *mama*. At that feast the belly of everyone in N'Titierte was as round as *tembo's* had been when he ravaged the women's shambas."

"And Job?" I prompted.

"When *tembo* fell and we saw he could not rise again, we went to Job, but he was already dead. Perhaps because of his age and his infirmity he had not been as quick and skillful as in his youth. Anyway, the beast had stepped on his back and he had died before *tembo* fell."

"He was smiling, *mama*. And he was as strong in death as he had been brave in life. None of us could loosen his fingers from the haft of his spear. We wrapped his spear up in the funeral mats with him. It was a good thing to do, *mama?* It is thus with his weapons that a brave man should be buried?"

"Yes, it was a good thing to do," I answered. How else could he have been buried? He lived a brave man; he died a brave man; he deserved a hero's grave.

CHAPTER
21

As a child, I was always disappointed with the endings of books. It seemed to me that characters who had such interesting experiences—I didn't finish any other kind of book —surely had more to tell. Now I can appreciate the problem of selection those authors faced.

I had almost four terms of service in Africa—not bad for a woman who was already forty before she ever saw the shores of the Dark Continent. There was nothing remarkably outstanding about my work, and I doubt if as a result of my twenty-odd years of service I could count as many Christian converts. To be perfectly honest, my evangelistic work had been only sporadic at best and usually the result of repeated instructions from those higher up. I never failed to feel silly when some black *boy* or *girl* bested me in an argument on religion and I had to reply in essence, "I know I am right just because I know I am right." Even an ordinary "ignorant savage" has a mind above that type of reasoning. Nor could I preach the religion of complete love, compassion, and forbearance, to say nothing of the brotherhood of man, when the white overlords of the territory, in whose hands lay all final authority, frequently ruled with as heavily mailed a fist as any feudal baron.

On the other hand, I am egotistical enough to say that I believe I accomplished more of lasting value than the average professional religious worker in the foreign field. When I returned to the United States for the last time, I left behind me a substantial hospital staffed with well-trained, efficient native workers, many of them far more capable than I, a corps of itinerant nurses for outstation medical work, and a school system that touched hundreds of villages, not only in the jungle along the tributaries of the Great River, but out into the boundless sun-baked plains of the The Hungry Country. I like to think that when the time comes that my people are not only ruled by white men but may live side by side with them, it will be my *boys* and *girls,* who are literate and who know some white man's trade, who will be best able to bridge the terrible gap between village life and white man's civilization.

At times I have been compelled to take part in something of which I disapproved. What might be called my last outstanding adventure in the Congo Territory was of this nature.

I do not like "explorers" who "explore" with million-dollar safaris, and whose sole "scientific" aim seems to be columnar miles of newspaper publicity and fat royalty checks from the books in which they tell the world how "famous" and "intrepid" they are. It was toward the middle of my fourth term of service that my dislike for these "explorers" came to a head. I knew it would be my last stretch in the Congo, for I was in my mid-sixties now and too often queasy with malaria. Aganza didn't look a day older, to me, than that first time I saw her. But Mata Kwan was a tall, handsome stripling, a student at Achimota College on the West Coast. He was bright enough, but Aganza and I, like mothers the world over, dreamed qualities into him that I am not sure he possessed. He was a really good average boy, perhaps, so to us he was perfect.

He spent his vacations with us in Big Bush, where he shed his white man's clothing and became one of the N'Titiertean bachelors, paying proper obeisance to the chief. I was glad for this, and I know Aganza must have been, for it was she who only a few years earlier had arranged for his circumcision and tribal initiation. Training at Achimota is aimed at native leadership, and I believe true leadership is mainly guidance by personal example in daily living. Mata Kwan's skin was black, and although he was privileged above all but the tiniest per cent of his brothers, he was a native African. We never tried to make him anything else.

The boy had completed his second year and returned to us for the long vacation when word came through from Monsieur l'Administrateur that we were to be visited by a pair of explorers. Monsieur, knowing that I would not divulge the contents of his letter, was extremely frank in expressing his dislike of this couple. They were just a simple outfit, he assured me, roughing it in the jungle with only about five hundred *boys,* an army of tents, radios, bathtubs, chemical toilets, and so on, to say nothing of the corps of Hollywood technicians who would operate their battery of movie and still cameras.

The white rulers of Africa have made it mandatory for a village to bring the white men who camp near it all the food desired. There is no getting around this law, and more than one village has been punished when it had nothing but empty granaries and locust-ravaged gardens to show the pale-faced stranger who popped up out of nowhere. It was impossible for N'Titierte to feed an army of five hundred people, so a system of food transportation would have to be set up with neighboring villages. All normal village routine would be disrupted, and the sole profit to the natives would be what little money the women received for their eggs and chickens and vegetables.

"I have witnessed that the Mrs. Explorer loves to haggle—'bargaining,' she calls it. Tell your women to bear this in mind when setting their first price," Monsieur wrote.

It was well that Monsieur warned us, for after the couple arrived, it became a regular morning routine for Mrs. Explorer to strut up and down before the line of women who had been compelled to strip their trees of the precious fruit. I have seen her scream, rant, and even kick the women in an attempt to beat the price of a stalk of bananas down from three cents to two cents. Not two cents a banana, or two cents a cluster, but two cents a stalk—the entire yield of a plant that some woman had tended carefully for two years. I tried to reason with her, but she informed me bluntly that some five years before she had paid two cents a stalk for bananas in Kenya Colony, and she didn't intend to be hoodwinked by these jungle savages. I too had once paid two cents a stalk, but that had been almost a quarter of a century ago, I remonstrated. Being only a missionary, I was naturally too soft with the Niggers; they needed someone like her to show them their place, Mrs. Explorer assured me.

Mr. Explorer was struck with the stupidity of the N'Titierteans. No matter how long he "reasoned" with a "Nigger," or how loudly, none of them understood either his English or his so-called French. None of them, that is, except Aganza and Mata Kwan. Jackie's pretense of stupidity was a protective armor that saved him many an hour of unpaid drudgery—and accompanying kicks. Aganza treated both the man and the woman with a fine disregard that would have been worthy of royalty, but Mata Kwan was at that age when dignity and curiosity fight for supremacy in a boy. He got in the man's way, whereupon the great explorer aimed a kick at the child and informed him that he was a dirty black bastard. I was furious, but my own temper was halted by the expression that crossed Mata Kwan's face. Had the two of them, white man and black stripling, been alone in the jungle, I believe the latter would have achieved manhood primitive fashion—by wetting his spear in human blood.

When the safari arrived, they moved onto my knoll without so much as a by-your-leave. It was the best site for a camp; that was why I had chosen it for a hospital compound. When I

256

asked the man and his wife to leave, the only answer I received was a series of exaggerated, knowing winks at each other. I chased them away finally, but it took some doing. They waved miscellaneous permits and letters from a battery of Belgian high and mighties in my face. I had my permits too, and I know with what facility and boredom Belgian officials can write these letters for importuning nobodies. We must have made a pretty spectacle—three mature persons behaving like children—but I held my ground and won out, for I had very sick people in my hospital, and relatives and minor patients in the rows of huts flanking the hospital buildings. That night the thatched roofs of one row of these huts burned. No one was injured, and the financial loss was not serious, but I am convinced that it was deliberate arson.

Such minor details cared for at last, I learned that our visitors were in N'Titierte to film a native lion hunt. Where else should they come but to this village whose men were reputedly the bravest lion hunters in all Africa? My villagers were proud of this reputation, which they had inherited from their forefathers, but in all the years I had been in Big Bush there had been no real lion hunt—only the one ceremonial dance. There were a few lions about, but the village had never, in my days there at least, been troubled by any old man-eater. So the N'Titierteans very wisely left the big cats alone.

One afternoon a delegation from the Council of Old Men asked me if I would tell my white brother and sister that the men who were experienced in lion-hunting were old; that the young men were brave, but ignorant and unskillful; and that the neighboring lions were exceedingly large and fierce. I couldn't help remembering Job as I listened to them, nevertheless, I delivered the message and was only laughed at for my pains. The laughter was a small matter—that I could have shrugged off—but they showed me a letter from no less a person than a prince of the reigning house. To have flouted that letter would have been to invite eviction from the Congo Territory, not only for myself, but for every missionary of my denomination.

That night the jungle throbbed with the voice of the big drums. I couldn't wait for a letter—it might take a month for one of our primitive postmen to find Monsieur l'Administrateur, and bring an answer back. I prayed desperately that someone higher up would tell these impossible people, "No!" I had my reply from Monsieur in less than two hours. This time he didn't try to be funny. He told me quite simply that the N'Titierteans must stage a lion hunt, but that I, as an American missionary, need carry no responsibility for it if I wished otherwise. He did not need to tell me that to risk being retired without pension after a lifetime of hard and faithful service was something he and Madame Petticoats could not face.

A village palaver hut is sacred to men and the intrusion of a female is a *faux pas,* if she be white, and a punishable misdemeanor if black. Therefore, I did not enter, but sat just outside the walls that evening and listened with a sinking heart as the old men translated Monsieur l'Administrateur's answer. These men were not cowards, but if some stranger came along and insisted that you wrestle with a grizzly bear, so that he might gain a few dollars and enhance his reputation for intrepidity, what would be your reaction?

For the next few days, N'Titierte was a beehive of activity. The old men who had participated in tribal lion hunts in their youth, but who had not held a spear in their hands for years, began practicing like young bachelors. The young men heard lectures on the strength, cunning, and unpredictability of the king of beasts. News of the projected hunt spread like magic, and several hundred young men and boys drifted into N'Titierte, some with spears, others with only sharpened sticks of thorn wood for weapons, all eager to prove themselves men in the time-honored fashion of their fathers.

Old rhino-hide war shields, which my generation had seen

used only in ceremonial dances, were brought out and mended, and the young men practiced for hours, first at carrying the cumbersome things and next at the art of hurling a spear and then falling and curling up under the shield so that no part of themselves was exposed.

Mock lion hunts were staged, with sometimes a half dozen old men playing the parts of surrounded lions. In short, an attempt was made to crowd into a few days what should have been the training of a lifetime. And all the while the "modest safari" of only about five hundred *boys* was devouring the gardens for miles around like a scourge of locusts.

Mr. and Mrs. Explorer were filled with impatience. Big Bush was but a minor incident in their intrepid lives, and they resented the days squandered on us. They were eager to get back to their base camp, where they were roughing it de luxe, with permanent buildings, exotic vegetable and rose gardens, airplane connections with the outer world, and many other necessities that would surely have made such dubs as Livingstone, Stanley, Burton, or Speke turn over in their graves.

For a week or so the cameramen took pictures of everything in and about N'Titierte with the exception of me and the hospital compound. It is a curious thing, but I have never read a book by professional explorers in which any word of thanks is ever tendered a missionary, yet almost all of us at one time or another have given these people hospitality, and many of us have stopped our work to render them assistance.

Mr. and Mrs. Explorer, on the other hand, were photographed in all sorts of ridiculous poses. For instance, there was one picture of the Mrs. dining with our chief. The later movie audience would not know that no morsel of the food set out ever passed the lips of the black man, for male black primitive Africa does not eat with women. *Cattle!* He would have felt himself degraded.

Finally preparations for the lion hunt were completed. The young men, who would have been warriors in the days before the white men forbade internecine strife, were instructed, as were the young boys. These latter, Mata Kwan among them, were to keep well in the rear, to thresh the tall grass with bamboo poles, and yell their heads off when the time came. Thus *simba,* charging for what looked like a weak spot in the circle of spears surrounding him, might be turned back.

And then an ailment of epidemic proportions hit the village. It might have been influenza, or it might have been something like to a communal case of buck fever. It broke out in N'Titierte, but it swept the camp of the explorers also. This was understandable, for the native African has the most delicate sympathetic nervous system imaginable. I have seen a "blood brother" shriek and writhe in what surely must have been real pain when a sworn friend had been clawed by a leopard. And in telling me of Job's death, more than one man said, "It was almost impossible to bear the anguish, *mama.*" Yet not a one of them had been injured in the least, or even very near the rogue until it was thoroughly dead.

Whatever the cause, half of N'Titierte, their guests, and the safari porters lay on their sleeping mats or dogged my every step with big, fever-brightened eyes. Foolishly, I was glad. Now this stupid farce would be delayed for a little while at least. Delayed until its fame spread farther and more experienced men might trickle in out of the jungle to share in the lion hunt.

I think Mr. Explorer would have waited a few days, but I underestimated his wife. Openly bored with us, she was eager to get back to East Africa: to the cocktail bars in Nairobi, to the tall tales of other "explorers," and to the chance meetings with the famous of the earth who form a steady procession through British East Africa.

She demanded that the lion hunt go forward, waving her omnipotent official documents under my nose. It went forward. I shall never forget that morning if I live to be a hundred. She and I stood on the peak of a forty-foot anthill and watched, I peering through my spectacles and she using the most up-to-date field glasses. The hunt was all over in half the time it took to show the film later. Mr. Explorer's white hunter had had a pride of lions under observation, almost under guard, for a week. Our men went immediately to the clump of thorn trees where they slept and surrounded them. It was an immense circle, at least a quarter of a mile in diameter, and for the sake of the camera those who would come into the picture were costumed in all the ornaments of fur, feather, bone, claw, copper wire, and other oddments they possessed. It would have been impossible for them to look less like a group of hunters on serious business.

They tell me that the actual "hunt" took only minutes, but the agony of each second is so clearly etched on my mind that in retrospect it seems hours. The edges of the circle were rippled, like a piecrust. The younger of the really experienced lion hunters were in the front. Their rhino-hide shields would make a brave showing on the screen, I knew, but I prayed that they would not fall apart if and when *simba* charged. It seemed to me that I could see some of the scrawny arms tremble under the weight of the heavy spears. Then there were the young men, in the prime of their manhood—good hunters for the most part, but knowing the king of beasts only through the old men's tales. They had shields of one sort or another, borrowed from their fathers and uncles, which they carried gracefully enough in the village ceremonial dances, but they looked tense and awkward now.

"Beautiful display of primitive savagery!" I heard the woman beside me exclaim. "It should photograph magnificently—if only heat devils don't obscure the film!"

I wish I had asked her the question that leaped to my tongue. "Primitive savagery—on whose part?" I might have had she not at that instant lighted a cigarette and given the match a careless flip. Fortunately it fell at my feet and I stepped on it immediately.

"Goodness, woman, what are you thinking of?" I burst out. "Just one spark in this grass is enough to kindle a fire that will burn for days and days. Destroy numberless villages and thousands of heads of game. Don't you care?"

She stared at me a moment, then gave a short laugh. "You do get worked up over these Niggers, don't you?" she muttered insolently. Nevertheless, she dropped her cigarette and ground it out.

"Satisfied?" she spit at me.

I wasn't, but what could I say?

Perhaps you have seen the moving picture of that hunt. If you have, all I can say is: Don't believe it! There was so much about it that was false, that was staged, that was Hollywood and not Africa. I peered this way and that until I picked out Mata Kwan, who had sulked for days. In spite of his gangling height and previous initiation, the old men had judged him still a boy, and he had been assigned to the outer circle of beaters and shouters.

At a signal the hunt began, covered from every angle by well-protected cameramen. Mr. Explorer was not even in the outer circle of boys, but was giving orders and shouting directions, busy as a housewife whose husband has brought the minister home to Sunday dinner. Then the circle began tightening and dividing itself into three concentric rings: first the older men, then the younger hunters, and finally the boys. And now and then one's eyes caught glimpses of a tawny figure in the grassy center. Then, high and shrill above the shouting of the boys, I heard an agonized scream.

Then it was all over, and—can you believe it?—there were three lions dead. Lions as full of spears as a dressmaker's pincushion is of pins. I wondered who had been hurt and how badly; I started down the anthill, but was stopped peremptorily. There were more pictures to be taken, and I must not get in the way. There must be a ceremonial dance about the dead lions, the man ordered. My N'Titierteans knew of no such

262

ceremonial, but they put on a dance nevertheless, with much stamping, shaking of spears, and whooping. The dancers already knew what I was still to learn, and the expressions on their faces were savage enough to please the most effete thrill seeker.

Then still more pictures! The intrepid explorer's parts in the lion hunt must be shown. There was the man, for instance, his gun supposedly jammed, casting it aside and struggling with a black warrior for his spear. The man won, of course, according to the finished movie, and he advanced with the innermost circle of experienced lion hunters, finally rising to his toes and hurling the strange weapon in best college athletic form. I don't know how many hundreds of feet of film the cameramen squandered before that celluloid hero was pictured just as they wanted him: virile manhood gone berserk in the excitement of the hunt.

Then—again I say, "Can you believe it?"—the woman was posed, aiming her gun at a dead lion propped up on stones about nine feet in front of her, its tail lashing about as a *boy* on either side of the beast alternately jerked hidden strings. Mr. Explorer was posed immediately behind his wife, grinding away like mad on an empty camera. And behind the two of them, a real cameraman recorded the couple's amazing courage. After a heart-chilling moment, Mrs. Explorer blazed away with her gun, a third hidden string jerked away a stick which had propped up *simba's* head, and the noble beast collapsed. It was magnificent—on the film.

Finally our visitors had enough; and in less than an hour the big tents were down and the man and his wife were swinging off down the trail in *tipoyes* that would have done credit to the palanquins of an Oriental emperor.

They were gone, leaving us to gather up our dead. I kept no record of the number of men and women and children who sustained minor injuries that day. Those whose muscles and bones were laid bare or mangled and crushed by the lions

263

came first. Barked shins and stubbed toes were disposed of hastily. Among the women there was an epidemic of nausea. I don't know what caused it unless it was the intensity of the hatred engendered by the visit of these two completely heartless, utterly selfish, egomaniacal members of my own race. I told the women to boil water and drink as much of the hot liquid as they could. They hated the taste, but it cured some of them; others lay in their huts, dull-eyed and gray-lipped, all night and for the better part of the next day.

At last all the suffering were cared for, and I turned to the four bodies lying beneath funeral mats under the thatched eaves of the palaver hut. The first face I looked into was that of Atakaa. He had four wives and probably a dozen living children. One boy and one girl were working and studying in my hospital. Atakaa had just entered the years of wisdom and dignity—that is, he was probably forty or forty-five years old. He had not been a wordy man, but even the chief listened when he cleared his throat to speak. N'Titierte would miss him.

The next man, they told me, was N'yan. He was old, experienced; by reputation he had been a magnificent lion hunter in his youth. He had hurled his spear, straight and true, but without much force; then when *simba* charged, in spite of his rheumatism the man had curled up and fallen under his shield as gracefully as a ballet dancer. But he was old and his arm was no longer strong. Moreover, his bones were brittle and they had snapped like dry twigs under the impact of *simba's* charge. I think he really died of shock. Everyone had liked him; they would miss him too.

The third face—O dear God! A dozen hands reached out to touch me—just to brush my body with their finger tips. A score of voices murmured gentle words. Then—then I could only stand and stare into the face of what had once been Mata Kwan. Mata Kwan, the boy who in a small way had taken the place of a son in my old maid's heart. Mata Kwan, the little Son-of-a-Goat.

"How did it happen?" I whispered to anyone who might know the answer.

"These many lions got away, *mama*," a voice equally low and tense replied.

Twinkling fingers tried to count for me the number of animals that had escaped.

"And each beast as it broke through the circle of hunters—" My voice faltered because I knew the answer.

But the facts were supplied me relentlessly, as the wretched always seem to bare their misery when sorrow weighs down upon them overwhelmingly. "Each beast as it broke through the circle of hunters left its mark upon some man."

"And Mata Kwan was brave; he rushed forward like an experienced hunter."

"He left his spear in *simba*."

I wondered—the child had carried nothing but a thorn-wood stick with a point he himself had hardened in the fire. Still, he would have tried; Aganza had made a man of him.

I turned suddenly. "Does Aganza know?" I asked.

"Yes, *mama*."

The stress of emotion and the pressure of work had been so great that day that only then did I realize that Aganza had not helped me in the hospital all afternoon.

"Where is she?"

My companions looked at each other, at my feet, at their own feet, and one by one slipped away from the palaver hut. All but one, an old man, who knelt and rolled the mat back over Mata Kwan's face. Then he uncovered the fourth boy— one of his own grandsons.

"The jungle has taken back what it lent for a little while," he murmured softly.

His voice and tone were calm, too calm. I knew his heart was as full of tears as my own.

CHAPTER

22

I WALKED back to my *dukas* like a woman in a trance, repeating monotonously: "I must find Aganza. I must find Aganza."

Inside I slipped to my knees in the dim half-light and hid my face in my arms. "O God," I wailed; and again and again: "O God! O God!"

It grew dark, and a sort of calm, if not peace, filled my heart. I got up and lighted my lamp and drew a shawl around my shoulders. I must find Aganza. But where would I look? Village folk do not visit back and forth in each other's huts. The women exchange gossip in the gardens, at the riverbank, or as they cook the evening meal before their huts, but when the animal hide or matting is dropped over their doorways of an evening, the privacy of those within is as secure as that of a monarch in his most secluded apartments.

There was a slight cough outside my door. I pushed the mosquito netting aside and found Jackie.

"*Mama,*" he began, and then looked about carefully, apprehensively. When he went on, his voice sank so low I almost had to push my ear into his face to hear him. "*Mama,* while you were busy with the injured this afternoon, N'Devli danced in front of Mother Aganza's hut."

So that was it! N'Devli, the witch doctor, cruel, malicious, and steeped in his wickedness, had at last found an opportunity to wreak his malice on me. For years I had laughed at him or merely pushed him out of the way. And his bitter hatred had grown with the years. His absurd gyrations, which passed for a dance—Aganza and I could both laugh at them. But what after the dance?

"Well?" I demanded of Jackie.

"They went down by the river, *mama*. They took the path that leads to the fetish houses."

"Come!" I said, and was ten feet away before I realized that my old gunbearer had not moved. I looked back over my shoulder, and he shook his head slowly.

"I am afraid, *mama*," he said softly.

Jackie was no coward. Although no African by choice ventures abroad after the sun has set, he had accompanied me on many an emergency nighttime trip. Now his eyes gleamed at me in the half-light. And was it the dry leaves above my head, or his breath, or his teeth, that soughed intermittently like the wings of a solitary locust in flight? Although he was a mission boy, and completely faithful to me as a servant, I could not force him to face whatever evil N'Devli the witch doctor might conjure up for the path that lay ahead. I wish I had said a word of comfort, of understanding to him, for in a way it was a moment of crisis in his life. I think it was the only time he ever failed me.

But I didn't. I turned and almost ran through the village of N'Titierte. A few dogs raised their heads and started to snarl, smelled my familiar scent, and grumbled drowsily before they tucked their noses under their paws again. Down the path beside the river I sped, the hidden path that led to the fetish houses. Something struck my face lightly and I brushed it aside without stopping although I was vaguely surprised that it did not possess the sticky quality of a cobweb. A minute later my feet crashed through a little heap of sticks in the center of the path. Then I understood. N'Devli wanted privacy for what-ever was to take place by the river that night, and he had placed the little fetishes, head level, feet level, which normally were more efficacious than white man's locks at keeping the unwanted away. Insignificant in themselves, they are symbols of the age-old terror that holds the superstitious in almost unbreakable bonds.

I went on more slowly now. I was tired. Tired to death! And I made less noise, but neither Aganza nor N'Devli would have heard me had I crashed through the brush like a rhino.

I once talked to a psychologist about what happened to Aganza that night, and he told me it was the most normal thing in the world. In moments of helpless anguish, every human being reverts in some part to the days of his childhood when another person solved his problems, bore the brunt of overwhelming responsibility, comforted him. Aganza's tempo-rary reversion to the religious ritual of her people was a grim-mer matter than anything that ever happens to you or me; but Aganza's youth had also been grimmer than yours or mine.

I stopped not more than a dozen paces from the two of them. The light of a crude torch danced weirdly over the fetish hut and these frantic human beings. I could see the head of a white cock dangling from a wisp of string about Aganza's neck, and the fowl's tail feathers protruding from the hut's tiny door. And I could smell fresh blood. A goat was pegged down on its side before the fetish hut, and Aganza, stark-naked, was groveling on all fours before it. N'Devli was bound-ing up and down and screeching eerily, like wind among dry bamboos. Each time he hit the ground he pricked her buttocks with the point of a spear. What was he trying to force her to do? To tear out the goat's throat with her teeth like a leopard? To drink the bubbling blood of the still living animal?

"Stop it!" I shrieked. "Stop it! Stop it, you fiend!"

Aganza moaned and collapsed on top of the goat, but

N'Devli whirled about in mid-air. He bared his teeth, snarled like a dog, and shook his spear at me.

I too leaped forward, and with no thought of what I did, but with surprising strength for an old woman, I wrenched the spear from the witch doctor's hands. The next instant I saw a knife high above N'Devli's head. Then, using the spear as a woman will a broom, I slashed downward as hard as I could. I heard bones breaking, and the witch doctor crumpled up at my feet. As I looked at him in the flickering light, I suddenly realized that he too was an old man. A very old man, with little time left for evil on this earth.

I pulled Aganza to her feet, and she shivered like one awakening from a trance.

"Are you all right?" I asked.

But she only shivered more violently.

I slapped her smartly on each cheek, and her head rocked back and forth as though it rested on a stem of rubber. Then her eyelids dropped and she breathed noisily through her mouth for a moment. It was like a death rattle, and for the first time that night I was afraid—afraid that Aganza was dying. I shook her by her arms, but she only stood there, swaying in the flickering torchlight. Then she opened her eyes, and I saw that she was herself again.

"Are you all right—now?"

"Yes, *mama.*"

At our feet N'Devli whimpered, and we both looked down at him. Then Aganza glanced at me quickly. I still held the witch doctor's spear in my hand, and maybe she thought I was going to kill him. Well! I had to wreak the insane fury that surged through me on something. Suddenly I began beating at the fetish house with the heavy thorn-wood handle of the spear; then, with the blade and the toe of my shoe, I shoved the debris into the river. That done, I leaned on my spear like a panting warrior, and, in the uncertain light, saw the ugly head of a crocodile rise, snap at something—perhaps the cock's body—and disappear again.

Aganza leaned over to untie the goat, and as she did so, the cock's head hung about her neck struck her hand. She flung it aside with a quick jerk that broke the string. Then, between us, we half carried, half dragged N'Devli back to the hospital. He wasn't badly injured—a broken collarbone and dislocated shoulder were all—but he was suffering from shock. I worked hard to save his life, and I stayed with him until the morning sun laced the walls of the infirmary hut. Then one of my nurses led me away and put me to bed.

To bed, but not to sleep or rest. Rather to such pain as I had never known before. To such pain as I had seldom seen others suffer. Nor did I need to be told what the trouble was. I was so full of malaria that for many years I had taken its recurring chills and fevers as a matter of course. It was my own fault; I had been careless about my quinine for too long. When I had it, I took it—if I remembered. When I was out of the drug, obviously I didn't take it. When there was only a small quantity in my stock, I gave it to someone else who needed it worse than I. This isn't heroism, but a fool's trick that every medical missionary to Africa has been guilty of.

For several days I had had pain in the small of my back, and it had seemed to me that my urine was taking on the color of bog water, but I disregarded the evidence of my senses. The explorers and their bogus lion hunt had turned my world upside down, and if they carried any report at all of me and my work to the outside world, I did not want it to be a smart-alecky description of a neurotic semi-invalid. Besides, I was in my late sixties and it was natural that I should have a little pain from time to time, pain that could be caused by any number of things—rheumatism, for instance.

Now my urine was almost black and there was no question about what caused the pain in the small of my back: black-water fever. Sentence of death! How often had I heard those words from the white hunters, the traders, the fellow missionaries who were guilty of the same carelessnesses as I. When I returned from my last furlough, I had remembered Dr. Mary's advice to bring a case of champagne back with me as a specific for blackwater fever, but somehow it had disappeared "by accident" en route up the Congo.

It was Aganza who saved my life. She drenched me with frequent and liberal doses of the nastiest brew any witch doctor ever cooked up. I don't know what therapeutic qualities it possessed, but I told her afterward that I had to get well just in order to describe that bolus to the American medical profession. Of one thing I am certain: no one would ever become a drug addict drenched with that hell's broth.

In three weeks I was on my feet again, shaky, weak, and perhaps for the first time in my life meekly submissive to authority. Black people suffer greatly from malaria, but throughout the centuries they have built up a resistance to it that stops it before it reaches the ultimate course it takes with white folk. And maybe the jungle African does have some sort of specific, I don't know.

After I had explained to Aganza just what blackwater fever is, she had sent word via the drums to young Dr. Early. He in turn had cabled my condition to America, and back had come a reply which had said in effect, "Go up to Big Bush and bring that old war horse out, by the hair of her head if necessary, and put her on a boat for home." Very well, I would go, not because I was ready, but because I must. Dr. Charles was coming up later to take over my work in Big Bush, and a young fellow, just recently out of McGill, would take over at Tani. He, this young fellow, was already an expert on—

But why should I detail his excellences? All the workers I had known in Africa seemed so wonderfully well prepared for the responsibilities before them. All but me. But God had helped me; God and an iron will which was perhaps my most valuable inheritance from my father.

Weak or not, I must pack. I grew a bit stronger day by day, but it was only a question of time until I would have another attack of the fever if I remained in Africa. I had escaped nature's death sentence once, but I wouldn't a second time. Everything was against me, my age, and—well, my work in Africa was done.

And yet, I knew that my accomplishments were not inconsiderable. When instructions came to pull me up by the roots, Big Bush was an outstation of which our denomination was proud. We had a compound of over thirty buildings, more than twenty of which were for the medical work. True, the dormitories and living quarters were mud-daubed wattle and thatch; but the hospital proper, the dispensary, and the two operating theaters were on floors and foundations of homemade cement and with walls of fired brick. Best of all, I had a native staff of over sixty men and women in training as nurses and midwives, and a handful of permanent employees, each one of whom was fully as useful as the ordinary interne in an American hospital.

Then there were the schools, which spread over hundreds of square miles. They were loosely organized, I know, and I have heard laymen criticize them as substandard, but one does not begin with perfection. Still, they opened the first few pages of man's recorded wisdom to boys and girls whose fathers' literacy had been a matter of reading the meaning of crossed sticks on a footpath, or of interpreting tufts of chicken feathers dangling from a bough overhead.

I started to pack, and although there were many hands to help me, there was much I must do alone. For my work really consisted mostly of unpacking and discarding. How could I, why should I, carry my treasures halfway around the world when I would never again really be permitted to use them? When they would be merely spread out for the unknowing and unappreciative to gape at? I could hear their remarks: "Just think of *savages* making things like that!"

No! I laid article after article aside. Aganza could use this, or Dr. Charles and his wife, or Jackie. Jackie?

There was never any question that Aganza would stay on at Big Bush. This was her hospital and these her schools, as much as mine. But Jackie had come from Tani with me. And before Tani—even Monsieur l'Administrateur had not known the name of the village where he had been born. What would Jackie want to do? I sent for him and asked him.

"This is my home, *mama*," he answered. "My wife is a N'Titiertean woman. My children know no other tribe. I am too old to go elsewhere, and my wife would raise her voice and chatter like a monkey outside the walls of the palaver hut if I demanded it of her. I would go anywhere with you, *mama*, even if my *cattle* complained all day and halfway through the night. But since I cannot cross the big waters with you, why should I leave N'Titierte where—" Jackie used an old Hausa saying that can only be justly translated by one of our equally old metaphors—"where my roots are down."

I too saw no reason for the old gunbearer's pulling up his roots. Transplanting is for youth and not for the gray-haired and brittle-limbed.

Jackie was already a rich man, but I heaped his arms with trivia that made him a black Croesus. I did not ask him to help Dr. Charles when the latter arrived. Jackie was by nature a good man, not a prig; he would help Dr. Charles without suggestion from me.

When my packing was finally completed, I had two little rolls of clothing; an elephant tusk, the price of Job's life (the other, from my Pygmy suitor, had been left behind when the big swamp swallowed N'zem); and a place setting of forged iron—knife, fork, and two spoons. The local blacksmith had made them for me out of nodules of iron that I had picked up from among the roots of the veld grass. I had used them for so many years that I knew the product of the silversmith's art was going to seem strange in my hands and on my lips.

At prayer meeting, the night before I left N'Titierte, my people expected me to speak to them, and I dutifully prepared

273

as nearly a formal sermon as I was capable of. Then the same fate befell me as did the preacher of the old story who pushed his notes too far back in the pigeonhole of the lectern and had to explain to his congregation: "God knows I prepared an excellent sermon for you, but now only God knows what I meant to say." The preacher had the advantage of me, for he could go on, "God willing, and my wife being successful with her hatpin, you will hear it next Sunday."

For me there would be no "next Sunday," and I stood before my people wordless. Several times I opened my mouth, but it was beyond my power to push sentences out from between my teeth. Then young Dr. Early, who had been sitting behind me on the platform, arose and asked my people if he might tell them a story. Their eyes gleamed with surprise, and he was already talking before they nodded assent. I was surprised too, but I sank back into the chair behind me with immense relief.

I can't put down for you just what Dr. Early said, but words were easy for him, and he had been properly trained to speak before all kinds of groups.

I have always enjoyed good sermons; nevertheless my heart was so full of tears that night that I scarcely heard what he was saying until I realized that he was talking about me—and borrowing the theme I had used when I faced the congregation in Tani my first night there a quarter of a century before. He used my old figure of speech of the woman at her cooking fire of an evening being stronger because of the protection of the flame dancing under her pot than the biggest man with the heaviest-headed spear who stood alone in the darkness.

The sermon wasn't long, but I could see the faces in front of me gleam with satisfaction as Dr. Early sat down beside me. The next minute I arose with the congregation, but I couldn't sing with them because my heart was suddenly flooded with such faith as comes to the best of us perhaps no more than once in a lifetime. The tears that had drenched my heart for days now overflowed, but they had become a woman's tears of thankfulness and joy.

Aganza put me to bed that night as though I were a child. I tried to tell her that if I had done nothing more than discover her, my life in Africa had been well worth-while. She smiled at me and patted my cheek gently.

It was cold and foggy when we started out the next morning. One of Jackie's sons went with us for a short distance as "dew drier." Aganza too trotted along beside my *tipoye,* holding my hand in hers. I kept telling her she mustn't come too far, but whenever I did, she only squeezed my hand the harder. She stood thus, silent while the carriers rested for a moment, but when they picked up the poles of my *tipoye* again, I knew she was saying good-by. They knew it too, for they stood waiting.

There were many words in her heart, I know, but as it had been with me the night before, they were fledgling words. Silently she put a hand into the bosom of her dress and drew out a little parcel wrapped in a segment of banana leaf.

"For her who bore you, *mama.* This is for her who bore you." Then she turned and plodded away.

I watched until she disappeared around a bend in the trail, but the old woman never looked back, not even once. Then I picked up the small green parcel. I could tell by my fingers what it contained: a handful of peanuts. Intrinsically worthless! But such a gift is the highest compliment one African can pay another; it is a mark of the greatest love and respect for one woman to so honor another's mother.

I knew what tribal custom demanded of me. Had my mother been living, I must go straight to her immediately, ignoring all other duties however pressing, and once there, lay the parcel of peanuts on her knees. My mother being dead, I must go to the little spirit house reserved for her— But what would people think of me? Good, Midwestern farmers, totally ignorant of the customs of people living sometimes only a step beyond their visual horizon? They would consider me absolutely crazy

275

should I do what Aganza expected. But then, why shouldn't I? I had brought the customs of these same farmers to Africa and had asked Aganza and her people to accept them. But couldn't there be something reciprocal in it? Why shouldn't I carry a little bit of Africa back to America?

I knew then as I swayed along in my *tipoye* that I would do it. When I reached home, I would go immediately to the little rural cemetery where my mother had slept these many years. There, before the "spirit house" that she shared with my father, I would lift up my voice and call upon my mother un-til—well, until Aganza, if she were with me, would be sure the spirit had awakened and was listening. Then I would tell my mother of this wonderful old black woman who so loved and honored her for the daughter she had borne. I would do all this, just as the custom of my black-skinned sisters demanded of me, and I would leave out no tiniest portion of the rite.

Feb 26, 1951 - Grace Stahl
thanks for hours of enjoyment.'